Don't Bite Vampires
Jeni Conrad

This book is dedicated to my dad, a wonderful support and an even better father.

Author's Note

As a teacher who has dealt with teens for many years, not to mention was once one herself, I wanted to bring up an issue in this series that many people struggle with. But for some, reading about it may be uncomfortable or even triggering. This story contains themes of an eating disorder. I am not trying to promote it or glamorize it in any way but rather trying to highlight the struggle a person might have with it and how damaging it can be. The issue does get resolved, but it takes several books to do so. If you or anyone you know struggles with an eating disorder, there is help. https://www.edreferral.com/

Contents

Chapter 1

When your best friend is a ghost it's important to set some boundaries. Even if those boundaries had been crossed a week earlier when you both shared a frosty kiss that shouldn't have been possible.

"And remember, absolutely no popping into my room uninvited," I repeated the first boundary in hopes that he'd listen this time. "Sometimes we need to go in there so I can talk to you about things without looking insane, but other than that, consider my room a sacred place."

We were at the skatepark on a cold Saturday morning. It was too cold and too early for most of the skaters to be hanging out there. Only two boys zipped around the cement while I sat on one of the picnic tables, snuggling into my jacket, pretending to talk on my phone. Brandon sat next to me, but, because he was a ghost, I appeared to be alone.

"A sacred place full of sacred girl things." Brandon grinned, his mischievous lips showcasing his near-perfect teeth and almost causing me to grin right back. Almost. I needed him to understand how important my words were and that he should listen for once. Also, I was determined not to get distracted by his lips. Again.

"However you want to look at it. And please don't tell me I have to go into details about bathroom time. You know basic rules of privacy, right?"

"I don't know why you're so worried about this, Hanna. I've been behaving myself. Mostly. You got number fourteen wrong."

I looked down to where he was pointing at my math homework and frowned. "I'm not worried. I just want to make sure I'm clear."

"Okay, no bedroom, no bathroom, no school. Where exactly can I show up? The few minutes in between walking to school and back? That doesn't leave a lot of time for me to regale you with all my interesting stories."

"Like what? I've asked you at least ten times how you died, and you refuse to tell me, always getting that wary look in your eyes and changing the subject." I erased my answer for question fourteen and studied it some more to figure out what I had missed.

"So then I could tell you about a super creepy house you need to check out."

"Exactly like that. Always changing the subject away from your-self."

He sighed and rubbed the spiked hair on his head, which sprung back just as soon as his hand passed over it. "I don't want to talk about my life. It isn't something I want to dwell on. Okay?"

"I thought we were friends now though? Don't friends talk to each other about difficult things so they can help each other deal?"

"We're friends?" He looked up with a hopeful smile that tugged at my heart.

"Of course we're friends! I wouldn't hang out with you so often if we weren't."

"Cool." He tried to hide how big his smile got but wasn't successful.

Feeling bashful myself, I returned to our other conversation. "Another boundary I need is one to keep me sane, and that is if there is another alive person around, it would really help me if you didn't talk so much. It's so hard not to talk back."

"Unless it's Noah, right? He knows about me." Brandon folded his arms and rested them and his head on the table, looking slightly dejected.

"Yes. Are you mad that I told him?"

He shrugged while still resting on the table, so I couldn't see his face. The fact that he was hiding his expressions said enough.

"Oh, I didn't realize it would bother you so much. I'd take it back if I could."

"Kind of late for that."

We sat quietly for a moment, and I tried to figure out a way I might make it up to him. On one hand, it had felt nice to come clean to another human being (an alive one anyway) about my secret. On the other hand, I could see how Brandon might have wanted me to ask permission before divulging a secret that wasn't completely mine.

"Are you embarrassed that you're a ghost or something? I know Noah has his weird secrets, but he's obviously different from other alivers. I can't figure out why it would make you uncomfortable for him to know about you."

He sat up and furrowed his eyebrows in confusion. "Embarrassed? Why would I be embarrassed? It's not like I chose to be dead. No, that's not it."

"Then what is it?"

His lips pressed tightly together as he studied me for a second before answering. "It's hard to say."

"Because you don't know? Because you have a sore throat? I didn't realize a ghost might need a lozenge or I would have stolen one from my grandma. Oh, wait, I can't do that. She's a ghost too."

Brandon rolled his eyes but wore a faint smile, so I knew he was at least partly amused by my lame jokes.

"Also, I have to add that I'm constantly surprised by your inconsistencies. You're not afraid to talk about being lonely or wanting my friendship, but you're so secretive about other things that don't seem as personal. Most guys aren't willing to admit when they're lonely."

He shrugged. "I'm dead. I'm not like most guys. I realize how short life is."

"So how come you can't tell me why you don't want Noah to know about you?"

"Maybe another time."

I frowned, noting the somber tone in his voice that was uncharacteristic of his usual teasing banter. "Fine. Be cryptic some more. Haha, get it? Cryptic."

"Hilarious."

"Is there a way I can make it up to you?"

"I already told you. We need to go check out this creepy house. There are *so* many ghosts roaming around it, it's unbelievable."

Familiar fear seized my chest. "How many? You know I can't contact one without attracting the attention of all of them."

"I know. I didn't say go in there and have a ghost party. I just said I wanted to show it to you. I'm thinking it's where a bunch of people died a long time ago. I say a long time ago because some of the ghosts are wearing clothes that were dated even when I was alive."

"Wow. That must be old."

"Exactly."

I sighed and put my homework into my math book to hold my place before putting all my stuff back into my backpack. "Fine. Let's go check it out. But if even one ghost looks my way, I'm out of there. You can chat with all the creepy undead people until you're blue in the face, but I'm not."

He rolled his eyes but couldn't stop a chuckle. "Again. You're hilarious."

As Brandon was a ghost, he was already blue and transparent, the same as how I saw all ghosts. It made it hard to see what colors they wore in life or what their eyes really looked like, but it was also mildly entertaining to see the world literally through their eyes.

As we walked out of the skatepark and towards whatever house Brandon had found, I thought about how different life was since I'd met Brandon. Before him, I refused to talk to any ghosts, even my grandma who had haunted my mom since I was little. They were too overwhelming and demanding. They always wanted me to help them find someone or somehow fix all their problems, but I had my own problems. How could I be responsible for fixing all of theirs? Not to mention, there were literally more dead people on Earth than living people.

But after meeting Brandon in the skatepark a few weeks ago and then needing his help to break a curse on my history teacher, I realized that perhaps not all ghosts are bad. I even started talking to my grandma and found out I'm a Seer (pronounced like see-er). I had been relieved to find out that she was one too and that she had lots of information to help me navigate my powers.

I still felt fear when thinking about talking to other ghosts, but I was starting to work through it. My goal was to get to the point where I could help at least one ghost cross over. My grandma had helped hundreds, and while that could in no way make a dent in the number of ghosts floating about and moaning in despair, at least it could make a difference for a few.

Plus, my efforts in learning more about my powers and how to help others seemed to make Brandon happier, and even if he wouldn't tell me how to help him, he was somehow super excited to help any other ghost we encountered.

I know how I sound, and like I told my ghost grandma several times—I'm not in love with Brandon. He's just my friend, and, so far, he's been the best friend I've ever had. So what if no one else could see him?

"It's just around the block here. I couldn't move very far without you around to help me with whatever spooky Seer powers you have, but I did glimpse the blue, shadowy movements from down the street. I've been dying to get a closer look."

I let that pun slide. If I acknowledged them all, he'd probably keep making more, which was a habit I didn't want to encourage. My dad made enough puns for all of us.

"Can we at least stay on the other side of the road?" I scanned the houses in front of us, feeling nervous about even being near a large number of ghosts.

Brandon chuckled, but he nodded anyway. "Sure. If that makes you feel better. In fact, we can even hide behind a car and peek through its windows like spies if you want to."

"I want to."

"Wow, ghosts have really got you spooked."

"Yes, no thanks to you."

The hairs on my neck started popping to attention as we walked closer to the house. It was falling apart. At one end, the gutter was coming off and weeds clawed up the siding. All the shudders, except one, hung sideways, and the grass was overgrown into a seed-sprouting field.

Chills came in waves down my back, surprising me with their strength. I had never felt the warning so strongly before. My teeth even chattered a few times.

As ridiculous as we looked to the houses behind us, we crouched next to a car that was parked across the street from the most haunted house I'd ever seen, including the one where I had helped Rose, a local psychic, capture nearly a dozen ghosts (which was a constant source of guilt for me).

The first ghost I saw was milling about the front sidewalk in her pajamas. She was singing a nursery rhyme but looked older than a child. I ducked further down behind the car, worried that she would notice my noticing of her.

As I peered through the windows that badly needed a washing, more ghosts winked into sight. Two boys on the lawn were playing with a ball I couldn't see. An older couple was holding hands and walking down the path. One ghost was hanging out a broken window with her body upside down and her head and torso dangled, arms waving freely in the wind. I counted seven more ghosts before they became so thick, I couldn't see them individually anymore.

"Speechless, aren't you?" Brandon whispered, trying to keep quiet in case the other ghosts might have super great hearing. It might have been a little silly, but I appreciated the caution anyway.

"A bit, yeah. How could there be so many ghosts in one place?"

"So many ghosts can only mean one thing."

"The house of a serial killer?" I wish I could have said it as a joke, but seriously, there were a lot of ghosts.

"Worse. Vampire."

I choked on a small laugh that wanted to burble out. "Vampire?"

"Why not? After what we saw in your front yard last week, do we not believe in vampires yet?"

I frowned, still staring through the car's dirty windows, trying to gather any information from the ghosts that I could. Despite displaying several different time periods of dress, they had to be related in some way in life since they had the same haunt in death.

"It's too far away to see if they have bite marks in their necks."

"Not to mention, ghosts don't physically manifest their death blows. If you could see mine, you'd have never talked to me in the first place."

"What a shame that would have been."

I had been joking but Brandon's tone was serious. "Yes, it would have been."

"When are you going to tell me about your death?"

He shrugged.

I glanced at him and frowned again.

"What are you looking at?" A deep voice asked from my right side, opposite of where Brandon was crouched.

"Holy—!" I might have dropped a few curse words that my mom would have surely chided me for. "What are you doing here? How are you so sneaky?!"

Caleb grinned, his perfect, white teeth dazzling me and probably the whole street at the same time. He was my sister's friend from school who, until recently, hadn't ever said a word to me, but a lot had changed in the last two weeks. Having him crouched so closely was nearly intoxicating after I got over the initial shock of his sudden appearance. His dark eyes were flecked with gold while his dark hair was cut short on the sides and long on top, swooped playfully away from his face. Physically, he was built like a Greek god, and while he was enjoyable to look at, it was his frosty, minty scent that really pulled me in. The smell somehow linked to a childhood memory I needed to get some more clarification on.

"Sorry. I didn't want to announce myself too loudly as it seems we are on some kind of covert mission here."

"Oh great," Brandon said from my left. I didn't have to look at his face to know he'd rolled his eyes. "Our favorite stalker."

"Right." I glanced between the haunted house and Caleb, not wanting to lose my hiding place, but also wanting to stand straight and act like a semi-normal person. "Yes. I was just checking out that house to see if...maybe they needed someone to come mow their grass for them?"

Caleb's chuckle rumbled deep inside his chest, and I wondered how it would sound with my ear pressed right up against his skin.

I probably had a blush creep across my face at those intimate thoughts because I could have sworn he knew exactly what I was thinking based on his teasing expression.

"And you need to hide from across the street because the grass is so tall, it's scary?"

"Something like that."

Brandon sighed. "Tell him to go away. I found this house first. He can go haunt somewhere else."

Caleb adjusted his crouching position into a sitting one, facing me with his long legs crossed and his knowing-more-than-they-should eyes studying me intently. "After all we've been through, you still don't trust me, do you?"

I pressed my lips in thought as I followed his lead and changed into a sitting position on the chilled sidewalk. To face Caleb, I had to turn my back on Brandon, but I didn't know what else to do. Plus, my legs were killing me from crouching for so long.

"Trust isn't something I can give away easily. Most people give the benefit of the doubt and trust first until it's broken, but I'm not like that. In fact, you're the one who warned me not to trust hardly anyone, remember?"

I was referring to the conversation we'd had in my bedroom last week where he'd snuck in and out much quieter than my ghost friend usually did.

Speaking of Brandon, he kept muttering quietly to himself grumpily but moved so he could feel more involved in the conversation, even though that meant sitting in the middle of the sidewalk. No one had walked by us yet, but, if anyone should happen down the street, they'd end up walking right through him. Not that they'd notice.

"Alright." Caleb nodded. "I can respect that, but please note that you *can* trust me."

"That's what the bad guys always say. Hasn't he watched any cartoons? Sheesh." Brandon folded his arms across his chest and shook his head.

As far as I knew, Caleb couldn't hear Brandon, so I had to ignore his comments, but honestly, it wouldn't have surprised me if suddenly Caleb could see and hear ghosts too. He was full of surprises like how, apparently, he was over three-hundred-years old or something.

"Just saying I can trust you doesn't prove I can trust you."

"Again, fair. What can I do to help you realize that I'm on your side here?"

"You can stop popping up from nowhere and following her around all the time." Brandon gave him a pointed look.

I really, really didn't want to react to his ghostly presence in front of alive people, but his comment was just too ironic for me not to laugh. It was exactly what *he* did all the time. I wasn't sure if he realized it or was just annoyed at Caleb for copying his game.

Caleb looked around for a second and raised his eyebrows. "What's so funny?"

"Nothing. Sorry." I spared a second to glare at Brandon, hoping he'd shut up for once. "Sometimes I just remember funny things and they make me laugh. Sorry."

Brandon gave me an annoyed look but at least he didn't say anything else for the moment.

"Hanna," Caleb said my name, and an involuntary thrill went through my chest.

"What?" I pulled back a little, feeling like I was in trouble for some reason.

"I know you can see ghosts. There's one with us right now, isn't there?"

I glanced at Brandon and then back to Caleb. "Maybe."

Brandon shook his head while staring at me intently. "Do you have to tell *everyone* about me?"

"Maybe if you'd be quiet, I could ignore you and no one would figure out you were here." I talked out of the side of my mouth like Caleb would somehow not notice I was talking to someone no one else could see.

Caleb, bless him, looked more amused than scandalized at my crazed behavior. "Your secret is safe with me. Remember? I don't want anyone else finding out what you can do any more than you do. You have no idea how many beings would kill just to have access to your powers. Seriously, you have no idea."

"Beings? Not people?" I couldn't help but notice his word choice.

"Yes, not people. Can we just talk about it already? You know what I am. You saw Mr. Tyler almost turn into a werewolf last week, and you see ghosts on the daily. Why is all this stuff so hard for you to accept?"

"I told you vampires were real." Brandon looked Caleb up and down as if they were both high school girls wearing the same dress at prom.

"But if he's a vampire, why can he be outside in the sun?" I shot back to Brandon with a sassy waggle of my head.

Both the ghost and I looked to Caleb for the answer. Ever the good-natured one, he laughed softly. "Right. All those legends. The pasty vampires can burn severely in the sun, but you've probably noticed I'm a bit darker. I have more melanin in my skin which serves to protect me from burns. Now, that's not to say I could spend all day at the beach and not regret it, but it's enough protection to handle a few moments of sunshine."

Brandon and I shared a look, trying to determine if we believed him or not.

"I mean, he's not burning up." Brandon pointed out.

"Yes, but that could just mean he's human."

Caleb shook his head, but his expression remained amused. "How else could I be so old and know about your grandma?"

"Lies and Google."

"What's a Google?" Brandon asked.

"I'll tell you later. Well? Looks like you're going to have to prove it to us." I followed Brandon's posture and folded my arms over my chest.

"Sure." Caleb's eyes met mine in a steady challenge. "Would you like me to bite you, or do you prefer the more tamer route as I sling you on my back and take a super-fast run through the forest?"

"This isn't *Twilight*, and I'm not Bella. How about answering some more questions? Like how well did you know my grandma?" I finally started voicing thoughts I'd had since last week when Caleb tried to help me fight a ghost curse afflicting my history teacher. "Did you know her well enough to be there on the night she died, maybe helping her young granddaughter hide in a kitchen cabinet?"

Caleb's only reaction was to raise his eyebrows slightly. "You remember that?"

I shook my head and sighed. "Of course, I remember that. It was the worst night of my life. So, was that you or not?"

"You don't remember who it was?"

"I was young. The details are fuzzy, but I remember how you smelled."

Brandon was looking back and forth between us as we talked. "What are you guys talking about? What night? How come you've never told me about this?"

"We've been friends for two weeks. Do you expect to know everything about me already? How about we start with how you died and then maybe I'll tell you about my worst memory," I told Brandon while keeping my eyes steady on Caleb.

"How I smelled, huh?" Caleb's slow smile spread across his face in a knowing grin, and I struggled to keep eye contact with him.

Blushing but pretending I wasn't, I narrowed my eyes into a glare. "Yes, it's like this frosty minty smell, the same one from the man who helped me hide."

"Fine. Yes, I was there." His smile faded, and I could have sworn there was empathy in his eyes, an expression I wouldn't have thought a vampire was capable of. "I'm really sorry, Hanna. I'm sorry I couldn't save your grandmother."

Brandon's eyes widened. "You guys are talking about the night your grandmother died? And *he* was there? How do you know he's not the one who killed her?"

Chills skittered over my shoulders at Brandon's words. Why hadn't I considered that?

Caleb's eyebrows drew together in confusion at my face which had probably turned to alarm. "What? What's wrong?"

"Are you sorry you couldn't stop her from being murdered because *you* murdered her?" I found myself asking, braver than I thought I was. I probably should have just ran away.

"What?!" Caleb raised his hands, palms toward me in a surrendering motion. "Woah! No! Why would you think that? I would never have hurt her!"

"Here's the trust thing again. How do I know you're not lying to me?"

As Caleb and I stared at each other, him confused and almost sad while I was determined to get the truth, Brandon spoke again, "I guess we could always ask her?"

"I'm so sorry, Hanna. I can't—"

I held my hand up so Caleb would stop talking. "We'll just ask her."

It was his turn to be confused. "Ask her?"

"Well, as you keep pointing out, I can talk to ghosts. My gran happens to be a ghost, and one that isn't ever too far away. We can ask her if you're telling the truth. Is there anything else you want to add to your story before we go?" I pulled my lips into a challenging pucker and continued staring at the vampire.

I can't believe I just used that word, vampire, but I guess I was starting to believe more of his story, or, at least, getting closer to accepting that there was more than ghosts that go bump in the night.

Chapter 2

Both Mom and Trina were home when we got to my house, complicating what I was trying to do—reunite my ghost grandmother with her long-lost vampire protector who also happened to be one of my sister's friends.

When I entered the front door with Caleb and Brandon trailing behind me, my mom greeted us from the kitchen.

"Hey, sweetie. Oh! You've brought a friend. Hello." Mom took a few steps towards us while drying her hands with a towel.

"Mom, this is Caleb." I gestured towards the tall high-school student who looked more man than teenager. Although, for the first time since I'd known him, he actually looked a little unsure of himself.

"Nice to meet you, ma'am." Caleb bobbed his head with the polite greeting.

"Oh, no need to be so formal. You can call me Mrs.—Ms. Sanchez." My mom's voice wavered, and her eyes were a little too shiny when she got to her title. Dad had left only six days ago, and it was probably the first time she'd had to change the way she introduced herself.

A few tears welled up inside my own eyes, but I blinked them away quickly.

Gran's ghost appeared next to my mom, and her gaze was instantly drawn to Caleb.

"Okay. Nice to meet you, Ms. Sanchez." Caleb nodded, his dark eyes sincere and showing more depth than I'd ever expected to see from a vampire.

Which was another reason I wasn't quite convinced he was who he said he was.

"Why does this young man look so familiar?" Gran's eyes darted to me before going back to study Caleb.

Trina took that moment to walk into the front room from where she'd probably been hanging out in her bedroom. "Hey, guys. Oh, Caleb, I didn't realize you were coming over today."

"Well, isn't this a fine, awkward kettle of fish?" Brandon chuckled.

"Er—Yes, we, uh..." I floundered for a few seconds.

"We're going to work on a school project together. I promised I'd help her with French. You know how I love to speak the language of love," Caleb filled in and added a wink.

Gran, Mom, and Trina all looked at me with wide, surprised eyes, and I blushed furiously. "Right. But it's just homework, nothing else."

I gave Caleb a hard glare.

Brandon thought the whole thing was funny and kept giggling. Although he did roll his eyes when he didn't think I was looking.

Lucky for him, my eyes saw more than I wanted to.

"Okay, well, no boys in your room. You know the rules." Mom gave us a stern look.

"Of course not. We'll just go work in the backyard. It's turning into a nice day, and I'm sure we'll have lots of supervision." I locked eyes with Gran and moved my head in what I hoped was a subtle gesture for her to follow us.

"Okay." Mom watched us go through the kitchen and out the back door.

Trina followed, and thankfully, so did Gran.

"I didn't realize you were so good at French," Trina said as we shut the door behind us and sat on the patio furniture.

Caleb shrugged. "It helps that I've spent a few years in France. You want to hang out later after we're done here? I'm sure you don't want to stick around while we're doing boring homework stuff."

I silently blessed Caleb's name to whatever god was listening. We needed Trina to leave so we could have a conversation with a ghost, and I had been searching for ideas of how to get rid of her, even though it was her friend sitting with me on the deck.

Trina's eyebrows made a little crease in her forehead. "I didn't know you'd been to France. I bet that was cool. You'll have to tell me about it later. I'll see if the others want to go for pizza or something. Have fun learning the language of love."

She gave me a smirk with her last statement before she turned away and went back into the house. My heart sank a little as I figured she'd probably confront me about the whole thing later.

"So, is she here?" Caleb looked around as if he could tell there was a ghost hanging about even though he hadn't noticed Brandon making faces at him nearly the whole morning.

I nodded. "Gran? How are you feeling?"

She finally stopped staring at Caleb and gave her focus to me. "I'm fine, dear. Just a bit confused by your friend here. He seems so familiar."

"Well, guess that confirms it." Brandon frowned and sat on the nearest empty chair.

"Do you think you've seen him before?" I asked gently.

Caleb's eyes bounced around, looking at me and then searching the air where I was looking. His tone was hushed when he spoke. "What's she saying?"

Gran was back to studying him. She walked so close and peered into his dark eyes that I wondered if he would be able to feel some of the coldness that I felt when a ghost was nearby. "I have, yes. I think he's been to the house before, but I've never really looked closely at him. I think—I think I might have known him while I was alive, but that's impossible. He looks so young. Maybe I knew his father?"

"She says you look familiar, but you're too young." I gave Caleb a sly grin. "I guess your liquid diet helps chase away the wrinkles."

Caleb shared my grin. "It does have its perks."

"Shouldn't we be more concerned about *where* he gets his liquids from? Maybe he feasted on your Gran's neck and watched the last moments of life seep out of her eyes?" Brandon muttered flippantly, almost as if he was talking to himself.

Gran caught the reference. "Wait. Are you saying he's a vampire?" I nodded.

Recognition flooded Gran's face. She fell to her knees next to Caleb's chair and put her hand where his sat on the armrest. "Caleb? Could it really be you? You don't look a day older."

Caleb's eyebrows drew together slightly, and he looked down at his arm. Perhaps he could feel some of her coldness.

"She figured out what we were saying and what you are," I still couldn't say the word to him out loud—it was too weird, "and then she seemed to remember you. She says you don't look a day older."

Caleb's eyes softened and, even though he couldn't see her, his expression grew kind and thoughtful. "I've wanted to apologize after all these years, Linda. I'm so sorry I couldn't save you."

I'd seen several ghosts cry during my life, but this was the first time I wanted to help one feel better. Usually, I ignored them, more afraid of the ghost than wanting to help it, but it was a whole different situation when it was my grandma. My heart went out to her, and I really wished I could hug her.

Even Brandon was saddened enough to stop with the sarcastic quips for a few minutes.

But Gran smiled at Caleb and patted his hand again. "No need to be sorry, dear. I'm sorry you've been carrying around this guilt for so long. There was nothing you could do. There was nothing anyone could do."

I relayed the words as she spoke them and was proud that my voice didn't waver even once.

Caleb shook his head. "I could have done something. It's pointless to have all this supernatural strength and not be able to help the ones I love."

I found myself feeling bad and awkward at the same time. This was a private type of conversation. "I would offer to leave the two of you alone so you could catch up and stuff, but I guess it would make it hard for you to talk to her."

Caleb smiled. "It's okay."

Gran stood, and I could have sworn she held her shoulders back just a little more than usual as if she'd lost some weight that had been pushing them down. "Hanna, dear, you have to convince him that it wasn't his fault. In fact, if it hadn't been for him, you might have died, too, and then where would we be?"

"Not sitting on the porch having an odd conversation between ghosts and vampires," Brandon pointed out, evidently not feeling so solemn anymore.

I told Caleb what she'd said and then added my own question. "What happened that night?"

Gran looked down at Caleb, and he stared out over the grass as if they were both thinking about how much to share with me.

"After all this stuff that happened, and now I have to sit here being an interpreter, I think I deserve to know." It's possible that I gave them a pouty lip as I crossed my arms over my chest.

"She does deserve to know, but since it's your story, I'll let you decide what to tell her," Caleb said to the grass.

I switched my gaze to Gran and stared her down. It wasn't that I didn't still feel bad for her, but I had the feeling she was hiding things from me, even though she'd given me plenty of ghostly advice over the past week about being a Seer.

She sighed and looked over at Caleb for a moment before looking back at me. "I would love to tell you the whole story, but I've forgotten most of it, and I just don't think either of us is ready to face that night. I'm sorry."

I frowned and looked back to Brandon who just shrugged.

"Okay, fine. What *can* you tell me about it? How did you die? Who killed you? Why did they kill you?" I gazed at her steadily, keeping my arms crossed.

Gran's eyes grew sad again as she pulled up the memory. "All I can tell you is that I remember being more afraid for you than myself. I remember telling Caleb to go to you first when he arrived. I remember..." She stared into space.

Brandon leaned towards me. "It's probably painful for her to think about her death. Do you think you should be asking her to do that?"

I turned my glare on him. "Don't you think we should find out as many answers as we can? Maybe helping to avenge her death will help her cross over."

"Are you ready for her to cross over?" He gave me a pointed look with an upraised eyebrow.

We both knew the answer to that, so I turned back to Gran, although my voice was softer than it had been. "It's okay, Gran. We can talk about it when you're ready, as long as you don't think we need to know something about it right now. Are any of us in danger from what happened to you?"

"No, we're not in danger. Probably. I'll think more about that night and see if I can remember more, but it'll be difficult since I've been burying these memories for twelve years, and ghost memories are even less reliable than human ones."

"Okay. Thank you, Gran."

She nodded, her eyes still distant and thoughtful, and wandered into the house, not bothering to use the door.

"Is she okay?" Caleb asked, sensing the change of atmosphere.

"She's struggling to remember that night. She needs more time. All she could tell me was that she was grateful for your help and was more afraid that I would get hurt than scared for herself. What kind of person could murder a kindly grandmother and then possibly try to murder her young grandchild?"

"Maybe we're not talking about a person here. Maybe it was a monster. Although I can say I feel mostly comfortable not thinking it was Caleb, just by your grandma's reaction. She seemed too happy to see him. Even if she couldn't remember that night, surely she'd know if she was supposed to be afraid of him."

Caleb studied me for a moment, probably mulling inside his brain about what he should tell me and what would be better left to my grandma.

Annoyed by his silence, I kept talking. "I mean, if this person, thing, or whatever killed my grandma, how do I know they're not after me, too? What if they come back to finish the job? Maybe they were trying to get rid of Seers, and, once they find out I am one too, they'll come for me? Surely you can't keep this information from me! Look at what happened last week. Mr. Tyler almost killed me and Gran. Do you want something like that to happen again?"

Caleb took a breath and his steady energy helped to ground me, sort of.

"Listen. I promise I'll always be there to protect you, even if you can't see or feel me around. Whatever happened to your grandma isn't going to happen to you because I killed the thing that attacked her. It's dead, like really dead, not like me or your ghost friend who keeps distracting you."

"He forgot to say handsome ghost friend, and oh, why didn't he tell us that from the start?" Brandon's voice rose as he talked. I had to admit, I agreed with him.

"Why didn't you just say that from the start? What kind of thing was it? Why did it attack her?"

Caleb chuckled, which I was able to both enjoy and get angry at, if that was even possible. His laugh rumbled deep in his chest and sent tickles through me.

"You still can't even say the word vampire yet, and you want to know more about the monsters out there? I'll tell you when you're a little more ready, when it's a little more important. Unless, of course, you're wanting to have nightmares as an excuse so I can cuddle into bed with you at night?" Caleb waggled his eyebrows.

"Ugh, I can't even with this guy." Brandon shook his head and rolled his eyes again.

I glared at Caleb, hoping my angry silence would make him uncomfortable enough to share his secrets.

It didn't.

"Alright, well. I think we've done what we came here to do. You now trust me fully and understand what I am, and we're all Gucci. You are going to be much smarter about who you hang out with and where you go, right?" Caleb stood as he spoke with a friendly tone that didn't cover up much of the bossiness.

It was my turn to roll my eyes. "Sure. Whatever you say."

"Wait, ask him about that house," Brandon said, bringing us back to what we had been doing earlier that morning.

"Oh, before you go." I stood as well because it felt weird to keep sitting while he was standing. "Do you know anything more about that house we were looking at? There were seriously a ton of ghosts out front."

Caleb's eyebrows scrunched as he thought. "Just because I'm old doesn't mean I know everything about everything."

"He does know something. I can tell from his face." Brandon gave me a flat look.

"But you do know some things."

Caleb chuckled. "It's true. I know a few things. I'm not one hundred percent sure, but I think that used to be an orphanage back in the day."

"A *murdering* orphanage?" Brandon opened his eyes wide and narrowed his lips in a scandalized look.

"Why would an orphanage have so many ghosts?" I mused, more for myself than the others.

Caleb shrugged. "Guess that's one for you to figure out. Well kids, it's been fun, but I've got to take my old-man nap and get out of this sun."

"I'm pretty sure that nap will be inside a dark coffin." Brandon nodded at me as if an expert.

"Probably," I said to the blue ghost wearing 90s clothes and then turned back to the tall, dark vampire. "Have fun sleeping in your coffin."

He grinned a predatory smile that put his canines on full display, and, while they weren't vampire length, they did look slightly larger than the average person's. Perhaps having proof that my grandma knew him, just as he looked now, should have been enough for me to fully believe and trust him, but my stubborn self wasn't totally buying it. I wasn't sure what would convince me completely, but I hoped it wouldn't come down to watching him turn into a bat or devour a bad guy using his sharp teeth.

Chapter 3

Trina confronted me the next day as I sat with blurry eyes in the kitchen, staring at a banana on the counter and wondering how many calories I should eat that day. She blew into the room with a flurry of energy that was uncalled for on what was supposed to be a relaxing Sunday morning.

After we'd talked yesterday, Caleb had spent the rest of the day hanging with Trina and her friends, or so I assumed since she wasn't home until late. Meanwhile, Brandon and I hung out, did homework, and talked about looking into helping another ghost.

Since it was still early, I hadn't bothered to contact Brandon or see if he'd come hang with me, yet. I needed a certain amount of wake-up time before I could be ready for his kind of energy.

"So, Caleb, eh?" She went to the fridge and pulled out the milk. "You guys best friends now or something?"

The bitter tone in her voice combined with the pointed look she gave me clued me in that it wasn't a good thing for us to be best friends.

"We're not best friends. Like he said, he was helping me with a French assignment." I tried to be soothing and lighthearted in hopes she wouldn't get offended or angrier at me.

She reached for a bowl and grabbed a box of cereal off the top of the fridge. "It's not like him to help with homework. I'm not even sure he gets above Cs, honestly."

"Huh, that's surprising."

"Why?" She tilted a manicured eyebrow at me as she poured milk into her cereal bowl.

I shrugged, trying to appear uncaring. "I don't know. He just seems more mature than other kids our age, and I figured that meant he'd be smarter, too."

Trina laughed. "Caleb? Mature?"

I mean, I couldn't tell her that he was at least old enough to have known Gran all those years ago, not to mention the real age he'd told me he was.

"Er, yeah, that's silly." I laughed, too. "I don't know where I got that."

As Trina put her spoon into the bowl, she paused and looked at me. "Listen, I just want you to be careful. Caleb has a reputation, and it's not a good one."

Boy, did I know that, but I appreciated her concern.

"I promise I'm not falling in love with him."

Relief passed over her face and into her tense shoulders.

"Wait... Trina, do *you* like him?"

A small smile peeked out of her lips, and she tried to cover it with a bite of cereal. "No, that would be stupid. So many other girls like him, he basically has his pick from any girl in school. There's no way he'd choose me over any of them, and now, apparently, you."

I chuckled at how far from the truth she was. "Oh, no. Not me. Nothing like that, I super promise you. He did tell me that he thought you were hot, though."

The blush on her cheeks confirmed my suspicions. "He did?"

"Yup." I left out the part where he had then gone on to say that hot and beautiful were two different things and that he thought I was beautiful. "Maybe he'll ask you to Homecoming."

I waggled my eyebrows at her, and she shook her head, laughing.

It probably wasn't a good idea to put suggestions out like that without knowing if there was any truth behind them at all, but it seemed like a fun thing to say at the time. Plus, it was a funny image of this old man vampire guy having to attend a high school dance with my gorgeous sister. Maybe I'd been hanging out with Brandon too much lately, but his voice popped into my head warning me about Caleb trying to gobble down all my sister's blood. Ugh, oops. Maybe I shouldn't have even suggested the idea.

Too late now.

"Do you think he'd do that?" She giggled again and then shook her head. "No. He hates going to dances. Even if he did go, he'd never ask me."

She picked up her bowl and moved over to the kitchen table, but I couldn't help but notice she still had that small smile on her lips.

I swiveled around in my stool to face her. "Hey, while we're talking... Are you going to go with Dad tonight?"

He'd sent us texts asking us if he could take us to dinner. It would be the first time either of us had seen him since he'd left without any kind of goodbye, and I wasn't sure how it made me feel. I mean, I knew I was angry, but, beyond that, I had too many swirling emotions. It had been easy to distract myself by dealing with ghosts and vampires, but I couldn't run from it forever.

Trina sighed and stirred her spoon around. "I don't know. I'm pretty mad, you know? What will we say to him that won't cause a scene in a restaurant? Plus, I kind of feel like he's trying to buy our love or something."

I nodded, having similar feelings. "But at the same time, he's got to know how we feel. He's got to know that what he did was wrong. Maybe he wants to apologize?"

"Since when do you remember Dad apologizing for anything?"

I frowned. "Never, but if he doesn't, we're probably going to hate him forever."

"I might hate him forever for what he did to Mom, apology or not," Trina muttered around the bite of cereal in her mouth.

"Me too."

Mom took that moment to whirl into the kitchen with the same energy that Trina had. Perhaps that was where she'd got it from. My mom was pretty and worked hard to keep up with her appearance. Trina and she both had shiny, long chestnut-brown hair, while I had inherited wavy blonde hair from my dad.

"Good morning, girls." Her eyes were puffy and red. It wasn't hard to see she'd probably cried herself to sleep.

Gran shuffled in after, her blue, transparent form looking rather, well, blue this morning.

"Hey, Mom. We were just talking about going to dinner with Dad today. Neither of us wants to, and we've decided we'll probably be mad at him forever," I said, trying to make her feel better, grasping at anything I could think of.

Apparently, that wasn't the right thing to say because she stopped working with the coffee maker and clutched at her chest. "Oh, no. Don't say that! He's still your dad and you can't hold that pain inside you. It'll only hurt yourselves."

Trina and I shared a glance.

"But it's not right what he did. Why should he get away with all of this while we have to play along and go to dinner with him while you are home alone crying and having to pick up the pieces?" I asked with a frown.

"Oh, sweetie." Mom wrapped her arms around my shoulders and rested her head onto mine. "Please don't think of it like that. He's not the only one to blame. Surely, I've had my part in this. Marriage is hard, and sometimes things just don't work out. Honestly, I'm not sure how to face all of it, but I do know that the choices we make now are important and we don't want to do anything we'll regret later. Your dad will always be your dad and he'll always be around."

Trina came over and wrapped her arms around Mom's shoulders, so we were all snuggled together. Her voice was muffled by Mom's sweater as she said, "We don't want you to be alone, though. We're also really mad at him."

"It's okay to be mad, but I still think you guys should go. I'll be fine. I promise."

I could still see Gran out of the corner of my eye, but she made no movements to come join our hug. It wasn't like we'd be able to feel her, anyway. Instead, a small smile spread over her lips, and I supposed that even though she knew we were all hurting, she was glad that we had each other to rely on.

We uncoiled from our group hug, and Mom gave each of us a faint smile. "We'll get through this. You'll see."

On my way to my room to get ready for the day, I munched on a banana and checked my phone. One banana was only around one hundred calories, so, if I ate it and something light at dinner with Dad, I would still fall in under the daily calories I was aiming for. No one had asked me to Homecoming yet, and, while the dance was already this next Saturday, there was still a chance someone would.

Coincidentally, the very person I wanted to ask me happened to text just as I hopped onto my bed.

Hey, are you busy today? I'm so sorry we haven't been able to talk much. My schedule is crazy! But I do have a few free hours this evening.

Warmth spread throughout my body as I read Noah's name and his message, but then I remembered I already had plans that night and my heart sank. Well, great. Here was another reason I didn't want to go with my dad.

Shoot. I wish I could hang out with you. I'd much rather do that than hang with my dad but it's the first time since... Well, let's just say my mom wants me to go and I probably should.

As I nervously waited for his response, I kept replaying my text in my head. Had it been too forward to tell him I wanted to hang out with him so badly? Should I have kept my cool more? Andrea would have known exactly what to say and how to say it, but when it came to boys I liked, I somehow always found myself guessing and floundering around with my words like a gaping-mouthed fish.

As I washed my face in the bathroom and ran a brush through my hair, knowing I'd better get my stuff done before Trina or else I'd never have a chance, I thought about how Brandon would have been making fun of me for feeling so anxious about texting Noah. He probably would make a joke about how Noah was just some dumb boy who was only thinking about one thing, and it was stupid to worry about what he thought.

The night before Brandon left, we hadn't made any plans to hang out today, so I was having a Brandon-free day. I'll be honest, it felt a little weird not to have someone to ignore all the time.

Then I realized how I was feeling about that and decided that missing Brandon was weirder. What was wrong with me? Just last week I'd been adamant about not even talking to ghosts, and now I was missing one.

My phone chirped and dislodged me from my thoughts. With slightly trembling fingers, I picked it up to read Noah's message.

I get it. It's okay. You really should hang out with your dad. I'm sure he misses you. I know I would. We'll find another time to talk. It's all good. Have fun with your family!

Smiling to myself, I sent a reply message, trying to be a cool person and not some clingy, love-crushed girl. **Sounds good. Thanks!**

Noah had said he'd miss me, and that thought placed a smile on my face for the rest of the afternoon as I got ready to go to dinner and did some homework, although I have to admit it was difficult to focus when all I wanted to think about was Noah's brilliant smile and toned shoulder muscles.

When Dad came to pick us up, he was actually three minutes early. As far as I could remember, Dad was rarely on time for stuff, certainly was never early.

Trina and I were sitting on the couch in the front room, and we raised our eyebrows at each other when we heard his car drive up outside.

"He's here, Mom!" I yelled down the hallway. "We'll be back soon. We love you!"

"Love you!" Trina hollered after me.

Mom peeked her head out of the bedroom door and put on a brave smile. "Love you! Have fun!"

"Yeah, right," I said, but probably more for her benefit than my own. I was sure it wasn't fun to watch your kids go off on a dinner date with someone who, until a week ago, had shared your bed.

We didn't wait for him to come to the door, although we probably should have made him feel the awkwardness of knocking on his own house's door just for punishment.

"Hey, girls," he said with a big smile as we met him halfway across the lawn.

"Hey, Dad." I don't know why I was feeling shy and uncomfortable, but I was. I mean, like Mom had said, he was still my dad.

He must have been feeling some of the same emotions because his shoulders were pulled back and tense. I could tell he'd worked hard to look decent for our date. He wore a polo shirt that was a bit wrinkly, probably from being stuffed in a suitcase all week, and his best pair of jeans. His wavy light hair had some product in it, and I couldn't remember the last time I'd seen him do that.

As for Trina and me, we wore just regular clothes we'd go to school in: holey jeans, nice shirts, decent hair, and makeup, and as always, Trina had that golden eye necklace she never took off for some reason.

We walked quietly towards the car, having too much and nothing to say all at once. The car ride to the restaurant was just as awkward. Trina spent most of it on her phone while I stared out the window and watched ghosts meander around the streets.

"So, how are things going?" Dad tried to start a conversation as he pulled out of our neighborhood.

Trina sat in front and gave him a meaningful look before going back to her phone. Feeling slightly bad for him, not a lot though but just a little, I sat up from where I was in the back seat.

"Besides the giant elephant in the car, so to speak, my week was pretty normal."

Okay, we all know that was a lie, but what was I going to say? My history teacher was really a werewolf, and since I had saved him from a curse and from a vampire who wanted to snap his neck, his pack owed me a life debt that I could use on myself or one of my loved ones? Or maybe I should have told him about the vampire who had saved me the night Gran died and who also happened to go to the same high school as I did and had befriended Trina with questionable motives?

"How was your week, Dad?" Trina said the last part with acidity in her voice.

It made me cringe, but again, he pretty much deserved it.

I was full of conflicting feelings, as was quite apparent by my paradoxical thoughts.

Dad sighed. "Honestly? It was terrible."

Trina scoffed and went back to her phone.

"What was worse? The guilt or the lumpy hotel mattress?" I asked, the memory of Mom's puffy red eyes in the forefront of my mind.

"Oh, girls. You can't know how sorry I am about this whole thing. Do you think I want to be a stranger to my own house? Do you think I want to hurt your mother? Do you really think I want to hurt you guys?"

I met his eyes in the rearview mirror for a second before he looked back to the road. There was enough pain there that I felt my heart melt a tiny bit. Perhaps it hadn't been so great for him either.

Neither of us answered his questions, letting the silence speak for our pain and conflicted feelings.

It was easier to ignore the awkward tension as we went through the routine of getting out of the car, entering the restaurant, being sat at a table, and ordering drinks from our server. Then the awkwardness was back.

"Are we allowed to talk about it?" I asked, looking over the top of the menu.

He'd chosen to take us to Trina's favorite Mexican restaurant, probably to try and butter her up some more. I had to admit, he had a lot of work cut out from him. She seemed to be taking the whole thing harder than I had, but that was probably only because I'd been so distracted by insane paranormal events swirling around me.

Dad put his menu down and gave me his full attention. "I'd like that. I want to know how you two feel and to answer any questions you might have."

Trina kept hiding behind the menu, but her fingers trembled, making the laminated paper waver. I wasn't sure if it was from holding back tears or holding back anger. Maybe both.

I decided it was better for all three of us if I spoke for the two of us. "We're angry and hurt, Dad. How could you do that to Mom? How could you do that to us?"

Dad took a deep breath to answer, but we were interrupted by a poorly-timed server who wanted to take our order.

We gave him our requested dishes and when Trina handed the menu away, I noticed tears had started pooling in her eyes, threatening to spill into her salsa bowl. I was so worried about her and the whole situation, I barely had time to think about the food I didn't want to eat. At least I'd had the presence of mind to order a salad, even if the shell around it was going to be fried tortilla and heavy on the calories.

Once the server had left, Dad took another deep breath and ran his hands over his bushy eyebrows. "I know that this might feel sudden to you girls, but the situation is complicated."

Trina rolled her eyes at his adult answer.

"We're not kids anymore, Dad," I interpreted for her.

"Look, I don't want to get into details that, from my side of the story, may put your mother in a... different light than you might currently see her in. In no way do I want to change your opinion of her, but I also want to tell you everything you want to know. I'm just not sure how to do both of those things."

"How about you just tell the truth?" Trina's voice wavered when she spoke, but at least the tears had started to dissipate.

"I will. I am! I'll always tell you girls the truth. I guess the heart of the matter is that your mother and I were not happy together anymore. As painful as it is to be apart, it was more painful to be together."

Trina huffed and shook her head.

"I don't think we believe you. It seems like you've underestimated how badly it hurts for our whole family to be broken up. How can you two living together hurt worse than that?" It was my turn for tears to prick my eyes.

Dad's eyes also got glossy. "That's why it took years for us to finally call it off. We stayed together for you girls, and I knew I had to stick around at least until you were both in high school."

"But you couldn't even last a week later than that?" I folded my arms across my chest and looked out over the other patrons in the dining room, hating all of the people who were laughing or seemed to be enjoying their dinner out.

"I–I...no, I couldn't. I'm so sorry." Dad looked down at his salsa cup, and I wondered if we were all going to be too distressed to even eat anything.

"Why did you guys always fight anyway? As far as I could tell, it was always over stupid stuff." Trina's eyes weren't shiny anymore, but there was still pain in them.

"There were a lot of stupid fights." I agreed with an eye roll but added a chuckle which seemed to lighten the mood slightly.

Dad looked conflicted, but a chuckle escaped his lips. "Yeah, there were a lot of stupid fights. I think we both learned things about each other and about ourselves that we need to work on. I should have listened to her more, but, by the time I figured that out, it was too late. The angry feelings of resentment ran too deep, on both sides."

Trina didn't crack a smile, but the fight in her seemed to have leaked out a little. "So, what are we going to do now?"

"I don't know. We'll figure it out. One day at a time."

Trina and I both scoffed at the expression we'd heard him say at least a million times, but we both knew that didn't make it any less true.

The waiter came and dropped off our food and somehow, we'd calmed down enough to at least try to eat dinner. My salad was huge, and I wondered how I was going to get by without eating very much but, at the same time, not make it obvious that I wasn't.

I happened to look up while taking a nibble of a chip with some salsa on it and saw Caleb walk through the front door of the restaurant. He pointed to our table while talking to the hostess who nodded and let him pass.

"What are you doing here?" I blurted out of my mouth before he made it to our table and before Trina, whose back was to the door, could see him.

Trina and Dad looked up from their food in surprise to see who I was so rudely talking to.

"Hello, Mr. Sanchez, I presume? Trina. Hanna."

I didn't know if Caleb needed to breathe or not, and that maybe he was just pretending for our sakes, but he seemed out of breath, for lack of a better way to describe him. His hair was disheveled on one side, his shirt looked dirty, and wait...

"Is that blood?" I asked, eyes wide as images of him massacring a bunch of innocent people flooded into my mind.

"Caleb?" Trina looked more surprised than I was, if that was possible.

"Oh," he grabbed at his shirt and looked down at the red smudges, "it's not mine."

"That's not what I was worried about!" I stood and gave him an alarmed, wide-eyed look.

"Right. Can we talk real quick?"

Trina stood up as well. "About what?"

"Oh, I'm sorry. I meant Hanna. It's er—about that French home-work. I think I might have given her the wrong answers." Caleb looked awkward instead of his usual smooth bravado, and for some reason, that made him more attractive, as if that's what I needed.

"Who is this? What's this about?" Dad stood as well, probably feeling like an odd man out sitting while the rest of us weren't.

I finally took pity on Caleb and decided it was best if we talked in private. "Oh, Dad, this is our friend from school. He's been helping me with French homework. Didn't you tell me your friend was prone to bloody noses?"

I asked the last part to Caleb who caught on and nodded. "Oh, yes. That's just what this is. I was trying to help him."

"So, we'll just go talk about the homework outside for a second. I'm sure I'll be right back," I said with the most reassuring smile and tone of voice I could muster.

I didn't give them any time to react as I steered Caleb out of the restaurant, past several patrons who gave us odd looks.

The cool air of an autumn evening greeted us as we walked out the doors, and it felt great on my skin which was warm from embarrass-ment and discomfort.

"Alright, what's the big deal? Why did you show up here looking like you've ransacked a village of innocent farmers and interrupt my already very awkward dinner with my dad whom I haven't seen all week?" I asked as we stepped to the side of the building, away from the door where people were going in and out.

Caleb, as if finally realizing he wasn't his usual put-together self, tried smoothing down his hair. "I'm really sorry to barge in here like this when you're with your family and everything, but I need your help."

"Help with what? I am *not* giving you a free meal." I gave him the strongest stare I had so he knew I was serious.

We might have been friends, but we were not that good of friends.

"What? Oh, no. You don't have to worry about that. I can take care of my own needs."

I glanced at the blood on his shirt. "I can see that."

He looked down at himself again and huffed. "I'm not that messy. Like I said, this isn't mine! I might have gotten into a bit of a scuffle, but that's not the point. The point is that I need your help with a ghost. Well, in the interest of keeping everything honest, my seethe needs your help."

"Seethe? What's a seethe?"

"It's kind of like a pack if we were werewolves or maybe like a big family if we were humans. There are two main seethes in our city. Most vampires belong to one or the other, except for a few loners, but they have to follow our rules while they're in town, or we'll run them out."

"Awesome. A vampire mafia. Just more fun things I needed to know."

"Oh, that's just the tip of the facts, darling." He flashed one of his canine smiles and my stomach tightened, but not from fear.

"Uh, okay. Anyways, what does your seethe need?"

"You see, there's this ghost."

I threw my hands up in frustration. "Of course, there is! Why can't I have one day to myself without any ghosts needing anything?!"

"Woah. Feeling a bit frustrated, are we?"

I sighed. "I'm sorry. Yes, but maybe it's not just from ghosts. My life is a crazy mess right now. Why do you need help with a ghost? Did you guys kill too many humans and now your house is terribly haunted, and you can't sell it and move to Transylvania where you belong?"

"Rude." He chuckled so I knew he wasn't mad. "No, but we do need to get some information from her. She was a human pet for one of the leading members of the other seethe in town, and we need to find out more information on him. We know where she is, finally, but we're having trouble talking to her."

"Wow, that's a lot to unpack there, but I think I'll start with–a human pet? That sounds terrible, and why don't you just have like a Seer or medium or someone on your payroll already? I'm guessing a seethe is pretty powerful."

He shrugged. "I can't explain all of vampire culture right now."

"Why not?"

"Well firstly, your dad is probably ready to come out here any second and beat me up, and secondly, I'm in a bit of a rush." He looked around the street as if looking for someone.

"Okay, just get on with it then." I waved my hand in the air vaguely for him to continue.

"Seers are very rare. There are probably maybe about five in total, worldwide. I keep trying to tell you this. So no, we don't have a Seer. The last one we knew of was your grandmother."

"Which is why you decided to enroll in high school and befriend my sister, isn't it? You were trying to find the next Seer. See? I'm not as dumb as I seem."

He smiled. "I never thought you were dumb. But yes, you're right. So, we need your help to talk to her, but there is one bigger problem."

"She doesn't want to talk to a vampire?"

"Well, I guess in a way, that's right. She's used up all her energy, and now she's just a raging ball of anger."

"You want me to talk to a poltergeist," I said this with a flat tone, trying to convey how crazy that was. Memories of the last one I'd seen came to mind, and I flinched thinking about all the books that could have hit me in the head while the ghost had made a roaring tornado of dangerous school supplies inside my history classroom.

"I wouldn't be asking you this if it weren't serious, if you weren't our only option, or if I had any other options."

He had regained some of his swagger during our conversation, but it was gone again, replaced with urgency, and if I didn't know better, I would guess, fear.

But what is a vampire afraid of?

Chapter 4

I fiddled with my hair for a moment as I thought. The last thing I wanted to do was get involved with vampires and human-pet ghosts. "I'll think about it, but you know you'll owe me a favor, right? Maybe even two."

"Name it. I'll be your slave."

I couldn't help but roll my eyes again. I seemed to be doing that a lot today. "I don't need a slave. What I need is information. There's this psychic lady I'm trying to find. I might have helped her banish a few ghosts last week. I've learned a few more things since then, so I'm thinking what I did was to help her curse—or maybe capture, not sure—the ghosts, and I need to make it right."

Caleb's eyebrows rose. "Wow. That's a bit much."

"You're telling me. I told you my life is a mess. There's just too much stuff going on, and now I need to help a vampire seethe with a poltergeist who will probably try to kill me."

"Right. Sorry."

"Can I have some time to think about it?"

"It's really not that kind of request. In fact—"

Our conversation was cut off by a newcomer.

"Hey, guys!"

We turned to see Noah jogging toward us through the parking lot.

"Oh, great." Caleb sighed and looked to the sky in frustration.

I, however, was pleasantly surprised to see him.

"Hey, Noah. What are you doing here?"

My crush of nearly two years glanced at the vampire I was standing next to and gave him such a disgusted expression, suddenly felt guilty for being caught with Caleb. Neither of them liked each other, but I still didn't have a clear reason why. It was obvious that Noah knew what Caleb was and that Caleb knew what Noah was, although I was still super fuzzy on the specifics.

"I'm just here to pick up a to-go order for my mom. What a coincidence that it's the same restaurant you guys are at! Wait, didn't you say you were busy having dinner with your dad? What's Caleb doing here?"

"I—" I began to explain but Caleb interrupted me.

"It doesn't matter what she's doing here with me. You're not her babysitter or her boyfriend or her owner or whatever you fancy yourself as. Now, we were just in the middle of an important conversation, and I need you to leave."

I scoffed and glared at Caleb. "Holy cow. Tone it down, will you?" Turning back to Noah, I tried to explain again. "My family is inside, and we were having dinner here when—"

Then Trina and my dad came outside the restaurant and headed in our direction. They had to-go boxes, so I assumed they'd finished up inside and had come out to find me.

"Hanna, what's going on? Is everything okay?" Dad asked as they approached.

Trina glared at me with intermittent glances in Caleb's direction.

I took a deep breath. "Yes, everything is fine. Dad, this is Noah from school, and you know Caleb. They're just my..." I glanced at Trina's icy glare, "I mean, *our* friends. And it was just a coincidence that we all showed up here at the same time. Guess this is a popular restaurant?" I chuckled, trying to ease the tension.

"Okay. Well, we got your leftovers. Are you ready to go?" Dad lifted the bag with the boxes in it to illustrate his point.

"Yup, I'll be right behind you guys." I gave them a reassuring smile.

"Hanna, please—" Caleb turned to me as they left.

I held my hand up, beyond annoyed with this vampire, even if he was as pretty as a Greek god. "I'll think about what you said and get back to you."

Noah smirked as if he had won something, but I didn't know what that could be since he had no idea what we had been talking about. Perhaps just the thought of Caleb not getting what he wanted right away made Noah happy.

"And Noah, I'll see you in class tomorrow, and just so you know, I expect you to clear a night in your schedule this week to explain all your weirdness that you've yet to get into. I'm pretty sure it's way past your turn."

And with that, I spun away, ignoring their protests.

Later that night, I sat in my bedroom, trying to decompress and let my brain catch up with everything that had happened within the last two days.

My life was a mess.

But all the supernatural stuff had gone to the backburner when we'd gotten home from our dinner to find Mom crying on the couch.

She had laughed it off, saying it was from watching a stupid romance movie and that she was glad we'd gone out with Dad and spent some time with him. Judging from the empty ice cream tub sitting on the coffee table, I had my doubts.

We'd spent the rest of the evening sitting with her on the couch, just being there for her and watching movies. Gran sat in the armchair while we comforted Mom, and I could see she was relieved that we were there for her. Trina hadn't said a word to me the whole time.

I'd gotten ready for bed and was scrolling through my phone to see what normal life things my friends were up to when a soft knock sounded on my door.

"Hanna, can we talk?" Trina's muffled voice came from the other side.

"Sure. Come in." Nerves fluttered through me at the impending confrontation, but I took a deep breath knowing that it was important to talk about things, even if they made me uncomfortable.

She opened the door, wearing pajamas. I'm pretty sure she was the only person I knew who had to have matching PJs. Well, except maybe Andrea. I could see her wearing the same kind of top and bottom sets that my sister wore.

"What's up?" I scooted back on my bed and crossed my legs so she had room to sit.

"I have some feelings I need to get out. I've tried to talk myself out of them and tell myself that I'm being stupid, but I can't help it."

For the second time that night, I saw a few tears prickle Trina's eyes. My heart went out to her, and I realized that maybe I wasn't the only one having a hard time.

"Your feelings aren't stupid. There is probably a reason you're feel-ing them," I said gently. "What's going on?"

"I just...It's about Caleb," and then she launched into a jumbled mess of words that took me a second to figure out. "I know you two are just friends and there's nothing between you because that's what you guys have said over and over, and I want to believe you. I mean, I have no reason *not* to believe you, you know? It's just that, when I see you two together, it looks like you're so comfortable with each other, and I get this feeling that you guys already know more about each other than Caleb and I do, and it's so frustrating because I've been trying to figure out his secrets for like two years, and then you get to school and you barely know each other a week, and he's showing up all messed up and asks to talk to you, and it's just so *frustrating*, you know?"

I blinked for a few seconds as my brain caught up to her quick words. "Wow, I had no idea you felt this way. You always make fun of girls who like Caleb, but it kind of sounds like you like him yourself."

I was hesitant to say those words outright, but she must have been dying to talk to someone about it for a while because she didn't freak out.

"Oh, yes." She sighed as if letting go of some old air that had been sitting inside her lungs for a while. "I tried hard not to."

I smiled. "You get credit for trying. Sometimes it's hard to ignore what your heart is saying, or sometimes screaming, as the case may be."

As I said the words, I realized I might know more about that situ-ation than I had two weeks ago. It was hard not to like someone when your heart wanted to, even if that someone was dead. Or undead.

Did Trina know he was a vampire? It didn't seem likely, but was it my duty to tell her, as her sister? Dating a vampire was like a big deal and probably super dangerous and well...What exactly was I supposed to say to still be considered a good sister but not a crazy one?

"Don't I know it. It's not fun to like a guy that everyone else likes, and who, apparently, doesn't even think of me as an option to like back. He's always super nice and flirty with me, but I get the feeling that doesn't mean much."

From what I knew of him, I had to agree, but saying that probably wouldn't make her feel better.

"Have you asked him how he feels?"

She laughed. "Of course not! I barely know how I feel! Just seeing you with him recently has started to churn up feelings I've been trying to keep tucked inside so they'll go away."

"Right. Maybe that's what you should do?"

She fiddled with her fingers in her lap as she shook her head. "No, I don't think that's a good idea. He would only try to let me down easy, and it would ruin our friendship. We wouldn't get to hang out anymore, and then it would be sad."

"Sadder than feeling lost like this and hopeless as he flirts with other girls?" I drew my eyebrows together in empathy knowing exactly how she felt.

It was hard to watch Noah and Andrea together, and I had to see that nearly every day. Perhaps I should have taken my own advice and asked Noah if he liked me, but that seemed stupid after seeing him with Andrea.

I didn't need an answer to that question because I already knew it.

Trina sighed and shrugged.

Then I said something I probably shouldn't have, but I was trying to make her feel better and grabbing at anything I could think of. "Oh, hey, he actually asked me for a favor so he's going to owe me one back. Do you want me to ask him to take you to homecoming? At least you can pretend for one night that everything is all sparkles and rainbows in love?"

She furrowed her brows, and her blue eyes focused intently on my face. "What kind of favor did he ask you to do?"

Oops.

"Uh—I, er...well, it's not sexual or whatever if that's what you're asking!" I held my hands up to wave the situation away. "It's just something his family needs me to do for some history information they need, and since I'm good with history and research and have a good relationship with my history teacher and all that, he thought I might be a good person to ask."

The lies intertwined with the truth in weird little circles, but I was doing my best under the circumstances. I hadn't been prepared for this conversation.

Confusion and maybe even some kind of pain crossed over her near-perfect features. "His favor is about homework?"

I had a feeling she wasn't quite believing me.

"Look. It's really nothing. I totally promise! Please just move on from that and not worry about it. What you should think about is that I can get Caleb to ask you to the dance! Don't you think that would be fun?"

And maybe he'd be able to show her a bad time without like eating her or whatever. He could be a terrible date, and then she'd be sad for a moment, but then get over him and go find a guy for herself that was actually alive.

That was turning into my tentative plan anyway.

She sighed and picked at a fingernail. "I don't know. I don't think I want our first date to be because my sister had to bargain with the guy I like to go out with me. It just doesn't feel that great, you know?"

She stood and her expression made me feel sad. "I'm going to try and get over him. You two really seem to get along though, so don't let me stand in the way of whatever you guys have got going on."

She left my room before I could respond, mostly because I had no idea how to.

Chapter 5

After I finally turned out the lights, put my phone to charge, and laid my head on my pillow, the tears finally started to flow. There were people out there with way worse problems than I had, but that didn't mean I didn't deserve to cry into my pillow when no one was around.

The worst pain came from seeing my broken family try to pick up the pieces and reassemble ourselves into something that could cope and move on from the whole debacle. It was hard to see my mom in pain but almost worse to imagine her going out on dates and having to meet strange men, wondering which one of them would become my new dad.

I closed my eyes for a moment to squeeze out some of the tears, hoping I could just get rid of the moisture that blurred my vision, and then I'd be done with it. Instead, I felt a prickle on the back of my neck and a brush of cold fingers on my cheek.

I didn't need to open my eyes to know Brandon would be there, breaking my number one rule by laying down next to me and using my own energy to materialize his fingers enough so he could touch my face, but I did, just to make sure it wasn't some other creepy ghost.

"Hey," he said softly when he saw my eyes glittering in the dark.

For some dumb reason, his appearance didn't reassure me or cheer me up. Rather, it had the opposite effect and emotion welled up inside of my chest and bubbled out of my eyes until I was crying so hard, I had to stifle a sob.

He cursed. "What? What did I do? Are you mad that I'm in your room?"

Probably without realizing it, he pulled more energy and pressed his palm against my cheek. He used his thumb to wipe away the tears, and we were both amazed to see that it worked.

A chuckle burst through my tears that kept flowing. "No. I mean, yes. You are breaking a serious boundary here, but no, that's not why I'm crying."

I'm not proud to say that as I spoke, my voice broke a few times. It's hard to talk and cry at the same time.

"Then why are you crying?"

I looked at his charming face with those soulful eyes, swooping nose, and the kissable lips that I knew could reveal a smile that would always brighten my day, and I felt sadness wash all over me again.

"Just lots of things. Aren't you sad that you died? What kind of wonderful life you could have had? What kind of pain did your family go through after you were gone? How did you exist for thirty years alone with only random skater kids to talk to who couldn't hear you or talk back? Your pain must be bigger than mine, and here I am, blubbering into my pillow."

Warmth filled his eyes and as his body became slightly more corporeal, I could see from the dim light coming through the window that his eye color was a cool green. For the first time in my life, I felt special, grateful that my powers allowed me to see him, and allowed him to get some of his physical body back, even only for a moment. And as selfish as it was, I didn't have to share him with anyone.

"If you're so sad, then why are you smiling?" A hint of a grin perked up the side of his mouth, and it made me want to see all of it.

"Did you know your eyes are green?"

He blinked twice and then chuckled. "That is not what I thought you were going to say. I mean, I guess I knew that, but it's been a few years since I've seen them or thought about it."

"Guess that makes sense." Surprised by my bravery, I pulled my hand out from under the blanket and gently touched his cheek with my fingers. "Can you feel that?" I said in a whisper.

"Yes." He took a deep breath and closed his eyes, barely leaning into my touch. When they opened again, I saw longing and fear in his gaze. "It feels really good."

"We shouldn't make a habit of this." I frowned, trying to draw myself down to reality. "It can't be healthy."

I started to withdraw my fingers, but Brandon used his hand that had been touching my face to grab my wrist and press down gently so I was cupping his cheek. I was surprised to feel some stubble there, and I might have giggled a little as I ran my thumb over the stiff hairs.

"Not bad for not being able to shave for thirty years," he said with a grin.

Smiling at the sensation of being able to see and feel my favorite charming smile, I finally noticed that my tears had mostly dried up. In his own way, Brandon had totally made me feel better.

"How did you die?" I whispered, still exploring the side of his face and the bottom of his ear with soft fingers.

His blinks were long and slow in a way that showed he was relishing my touch.

I had hoped that the physical sensation would distract him enough to answer the question that had been bugging me for two weeks.

It almost worked.

"If I tell you one thing about my death, will you promise to drop the subject?"

"For forever?"

He opened his eyes and nodded. "Talking about it will just ruin everything."

"Why?"

"Because it will." He released my hand, and I pulled it back.

The blue of his ghost-self slowly crept in as he stopped taking energy from me, and his body went back to being transparent. I was so sad to see the color leech out of his eyes that it kind of felt like I was watching him die all over again.

"Are you worried I won't want to hang out with you anymore if you tell me about your death?"

He sighed and rolled over so he was staring at the ceiling. "Something like that. Some things are too hard to talk about. I was sad enough in life, so, now that I'm dead, I want things to be lighthearted and fun."

I kept staring at his face, pulling my eyes down the slant of his nose, memorizing the way his lips moved as he talked, and noting the curve of his eyebrows as they expressed themselves.

"Then hanging out with me is probably not your best bet. My life is pretty much anything other than lighthearted and fun. How did you know to come here right now? Did you know I was sad or were you just popping in to be a pervy teenage boy?"

He grinned and rolled back over to face me. "I mean, I'd missed you all day, but pretend I didn't say that."

I smirked. "Okay."

"But it sounds stupid out loud, and it's hard to explain. Let's just say something felt off. I could feel that something was wrong with you, and I wanted to come and find out what it was, even if I had to face your wrath for appearing inside your bedroom uninvited."

"So, I guess I'm not the only one with powers." I raised my eyebrows in surprised appreciation.

"Maybe it's something ghosts around you can do?"

I shrugged one shoulder. "Maybe."

"You look like you feel better now."

"I suppose. Your big head is just too distracting to focus on anything else."

"I'm glad I could be of service."

Silence fell between us for a few seconds. I debated on whether or not to kick him out of my room, just to keep up with the rules and all, but I kept putting it off, enjoying the company and knowing he did too.

We stared at each other in the dark but we didn't touch. The power he was taking from me to manifest his body could have been dangerous. We knew so little about it. It was probably a good idea not to abuse it until we knew more.

"Listen, I've been thinking."

"Oh, here we go." I chuckled. "Let's hear one of your crazy ideas."

"How rude. It's not crazy. I just think we should try and do what your grandma says a Seer's job is and try and help a ghost."

Caleb's poltergeist situation popped into my head, but I wasn't quite ready to tell Brandon about it, knowing how angry he'd get that I was actually going to say yes to the vampire, even if it was for Trina's sake.

"Don't you think we should try and hunt down Rose first so that maybe we can learn how to set all those ghosts that I helped her capture free? *If* that's still possible, that is."

Guilt washed over me as I thought about her and what we had done. Since she had disappeared, it would have been easy to forget about the whole thing and move on with the other craziness going on, but the guilt wouldn't let me forget. The accusing eyes of the ghost boy from the 70s as he slid into her capture circle wouldn't let me forget either.

"Yes, definitely, and we will and are, but maybe it would be good just to start easy and practice learning how to help a ghost with its unfinished business in the meantime?"

"I guess. If we promise to start light. Don't even think of suggesting going back to that house that's so haunted I couldn't see the building through the ghosts."

He smiled. "Of course not. We'll start light. I'll even let you pick the ghost."

"How kind of you."

"I am the kindest."

I scoffed but still wore a smile. "Alright. I'll think about it."

"Cool. You probably need to get to sleep now, though, but do you mind having company on your walk to school tomorrow?"

"I suppose I wouldn't mind."

"How kind of you."

Chapter 6

The next morning, Gran met me in the kitchen as I grabbed a bottle of diet soda from the fridge. I'd asked Mom to start stocking the drink so I could use the energy without having to get the calories. I could feel the difference in my body when I had soda in me, and the diet part meant there were no calories. I had planned to allow myself around seven hundred calories a day, which was a good limiting number and should help me lose the fat around my thighs and butt. I was hoping that with good behavior, I'd be looking perfect for the dance this upcoming weekend.

Even if I still didn't have a date.

"How is Mom holding up?" I asked Gran as I caught her blue movement out of the corner of my eye.

"She's still sad, as anyone would be, but trying to do her best for you girls. I can see she's trying to focus on you two instead of her sadness. She does cry a lot while she's alone, though. She should probably start getting busy with other stuff instead of wallowing, but she won't listen to me."

We shared a knowing smile.

"I'm sure she'll rally in time, probably. Is there anything you think I should do for her?"

Gran shrugged. "The extra love you and Trina are giving her seems to help some, but all of this might be a thing she needs to figure out for herself. How are you doing with everything? I didn't see your ghost boyfriend at all yesterday. How did you manage to keep him away for a whole day?"

I chuckled and made sure to keep talking quietly so Mom or Trina wouldn't hear me from down the hallway where they were both getting ready. "I'm fine as can be expected. We aren't together every day."

Gran gave me a look.

"What can I say? He doesn't have anyone to talk to." I shrugged. "What should I do? He's quite the persistent one."

"Plus, you like him."

"I like him as a friend, yes. He's smart and funny, and he's nice to me which is more than I can say for most of my friends at school."

"Sounds like you need new friends."

"That may be true."

"So, have you started to work on what his unfinished business is? That is your job, you know."

"Funny that you would mention that. I've decided I'm going to try and help a ghost, like the right way and everything. I might need your help to figure out what to do, depending on the ghost's story and stuff. Do you have any suggestions about who I should start with?"

"You mean besides that ghost who follows you around all the time?"

I chuckled and took a swig of the soda. "Yes, besides that ghost."

"The best advice I can give you is to find one who seems mild-mannered. If you can find one that has died recently and has more of its memories fresh, that could help you figure out the issue quicker too."

I heard shuffling down the hallway and figured Mom was making her way to the kitchen. I whispered a "thank you" to Gran and went back to drinking my soda as innocently as possible, as if I hadn't been talking to an invisible being for the last few minutes.

It was definitely a Monday at school as the classes seemed to drag on. My brain was so slow to focus on school stuff that I felt like I had to give it CPR a few times to get in gear. P.E. was the same jog around the gym while I got to know Addy and Emma more.

History class was livelier and more fun than the other classes as we engaged in a heated debate about current events in the news. Mr. Tyler kept working like a totally normal teacher instead of a previously cursed werewolf teacher, however that kind of being would act. As I watched him challenge someone's point of view in a constructive way, I never would have imagined he had tried to suck all my ghost power energies away last weekend, thus almost killing me.

Time was funny like that.

Lunch finally arrived, and I met my friends at our usual table. I'd stopped to buy another bottle of soda and a banana, like I'd promised myself I could eat. Already the soda was helping me focus and operate better than I had without it.

"Hey, guys," I greeted as I sat next to Stephanie who had cleared a space for me. We were across the table from Andrea, Noah, and Randi. "Everyone have a good weekend?"

"Not as good as yours, apparently," Andrea said with a haughty smirk.

"What?" My mind went to the secret moment with Brandon from the night before, but there was no way she could have known about that.

"Noah told me all about your date with Caleb." Andrea glanced at Noah who looked slightly uncomfortable.

"Uh, okay." I gave Noah a look.

His soft brown eyes gave me a challenging stare back that seemed to say he wasn't too sorry for telling her, and that I deserved what scrutiny I got from hanging out with a guy like that.

"He said Caleb looked kind of beat up or something. What kind of kinky stuff are you all into?"

I laughed, not to be rude, but because it was so absurd. "Caleb and I are not into anything."

Noah gave me that look again.

"Well, not anything romantic or whatever. We're just friends. He asked me for some help with some research for his family history. It's not a big deal."

Andrea raised her sculpted eyebrow. "Sure. Whatever you say. It seems weird that he'd be into you anyway. I mean, he's got your sister, and she's a much more viable option for dating."

She must have noticed some of the hurt that crossed over my face at her words, because she added, "But that's just because she's older and stuff is all that I meant."

"Right," I said, trying to pretend I was unfazed by her words. "Anyway, we're just friends. Anyone go shopping for homecoming dresses yet?"

We hadn't talked much about the dance in the last week, or at least they hadn't talked about it while I was around. I didn't even know who had dates and with whom they were with. It was my (kind of) sneaky way of trying to find out if Andrea and Noah were officially going together. I probably should have assumed and forgotten about it, but the way Noah had been acting towards me, like he almost cared about who I dated, had me somewhat confused.

"Oh, I got mine ages ago." Andrea flung her hand into the air flippantly. "My mom took me downtown to Lola's Boutique, and we picked out the perfect dress. Stephanie, didn't you get yours from there too?"

"Yes. I love their dresses! Although mine isn't nearly as beautiful as yours is." The blonde cheerleader pouted her lip-glossed mouth. "I swear that color looks perfect on you."

Andrea smiled. "It really does."

"I'm going to wear a suit," Randi said, not surprising me. She liked to wear mostly men's clothes anyway. "It's a vintage powder-blue suit my grandpa wore in the 70s. It's like super gorgeous."

"Do you have a date, Randi?" I asked, trying to get closer to the real question I wanted to ask.

"No." She shrugged. "But it's fine. We're all going as a group, anyway, right?" She looked at Andrea for confirmation.

This was the first time I was hearing of this. Had they decided to go as a group but not tell me? I would have been hurt but not surprised.

"Actually, Noah and I are going together. We can go as a group to other dances. Homecoming is too important for that." Andrea fiddled with the ends of her expensively bought blonde hair as she scrolled through her phone, seemingly unaware of the effect her words had on Randi.

Or on me.

I knew I was being dumb. Of course they were going together. I had so much as expected it, but somewhere inside my naive little heart, I had held out a secret hope. Hope is stupid sometimes because it sets you up for disappointment and disappointment is *the worst*.

Randi's eyebrows scrunched in a sad confusion, and she looked down at her tray of food. "Oh, then I guess I've got a week to find a date."

"That'll be easy," Stephanie spoke up. "I'll help you."

Randi didn't look like she was as confident as Stephanie.

Noah watched my face as Andrea had spoken and kept staring at me as if he could read my thoughts.

I must have looked at least somewhat upset because he said, "Yeah, we're going to the dance together, but we can still all hang out. It's not like we're stuck with only one person the whole night."

"Right." I tried to cover my disappointment by popping the peel of my banana and taking a bite. I didn't really feel like eating, but my stomach was angry, and my arms felt weak.

"Besides, who knows? Maybe Caleb is planning on asking you out." Noah's smile was teasing, but there was a bitter undercurrent to his words.

"Yes, because I'm sure Caleb's *type* of people never miss a high school dance." I emphasized "type" so he knew exactly what I was talking about—vampires, I was talking about vampires.

I was getting a little more used to that word, though I still thought it was super weird and wondered where he got his blood.

It better not be from my sister.

Noah chuckled. "Yes, that might be true."

"I doubt he'd want to dance with any sophomores when there are so many cute senior girls." Andrea pulled out our math homework from Friday and gave me a look.

"But you would totally dance with him if he asked you." Stephanie smiled knowingly.

I pulled out my own math homework and handed it to Andrea without a word. I had figured she would want to check my answers again, so to speak—I guess we can call it what it is by now. She just wanted to get my answers so she didn't have to work, and I had brought the paper to lunch, even though I didn't need it until the last period of the day.

Andrea shrugged, but a small smile pulled at her lips. "Maybe."

Noah gave her a side-eyed look. "Too bad you'll be busy dancing with me and won't have time for that creep."

She started writing answers down on her paper that had been completely blank, which I happened to notice. "Maybe."

Noah frowned and stared at his fruit cup.

I suppressed an amused smile and turned to Stephanie. "Who are you going with?"

"Alex, of course." She smiled and had the dreamy look in her eyes that she always had when talking about her boyfriend.

"Of course." Randi rolled her eyes.

We chit-chatted throughout the rest of lunch. A lot of the conversation was Stephanie trying to get Randi to say who she wanted to go to the dance with, but Randi either didn't know or wasn't about to talk about it in front of all of us.

The disappointment from finding out Noah was going with Andrea settled down inside as I went through the rest of my classes. I kept trying to talk myself out of it because I really shouldn't have been surprised at all, but all my efforts only eased the sting a little.

It was time to face the reality that I might be staying home on the night of my first high school dance, without a date, probably shoving ice cream into my face on the couch with my mom while watching Lifetime movies.

Ugh. Maybe I could find a date on my own. Too bad Brandon was invisible... and dead.

As I stood at my locker at the end of the day, sorting through whatever supplies I needed for my homework. I was wondering if I should go find Caleb and agree to help out his seethe—but only because I wanted to help out Trina and get some possible answers about Rose—Emma from P.E. approached me.

"Hi, Hanna," she said and leaned against the locker next to mine.

"Oh, hi!" I might have been a touch enthusiastic with my greeting, so I reminded myself to chill out. It was just that I hadn't made any new friends for a while...oh, I take that back. I hadn't made any *alive* friends for a while, and I didn't want to mess it up.

Her brown hair was pulled up into a messy bun, and her eyes looked tired. As I thought about it, she had dragged a bit that day in P.E., but maybe she'd had a crazy weekend.

She looked around the hall as students milled about chatting with each other or slamming their locker doors or hurrying off to catch a bus. "I was wondering if we could talk."

"Okay. What do you want to talk about?" I shoved my stuff into my bag and shut the locker, giving her my full attention.

Emma chewed on her lip and glanced around us again. I was beginning to think she didn't want to be seen with me, but she leaned in a little closer and spoke quietly. "I'm not sure how to say this, but I've heard some rumors about you and was hoping that maybe, possibly, you could help me?"

I furrowed my brows, creating a line that was sure to wrinkle if I kept making that face. "Rumors? What kinds of rumors?"

She looked even more uncomfortable—if that was possible. Shifting her feet and glancing around the hallway, which was quickly emptying out, she said, "Uhm, I don't really want to make you mad or hurt your feelings or anything, and I wouldn't be asking you this if I knew what else to do. I don't know who else to turn to. You've been so nice to me in P.E., and I just figured it wouldn't hurt to ask, you know?"

As she spoke, her face became more pinched, and I could have sworn a few pieces of her hair popped out from her messy bun. "What are you talking about? Are you okay, Emma?"

She took a deep breath. "Okay, let's just say people are talking about you, and that you have some kind of dark side with spirits."

It was my turn to take a breath. "Say what? What exactly are those rumors? Who started them? Why would they?"

If Noah or Caleb had shared my secrets with anyone, I was going to beat them up, despite their questionable supernatural skills. How could they do such a thing? And why? If I had to guess, I would pick Noah, just because Caleb always seemed so worried my secret would get out, but it was hard for me to believe Noah would do that either. Was it possible it was neither of them?

Emma shrugged. "I don't know. Like I said, I would totally ignore them and not ask you about it or anything, except I'm hoping they *are* true and that you can help me."

I pushed the frustrating thoughts of the rumors out of my mind for a second and focused on my new friend. "Wait. You really do look upset. How do you think I can help you?"

She leaned in even closer, and I could see the warm brown swirls inside her dark green eyes. "Do you believe in ghosts?"

I laughed. I know I shouldn't have, but the sound just escaped through my lips.

She winced. "I knew I shouldn't have said anything. I'm so sorry!"

I grabbed her arm as she turned away. "Wait! Emma, it's okay. I'm sorry I laughed. It's just that," I glanced around to make sure no one was nearby listening, "my life is so full of ghosts, that it was funny to think of not believing in them."

Her eyes went wide. "Full of ghosts?"

"It's a long story. Do you have one troubling you?"

And that's how I ended up at Emma's house.

Trepidation crept up my spine as I rode in her car, an older Jeep that thankfully had its doors on or else I would have been chilled, and we turned down her street. It just happened to be the same road I had walked down with Brandon on Saturday—the same road with the *very* haunted house.

As Emma slowed the Jeep to a stop, my heart sank even more. Her house was literally next door to the ghost house.

No wonder she had ghost issues.

My heart hammered in my chest as I eased the door open and made certain I did not look at any of the ghosts in the yard nearby. I couldn't focus on them enough to count, but there was a mass of blue, transparent bodies in my peripheral vision. If there were so many outside, how many were on the inside? The thought made me shiver.

Emma's house looked totally normal, thank goodness. It was odd to see the contrast of the run-down place next to it. The shiny metal roof looked new, the yard was well-kept with autumn-colored flowers in pots on the porch, and a freshly painted porch swing swayed slowly in the cool breeze.

"Here we are," Emma said as we walked down the walkway towards her door. "No one is home right now so we don't have to be too quiet hunting the ghost or whatever it is you do. And you're sure you don't need to get any supplies or anything?"

"Nope. As far as I can tell, it doesn't really work like that."

"What do you mean? Don't you do weird seances and stuff all the time?" She unlocked the door with a key from her keychain, and we went into the dimness of her house.

"Uh, not really. Seriously, what kind of rumors did you hear?"

I followed her through the house and couldn't help but notice she flipped on every light that she could even though it was still early afternoon with the sun still slanting in through the western windows.

"I'm sorry. I don't like to spread gossip or whatever, but the word going around is that you've got some creepy occult thing going on. You love Ouija boards and seances. Some say that maybe you're even a witch."

I laughed again. The whole idea was just too absurd, ignoring, of course, that the truth of it struck too close to home. "What? I don't even wear black that much or dye my hair or whatever else usually means people are dark and stuff. How could people believe that nonsense?"

She shrugged and gestured to the couch. "You can put your stuff there. We're going to my room that just happens to be right underneath the attic."

Her wide eyes and trembling hands told me what she thought was in the attic. I had to admit, I wasn't feeling much braver myself. If this ghost had been loud enough that Emma knew about it, then it probably wasn't a kind, mild-mannered ghost who only needed a small conversation before feeling satisfied that its unfinished business was complete.

But this is what Grandma had been trying to prepare me for. As a Seer, I needed to help the ghosts that I could, so I had to start somewhere.

After putting my school bag on the couch, I followed Emma up the stairs, down the hallway, and into her room. Just before her bedroom door, the hatch for the attic loomed over our heads. I gave it a meaningful glare, trying to prepare myself for probably having to climb up in a minute.

"Please don't take offense at this, but I'm thinking people might believe some of the rumors because sometimes you seem a little spaced out. Like you're looking into another world?" Emma's face scrunched in an apologetic expression as she sat on the edge of her bed.

"Oh." I stood in the doorway of her room and looked around, unsure of what to say.

Honestly, it hurt to hear about these rumors. They were exaggerated, of course, but based on a truth that I had worked desperately hard to keep hidden.

Apparently the few people I thought I could trust, I couldn't.

"I guess it's pretty obvious that I'm a little different, at least," I finally said, noting that, as far as I could see at the moment, there weren't any ghosts inside the room.

Emma gestured to a cozy armchair that sat by her window. "You can sit for a minute. Don't you want to hear why I think I'm haunted?"

Her eyes did indeed look haunted and tired. She was right. I was here to help her, no matter what rumors went around at school. Maybe I could use them to do some good. Without the rumors, she wouldn't have known who to ask about her ghost problem.

"Right. I'm sorry." I sat on the edge of the bright pink cushion and gave her my full attention. "What's been going on?"

Emma took a deep breath. "I hope you don't think I'm too crazy, but I'm pretty sure there is a ghost in the attic above my room. For the past few months, I've been hearing crying. Not like boo-hoo, woe-is-me crying, but like absolutely heartbroken wails. They last almost all night, like, every night. At first, I was scared. I'd never heard anything like that, and then I went to check on my parents to make sure they weren't crying or that it wasn't my baby brother, but they were all sleeping soundly. Then, after a few days, I grew less scared and more sad. Whoever is up there is really upset. Now, I'm just angry. I'm *so* tired. I've gotten to the point where I can sleep through some of it, but it's really messing with my sleep. I can't fully relax, and it's driving me crazy!"

During the last bit of her story, her eyes were wide, and she flexed her fingers like claws to demonstrate her anger.

"I get it. I'd be angry too if something was intruding into my room and making me lose sleep."

Unless it happened to be a cute boy who died thirty years ago.

"So, you decided it might be a ghost because no one else was making that sound? Why do you think your family can't hear it?"

Emma chewed her lip in thought for a second. "Well, no one in my family is crying like that. During the day one time, I got brave enough to go into the attic and check to make sure there wasn't some homeless person up there squatting or something, but it was empty. And my room is the only one on this floor, right below the attic. My parents and brother sleep downstairs. One night, when the wailing was particularly loud, my mom came to check on me, but I pretended I was asleep. The moment my mom's foot hit the stairs to come up, the ghost quieted as if it was just trying to keep only me awake. That's when I got really angry."

I chuckled, trying to ease some of her tension. "That is annoying. Have you heard anything other than crying? Thumps? Like it's moving stuff around? Or has it tried to talk to you or anything?"

She shook her head.

"Hmm...I'll be honest here. There aren't many people that can hear or see ghosts. I'm impressed that you can hear it, but I'm also worried that it's using its soul energy to project its crying. The more energy a ghost uses, the less they are aware of themselves and can't remember who they were before they died. Usually, ghosts get angry, throw things, and can be pretty dangerous, but your ghost sounds like it's just really sad."

"The only time I've heard anyone wail like that was when Mandy down the street fell off her bike and broke her arm." Emma shivered at the memory. "That was intense."

"I'm sure. Have you ever seen anything? Like something floating? Or even maybe like their blue, transparent head poking down through the ceiling?"

We both looked up towards the ceiling as we spoke, just in case.

"No. Just the wailing. That's enough."

"I bet. Well," I stood up, "I think the only thing I can do next is to get up into that attic."

Emma stood as well and started to leave her room but stopped before she crossed the doorway. She turned around and smiled at me. "Listen. Even if you can't help or anything, or this is all just in my head or something, I'm grateful that you even believe me. It's nice to have someone listen to me and not think I'm crazy, even if I am."

I smiled back. "You're not crazy. In fact, if you're crazy, then I'm certifiable."

We shared a giggle and then she turned away, stepped into the hallway, and grabbed a nearby step stool. She carefully lined it up with the attic hatch and climbed. As she pulled on the cord, the door opened, and old wooden stairs clattered into formation.

If Emma hadn't been there and seemed so worked up about this ghost, there was no way I would have gone into that attic. If it were me, I would have bought myself a nice pair of earbuds and played loud music so that I could have slept, letting that ghost wail itself into oblivion, but I couldn't leave Emma to suffer. Plus, I had agreed with Brandon to try and start helping ghosts. This one seemed as good a place to start as any.

I stepped on the first stair towards the attic and turned to Emma who stood on the side. "I just had a thought. Have you tried earbuds with loud music?"

Her mouth tilted up on one side. "You're not scared, are you? Trying to get out of this by hoping I'll be fine with earbuds?"

"Of course not." I gulped.

"I did try that. It didn't help. I can't sleep with music and mostly I need total quiet. Believe me, I wish it had worked."

I nodded and ascended another step. The wood creaked underneath my sneaker, but it seemed sturdy enough. "Oh, I believe you. Guess there's nothing for it. You stay here so I can see if the ghost will talk to me. If you hear me screaming, I won't blame you if you close up the door and leave me to my death."

We laughed again together.

"Oh, don't worry. I wouldn't let that happen. I'd come up there to try and help and at least we'd die together."

I smiled, taking a second to enjoy friendly banter with a girl that didn't involve snide remarks that somehow always ended up putting me down, unlike some friends I knew.

"Alright. Let's go bust a ghost."

"You got this!" Emma pinched her fingers and waved her hands like she was holding invisible pompoms.

The wood creaked the whole way up the stairs, surely announcing my presence to anyone who was in the attic. When I got eye-level with the floor, I paused and peeked into the room to look around. It was the basic attic situation that most people had—boxes piled up in heaps over the dusty wooden floor, a few chairs stacked in a corner, and an old sewing machine leaned against more boxes. The only light came from a circular window nestled near the peak of the roof, facing the front yard. Thankful for at least some light and not wanting to go near the window at all in case I saw the ghosts from next door, I climbed the rest of the way into the attic. Even though I couldn't see any blue ghosts chilling out, prickles ran down my neck which was the best ghost detector I knew.

The first thing I did was call for some backup.

"Brandon? Can you hear me?" I whispered his name in case Emma could still hear me from down the stairs, and I pictured Brandon's cute face with that sneaky grin in my mind, hoping that the concentration would help further my call.

"What are you doing here?" Brandon appeared with a sassy stance and hands on his hips. "Are you trying to get a better look at that house? That doesn't seem like something you would do."

"No," I kept my voice quiet, "this just happens to be a friend's house from school who needs some ghostly help."

"I'm thinking you mean help *with* a ghost and not help *from* a ghost."

"Well, who better to help me with a ghost than a ghost?"

"You're just scared and wanted someone to hold your hand." He grinned that teasing smile I couldn't get out of my head. "Too bad I'm not too good at holding hands these days."

I shook my head in feigned exasperation. "Just help me find the ghost up here, okay? Emma says it wails all night. If it's using energy to wail loud enough that alivers can hear it, we might be dealing with a dangerous poltergeist here."

"What's a pol-er-eist?" a small voice asked from underneath a wooden table, causing both Brandon and I to jump.

Her blue form flickered for a second, but, as ghosts do when they're around me, she became more solid, empowered by whatever power I had to make them stick around better. Yay. Go me.

The table was in a darker part of the attic, further away from the window, but I could still mostly see her. She was young and small, no older than eight at the most. As she crouched under the table, I couldn't quite tell the timeline of her clothes, which usually helped me guess when a ghost died and how long they'd been haunting a place. Her face was sweet and innocent, and her long hair was curled around her face.

Both Brandon and I crouched down so we could see her better and hopefully try to ease her fears at seeing two strangers in her attic.

"A poltergeist," I said slowly and pronounced it again for her, "is a ghost who has lost memories of who it was before it died. Have you seen anything like that up here?"

Brandon and I shared a look, both of us knowing it was probably her and she didn't realize she was using up that energy, what was happening, or even that she was dead.

She shook her head, her curls bouncing. "This is my room. I'm the only one who lives here."

"What's your name?" Brandon asked in a kind tone that made my heart want to drag my body over to him and throw myself into his arms while gazing into his eyes lovingly.

I told my heart to shut it down and focus on the important things.

"Riley." Her voice was so small and weak, it was hard to think of her as the one causing all the wailing trouble. However, I did know kids were good at wailing when they needed to be.

"Hi, Riley. I'm Brandon, and this is Hanna. How old are you?"

The girl scooted towards us a few times but still stayed under the table. "I'm seven. How come you look all weird and blue?"

Brandon smiled and the empathetic look he gave her melted my heart. "I'm dead. I'm a ghost. See?" He pushed his hand through a stack of boxes, and it passed through entirely.

Riley's eyes went wide. "You're a ghost?"

"Yes. It's okay. I'm a good one. Can I tell you a secret, Riley?"

Brandon was doing so well with this little girl; I was afraid to interrupt in case I messed it all up. Even though I didn't have much experience dealing with strange ghosts, I was wise enough to realize the fragility of the situation. The last thing I wanted was an angry tornado of boxes like the one the history teacher ghost had formed in the classroom last week.

Guilt spiked through me as I thought of the teacher ghost, and how I had helped Rose capture him. I really needed to figure out how to fix that.

"What's the secret?" Riley scooted a few more times towards us, coming out from under the table by a few inches.

"You're a ghost, too," Brandon said with a soft smile and a gentle tone.

Riley scrunched her eyebrows together and blinked a few times. "Me?" She looked down at her hand and back up at us. "Does that mean I've died?"

Fear welled up in her eyes, and my heart went out to her. What would that moment be like when you realized you were dead? I'm sure it was far beyond my understanding.

And of course, during this delicate moment, Emma decided to check up on me.

"Hanna?" She called from the bottom of the stairs. "Is everything okay?"

Riley's eyes darted to the door in the floor. "Who is that?"

"I'm fine!" I yelled back as loudly as I dared.

At the same time, Brandon held his hands up in a calming motion. "She's just someone who lives downstairs. Nothing to worry about."

"What? No! I live downstairs! This is my house!"

Boxes started shaking around us, rattling whatever various contents they contained. Brandon and I shared another look, unsure how to deescalate the situation.

"Yes, of course! It's okay, Riley. We're just here to help." I crawled a few inches toward her, hoping to calm her down, but it was too late.

"No! I can't be dead! I don't need any help!" She blinked out of my sight, but the boxes kept moving violently, like an earthquake was shaking the house.

"It doesn't sound fine! I'm coming up to help!" Emma hollered, and I heard a creak as she prepared to ascend the staircase.

"No!" I yelled and dodged a stack of boxes that fell to the floor in a large crash. "I'm coming back down."

More stacks of boxes vibrated until they fell down. Getting back to the door felt like something from an action movie. When I kicked my legs over the side and got back on the ladder, Emma quickly scrambled down, giving me space.

"What's happening? This is new!"

I basically jumped down the stairs, and Brandon followed me, even though he wasn't in any real danger up there. "I'm sorry, Emma. I might have made things worse."

Together, we hastily pushed the ladder back up and closed the door.

"How?"

"Well, you were right. There is definitely a ghost up there. It's a little girl, and she doesn't know she's dead."

"Until we told her and made her mad," Brandon said as all three of us stared up at the door, listening to the chaos of angry boxes having a fit.

"How can a ghost not know they're dead?" Emma's green eyes moved to stare at me, and I felt terrible at having probably made her sleepless nights even worse.

I shrugged with a sympathetic tilt to my mouth. "It happens. In fact, most ghosts don't really know they're dead, but like the saying goes, acceptance is the first step to growth, or something."

A few more tumbles sounded from above us, but the fit was ebbing. She was calming down, or running out of energy, I wasn't sure.

"So, what do we do now?" Emma asked and turned towards her bedroom again. "I suppose this means I'm not getting a good night's sleep yet."

"Who is this chick anyway?" Brandon followed us inside the room but leaned against the door frame as he studied Emma. "Aw, Hanna, did you make a new friend?"

I wanted to glare at him and tell him to shush, but of course that would have looked weird to Emma, so I restrained myself.

"Honestly, I'm sorry, Emma, but I don't know. I'm still new to this whole thing, but I do know someone who can help."

With slumped shoulders, Emma sat back on the edge of her bed. "It's okay. It was worth a shot, anyway."

I sat down next to her, and the bed squeaked in protest. "Hey, I'm not giving up and neither should you. One thing we can do now is try to get more information about the girl. Can you find out who the owners of this house were before your family moved in? And maybe the owners before that? Try to find out if there was a little girl who lived here at one point, and if she died in a terrible accident or something."

Emma looked up from the holes in her jeans and nodded. "I can do that. It will feel better to do something productive."

"While she's at it, she could try figuring out what the deal is next door," Brandon added.

"I'll talk to my grandma and see if she can help us figure out what to do next. It might take a few days, but we'll get it, okay?"

She nodded; the brown hairs that stuck out of her messy bun waved.

"Until then, can you sleep downstairs on the couch or something?"

"Maybe. My mom hates when I do that, but I can sneak down there when she's in bed."

I nodded. "It'll be worth it if you can get some sleep. I'm afraid the ghost might be louder at night now. Sorry."

Chapter 7

After Brandon and I left Emma's house, I walked directly across the street, wanting nothing to do with the house next door. I didn't even look to check if any of the other ghosts looked at me or noticed another ghost was following me around.

Emma had offered to drive me home, but I'd told her my house wasn't far and a walk would do me good. I didn't tell her it would give me time to talk to the ghost that was quickly becoming my best friend and my ghost-talking-to partner, or whatever that position was called.

"When I suggested we try to help a ghost, this wasn't what I had in mind. I figured we'd start with an innocent old lady or something and definitely not involve someone you know from school. Aren't you trying to keep all of this a secret from the 'normal' kids?" Brandon used his fingers to quote the word.

I sighed and put my hands into my jacket pockets. As we walked, my backpack swayed in time with my gait.

"It just kind of happened. Besides, she knew to ask me about it because apparently rumors are going around now that I'm some kind of occult weirdo."

Brandon pressed his hand to his chest and gasped. "That Noah! What a turd!"

"It could be him, but it might not be. It could also be Caleb. Heck, it could even be my sister. She's caught me talking to invisible things a few times before."

"I don't think she would ever do something like that. Caleb seems too eager to keep your secret quiet. My money's on Noah."

I gave Brandon a look. "Of course. You never liked him."

He didn't bother to argue and shrugged. "So how are we going to help your friend back there?"

We reached the end of the street and passed the skatepark as we turned onto the next one. A few skaters were out since it was a sunny afternoon, but we didn't pay them much attention.

"I'm not sure. Hopefully, Gran will have some experience dealing with this kind of thing. We might even need to bring her with us next time."

"And have more people and more pressure put on the little girl? Not sure if that's a good idea. She seemed pretty skittish."

"True, but Gran is the expert here, and I don't know what I'm doing. Poor Emma probably won't get any sleep tonight."

Brandon nodded. "Probably not. That girl sure looked scared. Finding out you're a ghost isn't that bad."

"Maybe for you. Although, you weren't exactly happy when we met. You seemed really lonely. It's part of the reason I felt bad enough to keep talking to you."

"Oh, Gee. I'm so glad to be your charity case." He smiled a little though, so I knew he was joking. Maybe.

"You're welcome."

"I think you were just as lonely."

I remembered sitting with Andrea and Noah as she took my home-work answers, and I nodded slightly. "Perhaps. Now I need to go see a vampire about a ghost."

When we got home, I stopped myself from tossing my backpack on the couch and brought it to my room instead. It was a typical discussion between my mom and me, but I figured she didn't need any more stress and did what she wanted me to.

"Anyone home?" I called out as I walked back from my bedroom and towards the kitchen.

"Looks like it's all quiet," Brandon said, looking around.

As I walked by Trina's door, it opened, surprising me and my ghost.

"Oh! Didn't realize you were home," I said, glad I hadn't tried responding to Brandon yet.

"Yeah, but Mom isn't. I think she must be at a shoot or something." Trina fiddled with her golden eye necklace, and I was happy to see that she hadn't been in her room crying or anything. However, she did look a little distracted.

With Mom gone, that meant Gran's ghost was, too. She was haunting my mom, not our house. I could have probably summoned her like I was able to do with Brandon, but I hadn't tried that yet and figured I could ask her about Riley later.

Feeling a little guilty, I smiled sweetly at Trina. "Do you think you could give me Caleb's number? I need to text him about that favor and tell him to ask you to homecoming."

A few emotions flitted over her face—hesitation, frustration, and excitement. I guess the excitement won out.

"Don't tell him to ask me out. Just kind of suggest and hint and be more subtle about it, okay?" She pulled her phone out of her pocket and texted me his number.

I smiled. "Sure."

Brandon followed me into the kitchen as I grabbed a diet soda and then back into my bedroom. I didn't bother stopping him from coming in. As long as he didn't pop in randomly while I was getting dressed or something, it was probably okay.

I made sure to shut the door behind us so we could talk, albeit quietly.

"Are you sure you want a vampire to take your sister to a dance? What if he eats her?"

I sat on my bed, and he sat in his usual chair by the desk. I got my phone and copied Caleb's number to start my text. As old as he was, he probably preferred a message by the Pony Express, but I hoped he'd adapted to current times.

"I knew you were going to say something like that. If Caleb was going to eat Trina, he would have already done it."

"Maybe, or perhaps he's just waiting until she fattens up or something."

I gave him a flat look and he grinned.

"Hey, one of us has to be the practical one here."

"Yes, and it makes sense that it's the dead guy who does that."

"Exactly." He nodded.

I shook my head but couldn't get rid of the smile on my face. Then I got to work on the text message.

Hey Caleb. This is Hanna. I'll do what you need, but first, you've got to ask Trina to the dance and promise to help me find

more information about that missing psychic lady. Do we have a deal?

As I waited for his response, I started going through the stuff in my bag, figuring out what homework to do first.

"So, I'm not really sure what you're doing with the vampire. Did you tell me and my ghost brain forgot?" Brandon asked while poking at a pencil on my desk and watching his finger go through it over and over.

"Right. It's hard for me to keep straight about when you're around and when you're not." I continued to tell him about the time Caleb visited me during dinner, how he had asked me to help his seethe, and that we'd be up against a poltergeist. Then I explained that after talking with Trina and seeing how much she liked Caleb and how much I needed more information about Rose while having no ideas of where to turn, I had decided I'd need to help Caleb.

After I was finished, Brandon stared at me for several seconds. Then a whole bunch of questions poured out. "You're going to help vampires? Do you think that's a good idea? How are you going to handle a poltergeist? I mean, no offense, but we couldn't even handle that little girl today, and she's only partway to being a poltergeist. I'm sorry, but you haven't thought this through enough."

My phone chimed, saving me from having to answer all his very valid questions right away.

Be careful what you ask for. I'll pick you up at 10.

Not sure if he was trying to be funny or serious with the warning, I thought for a second, uncomfortable with the idea of sneaking out of my house so late on a school night. Again.

The last time I had done it was to help Rose in what I thought was banishing some ghosts. And now I was considering sneaking out to go meet up with a vampire so I could get scared by a ghost and probably make zero progress at all?

That didn't sound too good.

"What's that face? Have you decided you aren't too keen to hang out with vampires after all?" Brandon gave me a pointed look and crossed his arms over his chest.

"Maybe, but I'll never admit it to you. It'll just give you more reason to think you're right and that's annoying."

He pressed his lips together and nodded. "That's fair, but it doesn't change the facts."

"But I need to know where to find Rose. So far, Caleb has seemed capable of keeping tabs on people."

"You mean you."

"Yes, keeping tabs on me. Anyway, he would probably be a good asset for hunting down Rose, and I don't know how else to get him to help us."

"Did you try asking and telling him the situation without having to get into some kind of favor-deal with a seethe of vampires?"

I cringed. "No. I didn't think of that."

"I'm betting Caleb would like being on your good side too much to turn down a simple request like that."

Sighing, I rubbed at my eyes, careful not to smudge my eyeliner. "Well, it's too late now."

"You know I'm coming with you."

"I mean, it's not like I could stop you. You listen so well."

He grinned.

A few hours later, we were sitting at the dinner table. My stomach was hollow with not even enough energy to grumble at me. My hands were trembling, and my heart felt like it was frantically trying to beat itself out of my chest. I had done well the whole day, keeping my calorie intake well under 500. I could allow myself some food, I decided.

And Mom's chicken enchiladas looked so very good.

"Mmmm...does that taste as good as it looks?" Brandon watched me take several bites as the cheese dangled off my fork.

"Wow, this is amazing, Mom!" I said in way of answer to the invisible ghost who sat in Dad's empty chair.

Trina raised her eyebrows and widened her eyes at my eating gusto. "Guess you're finally eating again."

I shot her an angry look.

"Thank you, sweetie. I just felt like cooking today. Sometimes it makes me feel better." Mom's eyes were less swollen, but she still had a sad aura about her. Her shoulders were slumped, her movements were slower than usual, and she seemed almost fragile. But I knew better. She was going to rally from this.

We all were.

We smiled in support of her, all avoiding looking at Dad's empty chair.

For once, Gran hadn't commented on Mom's cooking, even though she was making one of Gran's highly praised recipes. Normally, Gran would have been trying to coach her through the whole process, but she hadn't. Instead, she was content to simply watch and wait.

It seemed Dad leaving had changed more than one thing around our house.

"So, did you hear from Caleb?" Trina asked, trying to appear nonchalant, simply finding something to talk about at dinner.

"Wouldn't you like to know." Brandon smirked. "Caleb and Trina sitting in a tree."

I ignored him, but Gran didn't. "What's this about Caleb?"

"I did. He didn't shut down my suggestions, so I'd take that as a good sign." I took a drink of water.

Trina's cheeks colored slightly, and she smiled down at her pile of rice.

Mom watched our exchange with interest. "What kind of suggestions are we talking about here?"

By the look of Brandon's face, he felt kind of bad for teasing Trina about Caleb in front of Gran. We had kind of forgotten their weird relationship several years ago.

"Oh, it's not a big deal." I waved it off with my hand. "We just thought it would be good for Caleb to go to a school dance with Trina. You know, to get him out of the house and to socialize more. He seems to keep to himself so much."

Trina looked at me oddly, but she should have been grateful. I was trying to cover up how much she liked him, for her sake and Gran's sake.

"Trina? Isn't he your friend? Why didn't you just ask him yourself? Aren't we all woke now in this generation or something?"

We both rolled our eyes at Mom's attempt to be more current with popular slang.

"I could, I guess." Trina shrugged.

"Sometimes it just feels nice to have a boy like you," I said, forcing my eyes not to bounce to Brandon.

Gran shook her head. "Oh, this is not a good idea. He's a vampire. Did you forget, Hanna?"

"That's true," Mom said sadly into her cup as she took a sip of water, probably trying to cover up the sadness in her eyes.

"It's just a school dance. It's not like they're getting married," I said more for Gran than Mom or Trina.

Trina coughed, almost choking on her food. "Definitely not getting married."

"Yeah, that's just a disaster waiting to happen," Mom said with a smile, so we burst into tiny giggles, choosing to use laughter as a release rather than dwell on the sadness in her eyes.

By the time I had finished my second plate, I felt terrible. My stomach was shocked by the influx of heavy, cheesy food, and guilt flooded through me. I didn't know why I had eaten so much, but it had almost felt like I couldn't stop myself, even if I had wanted to.

I dreaded what the scale would say in the morning and considered running into the bathroom to purge it all. My stomach felt wobbly enough that it probably wouldn't have been too hard, but Brandon and Gran would have probably followed me and that was not something I wanted anyone to know about, not even the ghosts.

"Wow, that was delicious, Mom," I said as I put my plate into the sink and rinsed it off.

"It sure was!" Trina slid her plate under my stream of water quickly, gave me a cheeky grin, and dashed off down the hall.

I shook my head and rinsed her plate too, and then turned back to Mom who was clearing the table.

"I'll just be in my room doing homework. Also maybe doing some research for a friend who I met today that needs help with finding out about her house and the people who lived there before who might have lost a little girl." I gave Gran a pointed look as I said the last part, hoping Mom wouldn't notice while she was busy clearing the table.

"Oh, that's terrible! Do you know how it happened?" Mom asked, bringing the leftovers to the kitchen counter.

"That's one thing we need to figure out." I twitched my head slightly towards my room while looking at Gran so she would know I meant for her to follow.

"Stories like that are so sad. Good luck with your research." Mom smiled and went back to the table to gather up more dishes.

"Thanks!"

Once we were in my room, Brandon took his usual seat while Gran sat next to me on the bed.

"So, we met a ghost today. We're going to try and help it!" I said with more energy than I expected, clueing me in on that maybe I *was* excited to try and help someone the right way. If I could help some ghosts get back to where they needed to go, I could get rid of some of the guilt for helping Rose.

Maybe.

Gran smiled and nodded her head. "That's great!"

"It is, except as is just like Hanna's style, she decided to start big and picked someone from school who was having ghost problems and get them involved, even though she is otherwise so desperate to keep all this a secret," Brandon informed Gran, so unhelpfully.

I sighed and gave Brandon a look. "I didn't mean to pick this one. She picked me."

Gran chuckled. "It's okay. What do we know?"

We told Gran about our ghost encounter, and in the back of my mind, I worried about the vampire ghost I was going to meet probably later that very night. I was too scared to ask her about poltergeists, worried that she would find out what I was doing and try to stop me.

"A little girl ghost." Gran pressed her hand to her chest and took a deep breath. "How terrible."

"It really is. I can imagine she has a lot of unfinished business." I nodded sadly.

"Yeah, so much we won't be able to help her get it all done and cross over," Brandon pointed out flatly.

"It's impossible to help every ghost with all their issues," Gran said.

I groaned and flopped back onto the bed.

"But," she continued, "it is possible to help them with the biggest one. No humans are completely whole when they die. There are just too many variables and life choices that can leave regrets and things undone, but there usually is only one, or maybe two at the most, issues that prevent people from crossing over. That's what you've got to figure out. That's how you help them."

"First step, get them to realize they're dead, right? Well, we already failed at that one. She freaked out. How do we get past that?" I asked, staring up at the ceiling.

"It's not easy, but I figured out that time is the best solution. If you let time sink in, and they start to pay more attention to the human world around them, eventually they figure it out. It just depends on the ghost for how long it takes."

Branon tapped his lip. "Hmm, would have been nice to start with an easier-to-access ghost. At this rate, we'll be over at your friend's house all the time, and since I've never even heard you talk about her before, I doubt you're close enough to get away with that."

"We'll just have to be?" I sat up and shrugged. "Emma is really upset about all of this. I have to help her."

Gran smiled. "That's the spirit. After she's accepted that she's dead, then you've got an even harder job of trying to get her to remember her life before death and come up with some ideas of what she might need to do or know before she can pass on."

"Great," I mumbled.

"Maybe some of the research Emma comes up with about her family and the people who lived there before will help?" Brandon said.

"Hopefully."

At nearly ten o'clock, I was a nervous wreck. I had snuck out of the house before with no problems, but Mom had decided to stay up late watching a show in the front room. Since our front room and kitchen were all in one big space, I couldn't sneak out the front or the back door without her seeing me. And even if for some reason she didn't see me, Gran would. I did not want to explain to Gran about going out to meet a vampire late at night.

"Isn't it time to go?" Brandon glanced at the clock from where he was laying on my carpet, his legs straight up against my bed and feet sitting on top of my blankets. Normally, I wouldn't have ever let anyone put their shoes on my bed like that, but I didn't even know if Brandon could take off his shoes.

"I'm not sure how to get out of here. Mom was still in the front room watching TV two minutes ago when I went to check and go to the bathroom." I was at my desk, in Brandon's usual chair, trying to sort through some homework which was where I'd been for the past hour.

Brandon had finally gotten bored enough to stare up at the ceiling for a while.

"It's probably not a good idea to stand up a vampire."

"Well, he shouldn't expect me to just be able to walk out of my house so late at night on a school night. Has he forgotten I'm still a minor?"

Brandon shrugged. "I don't know. He is an old guy, and they do forget stuff."

A light tapping sound came from my window.

Oh, right. My window.

"I'm so dumb sometimes," I said while shaking my head and walking over to the window.

As I pulled up the blinds, Caleb's grinning face met me from the darkness.

Like he'd done the last time he'd visited my window, he popped the screen off while I tried to quietly slide it open.

"Hey there," Caleb said, his voice purring from his chest.

My heart picked up pace, and I really hoped he couldn't hear it, but, from the grin on his face, I was betting he could.

"You know, it's not nice to ask a lady to sneak out of her house on a school night." I put my hands on my hips. "Especially when you're the one asking her for a favor."

Caleb stepped back so I could have room to climb out of the window. "I know. I'm sorry. It's just that daytime has too many people around."

Brandon stood next to me as I crawled out of the window, much less gracefully than Caleb had climbed in the week before. "Are you sure this is a good idea?"

I gave him a look that I hoped he understood to mean that we'd already talked about it, and he knew why I needed to do this.

He must have understood because he threw his arms up in surrender and followed me out of the window, although he didn't have to climb out, only walk through and step down onto the ground with a laughing smile in my direction.

Caleb helped me from behind by putting hands around my waist and steadying me. When both my legs were out of the window, but my feet were still several inches off the ground, Caleb tightened his grip, picked me up, and set me down onto the grass.

I dusted myself off, pretending that it was totally normal to be picked up by a vampire and pulled out of a window.

"If I get in trouble for this, Caleb, you're going to be in worse trouble." I glared as I adjusted my jacket and checked to make sure I still had my phone in my pocket.

"Oh, wow. What a scary threat." Brandon shook his head.

Caleb only smiled. "It'll be fine. I can use some vampire magic on your mom if you need me to, helping her forget that you were ever out at all."

That made me pause. "You can do that?"

He shrugged with that canine predatory smile. "Maybe."

"Have you ever done that to me? Have we snuck out like this before and you made me forget?"

"Maybe you danced the night away in romantic moonlight," Brandon teased me while cupping his hands together over his chest with a wistful expression.

Caleb's lips narrowed and his eyes focused on me in seriousness. "I've never done that, and I'll never do it unless it becomes important for your safety. Plus, it takes a lot of work."

"How very reassuring."

Caleb led us around the back of my house to the front, nearly melting into the shadows like a shadow himself. Next to him and a ghost who passed over everything silently, I felt like a bumbling, drunk elephant trying to make its way through a room full of cats in heat—that is to say, I felt loud.

When we got to the front, I hid on the other side of Trina's car as I followed Caleb to his car which was parked in front of the neighbor's on the other side of the street. I glanced back towards my house as we walked quietly. The porch light was on, and I could see the blueish reflection of the TV on the front windows. Everything looked normal so far. Hopefully, Mom would fall asleep on the couch for several hours and wouldn't come to check on my now-empty bedroom.

I paused when we got to Caleb's car. "This is your car?"

The black paint and silver rims glittered in the lamplight. I couldn't tell what kind of car it was, just that it had four doors and looked new and sporty. The windows were tinted, but it was hard to tell how dark since it was nighttime.

"If I didn't know Caleb wasn't your average teenage schoolboy, this car would confirm it. What kind of kid drives around in a Maserati?" Brandon scoffed and shook his head.

"I don't know what kind of car this is, but it seems very nice," I said, admiring its shininess.

Caleb opened the passenger door for me and smiled. "Eh, I've had a few years to save up."

"Right." I slid onto the leather seats and inhaled the chemical-clean smell of the inside.

Faster than he had any right to, Caleb was opening the driver's side door and climbing in. Brandon followed us and sat in the back, muttering something about how no one bothered to open the door for *him*.

"I just want you to know that I have a lot of reservations about this." I folded my arms as Caleb turned the car on. Or, at least it looked like he turned the car on since the lights and the console screen lit up, but I didn't hear any engine.

As quiet as its owner, the car pulled onto the street and zipped past the houses.

"As you should have." Caleb nodded, his eyes on the road before us.

"Not enough, methinks," Brandon muttered from the back.

"You're the one that told me to be careful about who I hang out with. I'm pretty sure you wouldn't want me to be with a vampire in the middle of the night who helped me sneak out of my house."

"You're exactly right. Except it's me we're talking about." Caleb flashed me another predatory smile and something inside of me did a little flip. I couldn't tell if my traitorous body was acknowledging his superiority as his prey or if it didn't care that he could tear us apart faster than I could get out a scream.

Brandon scoffed. "He's so full of himself. Can I steal some of your energy to scare him a bit, please? It would be so funny."

We still hadn't talked about Brandon taking larger amounts of energy from me so that he could manifest parts of his body into a solid form, but I figured we both didn't want our secret touches to stop and were afraid if we talked more about it, we'd agree that it wasn't the best thing to do.

"I suppose I should tell you there is a ghost with us. It might seem kind of weird, but he's basically my partner when it comes to doing stuff like this and trying to help other ghosts," I said to chase away the silence and because it felt like it might be an important thing for him to know for some reason.

At any rate, it would make it easier to reply to Brandon's peanut-gallery comments.

Caleb glanced at me and nodded. "Alright. I can respect your process. While we're being honest here, I should tell you more about this ghost and why she's important."

"Okay."

"Obviously, as talented as us vampires are, we cannot talk to most ghosts. Sometimes we'll get lucky, and one will use up enough energy to try and exact revenge on us, but mostly the ghosts are unknown to us."

"That sounds like it would be the opposite of lucky, but okay," Brandon pointed out sarcastically.

"So how do you know about this ghost? Why do you need to know about it? Is there something you need me to get from it or do you just want me to help it with unfinished business so it can cross over and leave you guys alone?" I asked, trying to better understand what I was supposed to be doing.

Brandon giggled. "These vampires are being haunted. Hah. Serves them right. It's probably from some poor victim they mutilated."

Caleb took us out of my neighborhood and onto the main streets of the city. Neon lights and streetlamps blazed by us as he cruised, apparently unconcerned with traffic laws.

"There are two main reasons we need your help. First, the ghost haunts an old church. It's since been turned into a homeless shelter, but the blessing on the grounds is still intact so we can't step foot on it even if the ghost would talk to us. Which brings me to the other reason, and that is we need you to find out the location of Dion's lair. We suspect this ghost has ties to Dion, and you need to get it to tell you."

Brandon sat up closer to the front and raised his eyebrows. "So the holy ground thing is true? Vampires can't walk on it?"

"Brandon wants to know more about the holy ground situation, and so do I. It's not just a legend?"

"The ghost's name is Brandon? It's a boy? Is he sitting on your lap or something?" Caleb looked over at me with amused eyes.

"I'm not an it or a boy. I'm a man, thank you very much."

I looked back and forth between Brandon and Caleb, unsure where to start. "Er, he didn't like that comment. He said he's a man. I mean, he isn't older than you, but he was born in the 90s."

"1990s? 1890s? 1790s? When it comes to ghosts and vampires, you may need to be a bit more specific," Caleb teased.

I rolled my eyes. "1990s. So, technically he's in his thirties so I guess that means he's a man? Not sure why that bit is important right now, and no, he's not sitting on my lap. That would be weird."

"Yes, that's the weird part." Caleb chuckled so I knew he wasn't too put out by this whole thing, but it wouldn't matter if he was. *I* was doing *him* a favor.

About twenty minutes, later we stood on the street next to Caleb's car and stared at a large looming building in front of us. Despite the late hour, there were lights on near the doorway and streaming out through the stained-glass windows. It was one of those old cathedral-style churches with spiky towers and dark stones.

"So... all we have to do is go inside there where I assume homeless people are milling about, find the ghost, which you said earlier was a poltergeist, and get it to calm down, realize its dead, remember its past life, and then tell me where this Dion's lair or hideout or whatever is, right?" I said while staring up at the glaring gargoyles.

"It's a she. Apparently, ghosts get offended if you refer to them as it." Caleb's eyes twinkled in the dark as he teased me.

"He's bypassing the part where all of this is dangerous, scary, and hard to do." Brandon put his hands on his hips, and his wallet chain swayed.

"I'm not sure I can get this all to happen in one night, that is if we even find the ghost right away. I'm going to need time," I said.

Caleb pinched his lips and the uncertainty I had seen from him last night at the restaurant made an appearance in his concerned dark eyes. "How long do you think you'll need?"

I shrugged. "I have no idea. I'm new to this. How do you even get a poltergeist to calm down long enough to talk to it instead of having it hurl a giant candelabra at you?"

Caleb shook his head and lifted his arms out in a partial shrug. "You're supposed to be the ghost expert here. All I can say is that my queen *really* needs this information as quickly as you can get it or bad things are going to happen."

Brandon frowned. "What kinds of bad things?"

I repeated his question.

Caleb broke eye contact with me and surveyed the street in front of us. "The kind that causes death and pain."

Chapter 8

"You should have reminded him what he's supposed to do in return for you doing this favor," Brandon said as he stepped through the iron gate and onto the official church grounds. The gate screeched ominously as I moved it open enough for me to walk past.

"You're probably right. I should have made him sign a paper and got it notarized before agreeing to do this."

The cobblestone walkway needed repair, and the closer I got to the building, the more I noticed that the whole place was lacking some generous funds and a caring carpenter's hammer.

"Definitely. At least we can be confident that we aren't going to be attacked by vampires while we're here."

"There are other things that can attack me. Maybe not you though, as you're already dead...in case you forgot."

"Thank you. I had almost forgotten." He gave me a teasing smile.

"Sometimes I think you do."

He let my comment hang in the air as we stepped past the giant wooden doors. We didn't shut them completely, and light spilled onto the stone stairs. Various smells hit me as we walked inside, but I was too busy being in awe of the high ceilings that rose far above us to notice the mixture of canned soup, musty fabrics, and rotting wood.

Most of the benches that sat in lines were intact, but some had fallen or were just simply missing. Piles of clothes and supplies heaped on top of several of the benches, and, although I couldn't see it from my angle, I imagined most of the bench padding was worn and holey. The front of the church where the podium and alter would have sat was an empty stage with more piles of clothes and supplies. Perhaps some of the heaps of clothing were actually people trying to sleep, but I wasn't about to go poke one and find out.

The lighting was dim from candles and lamps that ran along the outside walls of the chapel. It was enough to prevent people from tripping on anything or anyone but not much else.

If there was a person in charge there, they didn't come running to greet us. It was mostly quiet, except for a few people shuffling around and someone muttering to themself in the front pew.

"Now *this* is a haunt. Half these people are alive but are pretty much haunting this place already!" Brandon said as we looked around.

It was true that a few ghosts milled about, intermingling with the alivers. I could even see one that looked like a priest flash in and out on the stage, vocalizing some great sermon or something every time he appeared. I knew that my presence would increase his power and that he'd start to get more and more consistent.

None of the ghosts seemed like the one we were looking for. I hesitated to talk straight to Brandon while other ghosts were around, afraid they'd take note and try to talk to me as well, so I kind of talked to myself without looking at my ghost companion.

"So how do we find the one we need? All of these look too peaceful," I said quietly and nodded to a man who shuffled by me and gave me an odd look. I'm sure I wasn't the weirdest person in the place.

"Let's go search the other parts of the church. Perhaps she's in a back room somewhere." Brandon turned to the left, and I followed him into the dim sides of the chapel where we found a doorway leading into a darker hallway.

From what I could see, more piles of junk lined the hallways as well as several doorways.

"If I were haunting this place, it wouldn't be the main area," Brandon said as he strutted down the hallway, heedless of the danger and creepy factor.

I swallowed thickly, hoping no enraged drifter would try to attack me. It was an odd sensation being afraid of the alivers instead of the ghosts like I was used to.

A few piles of clothes murmured and muttered as we passed by, but thankfully none of them tried to grab me. The smell grew worse as we walked, and I wondered if some of the people kept buckets for their bathroom needs. We peeked into the classroom doors that were open as we went down the hall. Most of them were the same with heaps of clothes, random piles of mostly junk, and a few muttering forms. There were even a few ghosts wandering the hall or pacing in circles inside classrooms, but none of them looked like the ghost we were trying to find.

In fact, I realized Caleb hadn't given us a whole lot of information to go from. This search was starting to feel nearly as frustrating as it was scary.

"Maybe we should ask around? See if anyone has seen or heard anything weird?" I nearly whispered as we came to a turn to the right, and the dim hallway seemed to grow even dimmer.

"Let's explore what we can, and if we don't see anything crazy, then we can start asking around. I kind of love it here." His grin was barely visible in the lamplight.

"You would. Your creepiness fits right in."

Before we reached the turn at the end, a screeching wail rose from somewhere inside and sent the hairs on my arms and neck into standing at full attention.

"What was that?" I whispered as I turned back around towards the main area.

Several of the sleeping people sat up and looked around, indicating to me that this was a sound I hadn't been the only one to hear.

Brandon turned as well; his grin fully displayed on his face as we started walking back. "That has got to be our poltergeist. Isn't this exciting?"

I gave him a flat look that he missed because he was already walking quickly in front of me. "So exciting."

As we walked back down the hallway, more people were stirring, and I was surprised to find out that most of the heaps were people. I suppose if I was a homeless person, there would have been a lot worse places to stay at, as long as this was kept relatively safe somehow. However, from the looks on their faces after hearing that scream, most were having second thoughts.

Another wail echoed through the chapel just as we reached the main area. Several people started packing up their things while a few were staring wide-eyed at the ceiling, probably wondering the same thing I had: was this all in my head, or was this real?

"The banshee is back!" I heard someone harshly whisper to our left, talking to another squatter nearby. Both were scrambling to get their packs put together. "It's better to face the streets than to be here while she's awake."

"She's been quiet for days now. I wonder what woke her up?" The other squatter said as she struggled to roll up her sleeping bag.

Brandon and I looked at each other but we had very different expressions.

"That's got to be her!"

"We should leave," I said at the same time.

Instead of bolting to the door as several people were, he ran towards the heart of the chapel, his eyes darting all around the rafters as if the ghost we were looking for had somehow gained the power of flight in death. Which, after all the things I had seen, I supposed that could have been possible.

The lanterns and candles sputtered until they went out altogether, causing several more people to scream and rush to the doors. Light from outside streetlamps fought to come inside, but, since the moon was low still, there wasn't much to go by.

Essentially blind, I grabbed the nearest column and hugged it until my eyes could adjust. I had a small moment of clarity, and I couldn't figure out what in the world I was doing there. How had I gotten into this situation? How stupid was I, really?

The glowing ghosts were easily the first things I could make out. However, most of them seemed to have disappeared at the wailing as well. A few stuck around near the walls, but most were gone. Brandon, in all his excited glory, was still standing in the middle of the aisle, and, to my horror, started calling out into the darkness.

"Hello? Clara? Are you here?" He used the name Caleb had supplied us with as basically the only bit of information he could tell us—as helpful as that was. Anyone could have been named Clara.

"Brandon!" I hissed at him as loud as I dared, unsure if I was worried more about alivers hearing me or the dead wailing banshee. "What are you doing?"

"We'll never find her hiding behind a pole. Aren't we here to help?" He put his hands on his hips and stared at me.

I sighed and was about to come out of my hiding spot when the wail rose again, this time loud enough to hurt my ears.

"Aha! Clara! We're just here to help!" Brandon yelled back.

Then I saw her. A blue form zipped past the stage, empty now except for real piles of junk as all of the squatters had wisely evacuated the building. It seemed like this place had a reputation as an okay spot to sleep in until the banshee woke, and then it was time to find somewhere else to go.

"Get out! You're just working for *him*, aren't you?" Clara, I assumed, screeched from somewhere inside, her words echoing around us and making it nearly impossible to know where she was.

I ducked further behind the pole, afraid to keep my head out to see what was going on, but I forced myself to at least watch. Even if I was too scared to help her, the least I could do was watch Brandon do the work for me.

"Who's him?" Brandon spun in a circle, his eyes darting around the room to try and spot her.

"Don't pretend. He sent you in here; I know it!" Clara said, finally appearing on the stage again, sitting down and letting her legs dangle off the side.

My heart sank as I saw another ghost of a young girl, not too different from the one we had seen at Emma's house. I knew young girls died or were murdered or whatever horrible thing had happened to them, but it was another fact entirely to see their ghost form, unable to prevent myself from going into dark places of my imagination.

I found myself easing out from behind the pole and taking a few tentative steps towards the front.

Brandon still stood in the middle of the aisle, and he faced Clara, hands on his hips. "Clara? Is that you?"

She shrugged, and her light hair fell off her shoulders. I couldn't tell what color it had been in life, but I could at least tell it had been light, stringy and unwashed. Her dress was tattered and basic. It had short sleeves, narrowed at the waist, and ended at her knobby knees. Whatever she had been, she hadn't been well fed.

Slowly, I made my way until I was standing next to Brandon, probably about six feet away from the stage.

"We're here to help you. It's our job to help others find and finish their unfinished business," Brandon explained gently.

Clara didn't say anything, and Brandon and I exchanged looks again.

It didn't seem like a good idea to disrupt the peace I was sure was temporary and try to go for the first step Gran had laid out for me—letting her know she was dead. So, I tried a different tactic.

"Clara? Do you know where you are?" My voice felt weak and quiet compared to the high ceilings above us and the thick darkness.

Thankfully, my eyes were adjusted enough to at least see the vague shapes of things.

Clara's eyes were unfocused and had trouble staying on any one object at a time. I wondered if this were a common characteristic of poltergeists, or ghosts who had lost most of their human selves by using up their energy to connect with the material world. It would be helpful to know how to spot a poltergeist without having to see them throw something.

"I'm where I always am. It's where *he* wants to keep me. It's cold." She gripped her elbows and shuddered, probably lost in the memories of wherever it was that he had kept her, whoever he was.

Just because she haunted the church, didn't mean that's where she had died. Ghosts had different haunts for different reasons. She could have come here once as a kid, and the place was so stuck in her mind, it had ended up being her haunt.

"You're in a church. Do you know where you lived—er, live?" I advanced a few steps, wanting to establish some kind of personal connection. It seemed like a better route to take than to tell her she was dead straight out.

Brandon followed my lead but was smart enough to hang back slightly, not wanting to overwhelm Clara.

"Here."

"You live *here*?" I looked around and couldn't see much but dark, grey shapes.

She shrugged again, but her blue form seemed to flicker a few times, almost like a web page refreshing itself, and I started to worry we'd lose her.

Brandon must have had the same idea because he jumped into a question that she was not ready for. "Do you know someone named Dion?"

I didn't even have time to read the expression on her face before she disappeared with another enraged wail. I suppose I didn't need to see her expression after hearing that. It was clear how she felt about Dion. Perhaps it was the same "him" she kept talking about.

"I *knew* he sent you! He always sends humans to do his bidding. Get out!" She screamed, and I felt items around us shaking and trembling. Discordant keys from the old organ blared, and the walls groaned.

"We need to get out of here!" Brandon yelled over the screaming and cacophony.

I hesitated, but Clara screamed, "Leave me alone! He'll never use me again!"

Something that felt small and hard, like a book perhaps, smacked into my leg. Cursing, I turned to leave but was unable to run well in the darkness and with the stinging pain from my shin. "That hurt!"

"There's a pile right in front of you," Brandon said loudly, and I followed his trail through the darkness towards the door which was still slightly cracked open. The glow of streetlights beckoned me to safety.

The rumbling and screaming grew louder, and I wasn't sure if Clara was trying to stop us from leaving or was too mad to realize she was hindering our efforts to do as she had asked. Before we were but ten feet from the door, a creaking and screeching of metal was the only warning I had before an entire pew was wrenched up from the floor.

"Duck!" Brandon yelled, and I dropped to the floor immediately, landing on top of a stinking pile of some type of fabrics, clothes, or blankets or something.

Air stirred over my head as the bench swished by, going completely through Brandon and crashing into the nearby pillar. The building groaned in response, and I worried the whole thing would come down on our heads.

Struggling with my hurt leg, I slipped on the fabric and fell into the stench again.

"Get up!" Brandon said, urging me on with his hands and arms going in circles.

"I'm trying!" I finally freed myself from the cloth, and my sneakers found purchase on the stone floor.

The screams of the ghost followed us as we finally made it past the door and ran down the walkway. Once we were past the iron gate and standing on the sidewalk, I finally dared to turn around, fully expecting the structure to collapse.

The church was still groaning as wood strained to support the weight, but it must have been tougher than I'd thought because it didn't fall to the ground like a stack of very heavy cards.

"You know, it's times like these that I wish your grandma were still around to do this kind of stuff," Caleb said, suddenly standing next to us with crossed arms as he appraised the struggling building.

I wanted to punch him, but, instead, I restrained myself and rubbed my leg where I'd been hit. "Me too."

Caleb surprised me by laughing. "That's not how I thought you'd respond. I figured you would have hit me or something."

I glared and turned away, looking for the nearest place to sit down and assess my leg. "Shows what you know."

Brandon chuckled and followed me. "You were so going to hit him. I saw your fist clench."

I didn't bother to tell him to shut up.

Noticing my limp after a few steps, Caleb swooped me into his arms and walked down the sidewalk, away from the church that had started to settle but still emitted a strange, angry keening that sounded too human to be anything else.

"Ugh, this guy," Brandon muttered somewhere behind Caleb's broad shoulders.

"You don't have to pick me up. I can walk."

"You're limping and bleeding. Walking could cause more damage. We should at least check it out first. I'm sorry I couldn't go in there with you. That does make me the most nervous about this whole thing." Caleb's voice rumbled from inside his chest and the vibrations tickled throughout my body.

Something about vampires made them hard to resist. It must have been some kind of survival situation to lure humans in. It was kind of annoying.

"I just got hit in the leg by a book or something hard," I said as he gently placed me on a bench a few paces away from the church.

"Well, he's right about one thing. It's stupid to send us in there alone. We should take someone who can protect you next time." Brandon walked around the bench and stood on the other side of me.

"Brandon says we should take protection from someone who can walk on the grounds next time, and I have to agree." I pulled up my jeans, gingerly trying to avoid having the fabric touch the wound.

Caleb and I both winced when we saw the damage.

"What? The ghost boy can't protect you?" Caleb's grin told me what he thought of my "ghost boy" and that he was teasing me for having one around all the time.

I blushed but hoped the darkness of the night would help hide my rosy cheeks.

Brandon snarled. "How rude! He should try being incorporeal and see how he feels!"

"Brandon protects me in his own way," I said for the benefit of both, "but it might help to have someone with a physical body next time."

"Noted." Caleb pulled a handkerchief from his jean pocket and used it to dab at the blood running down my shin.

"Is this going to put you into bloodlust, and you'll suddenly lose control and drain me until I'm as dead as Brandon?" I asked, unsure if I should be letting a vampire doctor me up.

Caleb grinned, displaying his canines. "You make that sound like it would be a bad thing. The pleasure a human feels as the venom from a vampire's fangs spreads throughout their body can only be rivaled by one other experience. And, let's just say, it feels pretty good to die that way."

"Ew," Brandon said and retched dramatically. "This guy is so gross."

Cheeks still blushing, I focused my attention on my leg.

"Brandon and I agree that you're gross."

Caleb chuckled, the sound warm and deep. "Just telling the truth, but, like I keep trying to get into your skull, I'm not a danger to you. If anything, I'm one of your strongest assets. I had hoped talking to your grandmother would have helped you establish that, but it appears you'll need more convincing."

"I'm sorry. It's just that vampires are evil and suck human blood. What else am I supposed to think? You're the one who keeps telling me not to trust people easily!"

With deft fingers, Caleb wrapped the handkerchief around my shin and tied it snuggly.

I hissed as it came in contact with the wound but didn't pull my leg away. It was probably a good thing to have it covered up and have something to keep more blood from soaking into my jeans. As it was, I was going to have to throw these jeans out because whatever had hit me had ripped them open. It was going to be difficult to get all of the blood out anyway, which made me sad as they were one of my favorite pairs.

"Right, but that doesn't go for me. If it helps, I don't drink human blood unless it's from a blood bank or from someone willing, someone who I didn't use my influence on, and even then, it's only a little. I'm old enough to have more restraint than the new ones who can't stop feeding until there is nothing left."

"I suppose that's kind of reassuring?" I didn't bother to pull my pant leg down and left it bunched up.

"So, what did you learn from the ghost? Anything helpful?" Caleb asked with hopeful eyebrows.

I sighed and shook my head. "It's much harder than that when talking to a ghost and even more harderer when talking to a poltergeist. There isn't much left inside of her except the fear of some *him* she kept talking about, and that's pretty much it. You wouldn't happen to know who she was talking about, would you?"

"From the way she reacted, my money's on the Dion guy." Brandon frowned.

Caleb sat back on the bench and both of us stared out into the quiet street. A few cars had driven by as we'd talked, but for the most part, there weren't many people out at this time of night. I wondered for a second where all those homeless people had gone after being yelled out of the church but figured they knew the streets so well, they had backup places to stay, hopefully less haunted ones.

"She probably is talking about Dion. He wasn't very nice to her, which is one reason we want to find his lair. He's giving vampires a bad name."

I gave Caleb a flat look. He glanced at me and laughed. "I mean, a worse name than we already have."

"Why do you guys need to know where his lair is and why are you in such a hurry? I'm sorry to say that it's going to take me some time, even if I didn't have school and other things happening in my life except pleasing my vampire masters."

Brandon snorted and Caleb's mouth pulled up on one side.

"Actually," Caleb said and dropped the half-smile, "he's got one of our own. Somehow, he's kidnapped our queen's niece, and every second he has her is another one in which she could be murdered. He's most definitely torturing her at the very least."

Brandon shook his head. "Oh, vampire politics. I'm betting we don't want to get involved in that mess."

"Why?" I asked.

"She's the queen's niece. Does he need another reason?" Caleb's eyes were sad as he looked out into the night, and I wondered how close he was to this girl, or if it was just loyalty to his seethe that was making him so upset. "What's worse is that if we don't find the lair soon, my queen is going to go berserk. She'll do anything to find her niece and that could mean some bloodshed at the least, or a full-out street war at the most."

"Is there another way to find where his lair is? Are you sure that's where he's keeping her? Why does Clara know where it is? Maybe he's changed it since she was alive and there?" I didn't mean to throw so many questions at him, but I felt they were all important to know.

"I promise we're working all the angles we can. We've got trackers out there following around the members in his seethe, hoping they'll give him away. We've captured and tortured a few, but vampires don't give up information like that easily. Some of them even enjoy the pain, having something to feel during this unending existence."

Brandon shuddered. "The more I learn about these creatures, the less I like them."

Chapter 9

By the time Caleb drove up to my house, it was past midnight.

"Do you need my help sneaking back in?" Caleb leaned towards me in his car, the leather seat creaking quietly.

I shook my head. "No. I can walk fine, and I'll just go back the way we left, but all this better be worth it. Remember what you agreed to do with my help?"

Caleb sighed and sat back in his seat. "Yes. I remember. I have to take Trina to the dance this weekend."

"She likes you, you know. Poor girl." I gave a small smile, so he knew I was kind of teasing.

"I know. It's a tragic side effect of being around someone as gorgeous and amazing as me."

"Ew, again." Brandon rolled his eyes. "I'll be outside."

As Brandon fazed through the back doors of the car, I opened my door. "Right. Yes, maybe you could take her out, but be a terrible date so she can get over you and move on. It might make her sad in the short term, but at least she won't be heartbroken in the long term."

Caleb frowned and nodded. "The last thing I want to do is hurt either of you."

"And you also agreed to help me get more information about that psychic, remember? I need all the help I can get figuring out where she went and what she's up to."

He nodded again. "Yes, we should be able to find something out. Thanks for your help, Hanna. This means more to me and my seethe than you'll ever know."

I smiled and nodded back before stepping out of the car and promptly falling to the ground.

Caleb was near my side before I could figure out what had happened. "What's wrong? Are you okay?"

I felt detached and dizzy, and when I shook my head, the confusion only got worse.

"Oh, great. Please don't tell me you fainted because the vampire was so handsome," Brandon said and then looked down at my leg and cursed.

Caleb was already examining me and cursing as well. "You've lost too much blood, Hanna. I hadn't realized it was bleeding so badly."

I stared numbly at my leg and blinked slowly as my brain was unable to process much at a time. "That's probably not good."

"Try the opposite of good. You should go to the hospital," Caleb said while frowning and gingerly removing the handkerchief he'd put there before. It was soaked and dripped dark spots onto the pavement.

"No way. My mom will know I've snuck out if she doesn't know already."

"Having your mom find out you did a totally normal teenage thing is a lot less bad than you dying," Caleb said flatly.

Brandon huffed and folded his arms across his chest. "Don't be a hero or something. Let him take you to the hospital."

Caleb disappeared for a second and came back, presumably from his car, carrying a first-aid kit. "I should have used this from the start. I'm sorry, Hanna. I forget how fast humans can bleed."

"You mean when you're not sucking the blood from their necks?" Brandon muttered.

Ripping open a big square of gauze, Caleb pressed it to my wound and caused me to hiss some more.

I stared into the dark sky, not wanting to look at my injury anymore. "Who knew a book could cause so much damage?"

"Hanna, can you walk?" Caleb's dark eyes shined from a nearby porch light.

"Let's see." I tried to gather my good leg underneath myself to push up with Caleb's help, but, for some reason, it wasn't listening. I gasped in pain and fell back down.

Caleb caught me and helped lower me back onto the cold pavement, cursing again. "We've got to take you to a hospital."

"No, no, no." I shook my head and then watched the world swirl around me in dizzy circles.

"Stop being stubborn, Hanna. Let the man get you some help. You should just be glad he isn't trying to suck up all the rest of your blood as it is!" Brandon leaned over and tried to catch my eye.

"Oh, that's a good idea. Caleb, just loan me some of your vampire magic, and I can heal right up without going to the hospital, scaring my mom, and making sure she doesn't ground either me or Trina from ever seeing you again."

I did feel a little drunk as I talked, but the idea was too good to pass up. Or... at least that's how it felt at the time.

"It doesn't work like that, doll," Caleb said, but his eyes told me he was considering it. "But... I do need you to be able to come help with this poltergeist and having you grounded or locked up inside the hospital wouldn't be great."

Brandon threw his hands up into the air. "Is everyone crazy? Since when is it a good idea to get that kind of help from a vampire? What is the world coming to?!"

"Yes, we don't want me locked up. It's that easy," I muttered sleepily and then the world went dark.

I woke up inside my bedroom. The only light came from the desk lamp, casting a dim glow over the familiar objects around the room.

Caleb was sitting on the bed next to me while Brandon paced back and forth across the carpet.

"What happened?" My voice was groggy, and it was hard to blink without letting my eyes close again for a while, but I felt way less drunk than I had.

"You crazy girl! He did exactly what you suggested. If I weren't dead already, you would be the death of me!" Brandon shouted while still having the presence of mind to keep his voice hushed enough to not draw Gran's attention who was probably in a nearby room or down the hallway.

Caleb was much calmer, and he smiled kindly as he moved a strand of my hair off my forehead. "I promised your grandma I'd take good care of you. It wasn't ideal, by any means, but I gave you some of my blood. It doesn't take much for the vampire magic, as you call it, to work through your body and help speed the healing process. I wouldn't go run a marathon right now or anything, but you should be feeling fine by the morning."

"I'm not sure if I should thank you or curse you." I blinked slowly, waiting for my brain to tell me how to feel.

"I mean, it was your idea." Caleb's smile turned from kind into teasing as he stood and tucked the blankets in around my arms. "My blood will be out of your system in a few days with no lasting effects."

"Are you sure she won't turn into a vampire?" Brandon had stopped pacing and was staring at Caleb with fiery eyes.

"Are you sure I won't turn into a vampire?" I echoed Brandon's words, finding out that I very much needed the answer to that question.

"Not to worry, doll. It takes much more than that to turn into a vampire, as cool as a Seer vampire would be," Caleb said with an appreciative nod.

"I feel so reassured."

"I'll check in with you tomorrow." He smiled and slipped out my window silently. He was even able to close the window behind him and pop the screen back in place so quickly and efficiently it could have all been a dream.

Brandon huffed and went back to pacing. "That was not smart. He says nothing will happen to you, but how can we know he isn't lying? You heard him. He'd be glad to see a Seer vampire."

"It's better than going to the hospital and getting in trouble, isn't it?" I said, snuggling deeper into my blankets and finding my eyes felt heavier by the second.

He shook his head. "I'm not so sure about that."

"You'd better go before Gran finds you in here. Then she'd probably move in, and we'll never get time to ourselves." My words slurred, and my eyes drifted shut.

I felt a cold brush of air and a soft kiss on my forehead. "You're lucky I don't have anyone else to hang out with, or I'd leave you to deal with your crazy vampire drama all by yourself."

I slipped into sleep with a smile on my face.

Chapter 10

T he next morning was Tuesday, but I felt like I'd lived a whole week already. I was tired, but somehow not sore or weak. In fact, I almost felt good.

As I dressed, I examined my leg, and weird memories flooded into my head. I remembered most of it, but it grew fuzzy after I'd gotten into Caleb's car. I was able to piece enough of it together to realize, with overwhelming horror and embarrassment, that I'd drank vampire blood, and what was worse, the idea had been my own suggestion.

My stomach twisted at the thought, and I shuddered. However, as I inspected the pink skin on my calf, I had to admit there were curiously blessed properties of drinking the vampire magic, or whatever I had embarrassingly called it last night.

No wonder Brandon had been so beside himself.

My leg was completely healed, and I felt no side effects of having lost so much blood. The only thing I could do was hope Caleb had been honest about the chances of me turning into a vampire and that the blood would be out of my system in a few days.

Guilt accosted me as I stood in the kitchen, staring at the contents of the fridge and seeing the leftovers of last night. How had I let myself eat so much? In the light of the morning with semi-renewed energy, it was unfathomable to me that I had allowed myself to eat such a cheesy, calorie-laden meal. I couldn't keep doing that or I'd end up huge.

I grabbed a diet soda and skipped the banana that morning. I didn't deserve to eat anything for a while.

As I headed to the table where my backpack was sitting, Mom whirled into the kitchen. She was humming as she got out the coffee can and started fiddling with the machine. It was probably the first time since Dad left that she didn't have puffy, red eyes after waking up.

Gran was nowhere to be seen which kind of surprised me. She'd been hovering closely all week. Perhaps even ghosts needed a break sometimes.

"You seem happier today," I said as I zipped up my bag, making sure I was ready for the day. Usually, I did that the night before, but I'd had other things on my mind.

Mom turned and flashed a smile at me. "I do feel better. I can't explain it, but this morning I felt different when I woke up. Don't get me wrong, I'm still upset and sad, but it's like I saw a peek of sunshine through the clouds. It also helps that I've got my first personal photography booking from my website last night. It's just one session, but it fills me with hope for the future, you know?"

"Really? That's so good!"

"What's so good?" Trina wandered into the kitchen, looking sleepy. Her hair and makeup were done but she was still wearing her pajamas.

"Mom got her first solo booking!" I offered before Mom could, maybe as excited as she was, but not for the money. I was just glad something could pull her out of the sad funk, even if just for a moment.

"Perfect! I need a homecoming dress. Honestly, I'm behind and should already have one hanging in my closet ready to make me look gorgeous this Saturday." Trina got a mug out of the cupboard and waited on Mom to get the coffee ready.

"Oh? Did someone ask you yet? I thought you said you hadn't gotten a date?" Mom asked as she opened the fridge and shuffled around inside.

Trina gave me a knowing smile to which I returned somewhat wobblier than hers had been. "I have a feeling I'm going to get asked very soon, but if not, I can still go anyway. It's my senior year. I shouldn't miss out because a dumb boy doesn't know he should ask me out."

Mom chuckled and put some bread in the toaster. "True enough. I love my strong, independent daughters."

We both beamed at the compliment.

"Unfortunately, money is really tight. Your dad is going to help us out, of course, but I have no idea how much money I'll be making from my new business, and, for a bit, we might be living off of credit cards. Plus, as much as I didn't want you girls to have to worry about it, I've come to the decision that you both are old enough to be included in learning about the family's finances, and you should know that part of the reason your dad and I were fighting so much was because we were struggling...how do I put this? We had different ideas on what we needed to spend money on."

I glanced at my phone, knowing it was time to leave for school if I wanted to enjoy my walk without having to run, and from the state of Trina's dress, it was obvious I would have to wait longer to catch a ride with her.

"Oh! That's terrible." Trina frowned into her mug.

"We'll get through it, Mom. I know we can." I went over and gave her a quick peck on the cheek. "We'll do this together. I'll see you after school."

Mom gave me a soft smile, but I could tell that talking about money had brought the gloomy cloud back into her eyes.

I found myself alone with Emma in our section of the locker room before P.E. I swooped in to ask if she'd learned anything more about her ghost but made sure to keep my voice quiet so the other girls in the locker room wouldn't notice our odd conversation.

"How did you sleep last night?" I asked by way of broaching the subject.

We were both rummaging around our lockers and getting changed into P.E. clothes. The familiar smell of old socks and sweaty bodies floated around us as chatter from other girls echoed loudly.

"Not great." Emma's eyes were red around the edges, despite the eyeliner she'd tried to use to cover it up. "I tried to sleep on the couch like you said, but I couldn't get her cries out of my head, even if I couldn't directly hear them. It's like my brain was waiting for it all night. So, I went back to my room and sat on the bed, just waiting to hear the cries. But they never came. Are you sure you didn't get rid of her?"

I chuckled as I laced my shoe. "You saw how angry she was when we left. No, she's still in there. She might have worn herself out and needed to take a break. Were you able to find out about her family or the people who lived there before you?"

Emma kept her voice quiet. "I asked my mom what she knew about the people we'd bought the house from, and she told me this terrible story. I guess that's another reason I couldn't sleep. I couldn't stop thinking about it."

"Does it have to do with the girl in the attic?"

"It might?"

Addy popped around the lockers and was slightly out of breath. "Phew! I thought I was going to be late for sure."

Emma and I both were startled to see her for some reason. She shared the same space as we did, and she was there every day just the same as us. We had been too wrapped up in our spooky conversation.

Checking the time on my phone, I gave Addy a friendly smile. "You've got two minutes to change. You'd better hurry."

She cursed and began frantically getting her stuff together. Out of politeness, we waited even though we were fully dressed and ready to go.

The room emptied out around us, and we could hear Coach Reed's sharp voice every time someone opened the door to the gym.

Finally, Addy was ready, except for her shoelaces being tied, and we rushed out into the gym just as Coach began class. "Okay. You all know the drill by now. Five minutes to stretch and then we're jogging around the gym."

As we sat in a circle, Addy nimbly tied her shoes. "So, how are you guys today?"

Emma glanced at me, and I shrugged while extending one leg out and feeling the stretch along my leg as I touched my toes.

"We were just talking about the family who lived in my house before us. My mom heard this terrible story, and I still can't quite believe it."

"Really?" Addy began stretching her legs as well.

Emma nodded and pulled her feet towards herself to stretch her inner thighs. "Apparently, the family who lived there had two little girls."

I raised my eyebrows. "Two? Are you sure?"

Addy gave me a confused look that Emma and I ignored, probably cluing her in that something more was happening than we were saying, but I'd said the words before I thought about them.

Emma nodded and glanced at Addy before continuing. "There were two girls, both sisters, obviously. The crazy thing is that the older sister disappeared when she was eleven, which was about ten years ago or so."

"What do you mean she disappeared?" I switched legs and kept stretching.

"That's just it. No one knows what happened. The family went to bed like usual one night, but the next morning, the oldest girl was gone. Just missing. There was no evidence of a break-in, and she didn't pack any of her stuff, so it didn't look like she ran away or something. She was just gone."

"That's terrifying." Addy scrunched her face in worry.

"Tell me about it. Afterward, the younger sister was never the same. She was so upset that she cried in her room for days."

"Interesting," I said and looked up towards the gym's too-bright lights.

"Interesting? Seems like an odd response," Addy said. "It's more like horrible. I mean, I've heard of bad things happening like that on TV shows and stuff, but you don't usually hear about it in real life. There's no wonder the younger sister was never the same."

Emma gave me a pointed look and nodded. "You're right. It is terrible."

I gave them an apologetic smile. "Definitely terrible."

It's not like I was heartless. I just had my focus on working with the ghosts, that's all. Obviously, I wasn't about to explain that though.

Coach blew her whistle, and we jogged around the gym, talking about more normal things for the rest of the period.

After class, Emma and I got dressed slowly, letting Addy get ready and move on so we could talk some without her.

"See you guys later!" She waved and dashed out of the locker room to go to her next class.

Emma swung her backpack onto her shoulder and shut her locker door. Talking quietly, she said, "So I'm thinking the younger sister is my ghost."

I slid my feet into my flats and wiggled them around a bit to get them on right. "She could be. Do you know if she died later or something? Does your mom know the name of the family? Maybe we can look them up online."

Emma nodded. "I'll see if I can ask her. They probably had to sign some stuff when we bought the house, right? Maybe their family name will be there."

"As much as I'm sure you want to get rid of this ghost as soon as possible, I'm thinking it's best if I don't disturb her until we have more information," I said quietly as we left the locker room and entered the chaotic halls.

"That makes sense. I'll text you what I find out after school, and we can go from there."

Chapter 11

The next few classes went by slowly as I kept thinking about that family and how sad it would have been to lose a sister like that. I know that if something had happened to Trina at eleven years old, I wouldn't have ever been the same either.

Noah might have tried to talk to me a few times in history class, but I was too distracted to give him much thought. Plus, I was still mad. I felt dumb for being mad about him taking his obvious girlfriend to homecoming, so I decided that being distant and distracted was better than being angry and short-tempered with him.

Mr. Tyler didn't do anything out of the ordinary for a history teacher like sprout fur or howl at the ceiling. Part of me was beginning to wonder if I'd imagined the whole werewolf thing.

When the bell rang for lunch, I headed towards my locker at a slow pace, totally certain I did not want to hang out at our table while having to watch Noah and Andrea swoon over each other. I thought about where I could go as I walked, trying to ignore the hollowness in my stomach and the trembling of my fingers.

As I was putting my stuff away, Caleb popped out of nowhere. I didn't even see him walking down the hall towards me.

"How's your leg? How do you feel?"

I shrugged. My irritation with Noah and Andrea coupled with the frustration of feeling hungry while having totally eaten like a pig the night before was making it hard for me to feel like the most pleasant person in the world.

"Did you ask Trina to the dance yet?"

Caleb leaned back on the lockers next to mine and fiddled with a pen. He could swirl it deftly around his fingers without even thinking about it. "I will. I have to say, it's kind of weird how badly you want me to do that. You could have probably asked for lots of things, and my seethe would have figured out how to get it for you. Even a new car or some cash or something, but the first thing you ask for is for me, a blood-sucking vampire, to take your sweet sister on a date."

I frowned and didn't need Brandon to be hanging around to hear his teasing voice in my head. *He's got a point, you know. Vampires are bad news.*

"I just want my sister to be happy. What's so wrong with that?"

Caleb's eyebrows rose at my snippy tone. "Nothing, but are you sure it isn't to make yourself feel better at the guilt of hanging out with me so much?"

I kept frowning but didn't bother to answer his question. We both knew the answer.

"Why don't you go ask her right now?"

"I thought we could spend lunch researching that ghost. Unless you don't want to hang out with me, that is." He gave me a teasing grin.

"I don't actually. I'll go do the research, and you go ask Trina out. And since you mention cash, maybe you could slip me some so Trina can get herself a pretty dress without knowing it was you who paid for it."

Caleb chuckled and stood straight. "You drive a hard bargain."

"Listen, if you're as old as you say you are, and you drive that insane car, I'm sure you could spare a few bucks. Besides, if she looks good, you'll also look good with her on your arm."

Chuckling again, he pulled out his phone. "Fair enough, but there is one condition."

I eyed him skeptically. "What?"

"You have to buy yourself one, too."

Huffing, I shook my head. "I don't even have a date. Are you trying to get two dates to the dance?"

He flashed his white teeth at me in a way that sent tingles down my arms. "I wouldn't worry too much about not having a date. Plus, it just wouldn't be fair. Dressing up is fun to do sometimes, and I have a feeling I'm not the only one who would want to see you. Now, give me your info."

Sighing, I gave him my digital payment account information. He sent me the money and left to go find Trina, supposedly. I almost felt guilty taking money from him, but it was for my sister, and I was certain he had plenty to spare.

On my way to the library, I stopped by the vending machines. I knew I couldn't have food or drink inside the library, but I put in a few quarters and got a packet of mints. They weren't going to make me huge, but they might help my stomach and mouth feel less like eating all the carbs I could get my hands on. Plus, they'd give me pleasant breath at the same time.

As I entered the library, I took a deep breath through my nose, feeling the tingles from the mints and enjoying the peace after the chaos of the lunchtime sounds and smells. There were a few kids in there, some reading on their own, others sitting together at a table playing a card game.

The research I needed to do was probably all online, so I went to the computer section and picked a seat far from anyone else. I could have probably done the same kind of searches from my phone but going to the library was an excuse to be busy during lunch. Also, it might have been a tad easier to scroll and type on the computer than it would have been on my phone.

As I sat, I tried to look around the area for any ghosts, afraid I would accidentally stumble into one if I wasn't prepared for their presence. The last time I'd been in the library, a random lady ghost had dropped a real-life physical book on my desk. The book had happened to have the information I needed to help Mr. Tyler, but I hadn't seen the lady since.

I stared at the white screen of the internet search page and tried to figure out where to start. Deciding I needed someone to bounce ideas off, I closed my eyes and mentally summoned Brandon. I wasn't sure it would work without saying his name out loud, but the hairs on my neck prickled right before he appeared in the chair next to me.

"Oh, the library. How fancy. Couldn't go a half a day without needing me?" He batted his eyelashes prettily.

I obviously couldn't hold a conversation with a ghost in the middle of the library, so I pulled up a note-taking app on the computer and typed a message to him.

We need to find out more about Caleb's ghost. I figured having you here might help me come up with ideas, or at least have someone to bounce ideas off of.

Brandon's eyes scanned my words as a grin grew on his face. "Don't lie. You missed me."

I gave him a look, went back to the computer screen, and pulled up the internet again. Inside the search bar, I put the name of the cathedral and Clara's name, trying to see if there was a link between the two.

There wasn't, at least not that I could see from the first two pages. Most of it was talking about the history of the church and the services it offered as a homeless shelter. No one named Clara was associated with the church in any obvious way.

But vampire secrets were unlikely to be obvious.

"Try searching for Dion and see what comes up." Brandon looked around the library, seemingly interested in how it had changed since he'd been there last.

I figured a prominent vampire wouldn't have his own website or was going to be easily searchable, but I didn't have much to lose so I typed in his name.

A few companies included the name and, of course, its origin in Greek mythology popped up. There was even a songwriter with the name, but, no surprise, nothing about vampires.

"Okay," I whispered to myself and Brandon, "that's not helpful. But what about..."

I typed Clara and Dion in the search box. There was nothing significant at first, but I had no idea what else to search for so I kept scrolling through the pages. Usually, if I didn't find what I was looking for in the first two pages, I gave up. However, I kept going this time, trying to search my brain for other things I might be able to look up, for any clue that might help me with this screeching poltergeist.

Six pages in, an obscure article caught my eye. When I clicked on it, Brandon leaned into the screen to see what I was looking at.

It was an eight-year-old article from a local newspaper. The title was "Missing Girl's Body Found", and the internet search had flagged the name Clara in bold.

Brandon and I read it quickly, our eyes zipping over the words.

Thanks to an anonymous tip, authorities discovered a young girl's body that appears to have been dumped in the East River. The body was washed up on the shore and resembles that of a missing girl from the area. It has not been confirmed, but sources speculate this may be Clara Sharp who disappeared from her own home four years ago. The cause of death is not known at this time, but there appeared to be savage marks all over the girl's neck and arms. There were also marks on her ankles and wrists, indicating she may have been shackled for a long period of time.

My eyes were wide as I met Brandon's. Quickly, I moved to the note app and typed my thoughts.

That's got to be the girl from the church. The East River isn't far from the church, either.

Brandon nodded as he read my words. "Vampires are too smart to dump bodies in the river. What do you bet she was escaping, weak from being held captive for so long, and fell in? She couldn't survive in her weakened state and drowned."

I nodded, but kept my eyes on the screen, trying to keep anyone from thinking I was having a conversation with something that wasn't there.

This story feels familiar in some way. Emma's ghost had lost an older sister and, while we don't know the family name, I'm wondering if these two girls might be connected. How tragic would it be if this was her sister?

"Vampires are monsters. I keep trying to remind you. I wouldn't put any of this past them," Brandon said.

I never said they weren't. I just happen to believe they might not all be the same, just as humans aren't. We need to find out the last name of the family who lived in Emma's house. If they are sisters, it might help us figure out how to help them. Even though Caleb only wants us to get information from Clara, I wouldn't feel right letting her haunt that church after we get what we want. We've got to figure out a way to help her cross over too.

"That would be ideal, yes, but how do we do that?"

I allowed myself to share a worried look with Brandon, hoping if anyone noticed, they'd just assume I was staring off into space.

Shortly after that, the bell rang. I said a discreet goodbye to Brandon and headed to class. It was difficult to concentrate on anything and having math at the end of the day made it worse.

I got to class before Andrea and decided to take a seat in the back, hoping the teacher wouldn't notice I was so distracted. My thoughts kept tumbling around, trying to connect pieces. Why would the vampires want to abduct this specific girl? They could probably get their hands on any random human they wanted, focusing on homeless people and runaways who wouldn't be missed. It didn't make sense for them to take a girl who had been sleeping soundly in her own home.

It was easy to picture a vampire sneaking in and out of the house without evidence after having seen Caleb creep in through my own window. It wasn't a question of who spirited the girl away, but rather *why*.

Maybe Caleb would be able to answer that.

Andrea whisked into the room just as the tardy bell rang. There were a few open seats, but Andrea chose the one next to me. She shot me a small smile as she sat down, but we didn't get to talk as Mr. Mink started class.

He called for us to switch our homework papers from the night before. Andrea gave me such a sweet smile as we exchanged homework that I felt a little creeped out. Then I looked down at her empty page and realized what that smile was trying to convey.

I hadn't been there at lunch for her to take my answers, and she had probably planned on having me fill it out while we were supposed to be correcting, not even attempting to try and do her own homework. In the past, I might have been tempted to do as she wanted and fill in the correct answers as Mr. Mink read them out from the front of the room. Instead, images of her and Noah dancing romantically while staring into each other's eyes as disco lights and loud music bounced around the room entered my brain. I folded my arms over my chest and sat back in my chair as Mr. Mink began reading the answers.

She shot me glances of dismay at first, and I gave her a smug smile. Then she looked down at my paper and turned back to me with a spiteful grin. I watched in frustration, mostly with myself, as she started changing the answers on my paper, so they were wrong. I had written with a pencil, so it was easy for her to change it up. Then she got out a pen and put crosses over each math problem, making it impossible for me to try and correct them in the short time before Mr. Mink would be there to pick it up.

How had I not seen it coming? Of course, she was that petty.

I gave her a steely stare as we exchanged papers, hers blank and mine covered in angry x's. She smiled sweetly again and hastily scribbled in some of the correct answers before Mr. Mink called for us to pass our papers forward.

Anger coursed through me as the teacher started the lecture for the day. I thought of all kinds of things I could do—the worst of them being nothing short of having a certain vampire friend attack her one night. I could have told Mr. Mink the whole story and what was happening, but I might have gotten in trouble for helping her for so long. Plus, that just didn't seem like enough punishment for her.

I was fuming and shaking with nervous energy as class finally ended. There were so many things I wanted to say to her, but I was worried I'd mess it all up. Confrontations like these always made me nervous, but I was too upset to let this one slide by. I had to say something.

"Andrea, that wasn't cool. I've helped you so—"

She shut me down with a flipped hand in my face. "Stop. You're pathetic. You think you can bend some rules when you get something out of it, but then follow the rules when it suits you. You know what? Since you're so desperate to hang out with us that you'll let me copy your math homework every day, let me help you take that issue away. Consider yourself blocked. Now you don't have to worry about sharing your answers. You're welcome."

She flipped her blonde hair in my face and strode out of the room, leaving me staring after her in angry surprise.

Lots of witty comebacks flooded my mind once she was gone, and I cursed at myself for being so slow—slow at the comebacks and slow for thinking Andrea could have been my friend.

I grumbled to myself all the way to my locker as I shoved things inside.

"Guess who asked me to homecoming?" Trina did a little twirl before bumping into me, nearly toppling me over.

"Er, Santa Claus?"

"Hah, so funny. I guess you were able to get through to him, after all. What did you say to convince him to go to a dance? Seriously, I don't think he's gone to one his whole high school career."

I smiled despite my recent anger, glad that she was so excited and that I had a part in helping my sister be happy. Or at least, for now. "It was easy when he already wanted to ask you out. He said he's been waiting for a good time, and this seemed like a good time."

She sobered slightly and leaned back on the lockers. "Now to only find a good dress that is somehow super cheap, or even better, free."

I shut my locker and tried to relax my features. Lying should have been second nature to me at that point, having to hide my ghostly powers for all my life, but I still wasn't good at straight-out lying, especially to my sister or my mom.

"Listen, I've been saving some money up from birthdays and odd jobs and stuff, and I think I have enough that we can both get a nice dress."

"Both of us? You would do that for me?" Trina pressed a hand to her chest and pulled her eyebrows into a touched expression.

"Of course. It's no big deal."

"So," she leaned in closer with a sneaky smile, "did you get a date? Did Noah finally ask you?"

Frustration burned through me at the mention of his name, and I may have growled.

Trina backed up and laughed. "Oookay. Guess that's a no."

"Sorry. It's been a day. Why don't we go shopping? We don't have much time to find the perfect dresses." I shut my locker and zipped up my bag which held more homework to do than I wanted to face, including a new set of math that I had no idea how to do after I had completely spaced out the whole lecture, thinking about the best ways to torture a certain blonde cheerleader.

The drive to the mall was pleasant enough. We could have ordered some nice dresses online, but there wasn't enough time to see if they fit, possibly needing to send them back. We'd have to buy dresses the old-fashioned way.

While we were there, the warm smells of the pretzel store wafted down the main thoroughfare. It smelled so good, I had to close my eyes for a second to savor it. Trina and I both looked at each other and grinned, not even having to verbally confirm what we were both thinking.

Pretzels, bread, and carbs weren't good for me, but it was like I couldn't help indulging for a moment. I had been good all day, and a pretzel with a diet soda wouldn't make me gain weight, probably.

When the salt hit my tongue, combined with the warm, soft bread, I knew I'd made the right choice. I'd worry about the consequences later.

After a few hours of trying on several dresses, Trina trying on way more than I did, we finally picked one each and paid with it using my Paypal account and Caleb's money.

I was nearly exhausted by the time we made it home, and I plopped onto my bed to take a nap, ignoring the pile of untouched homework staring at me from inside my backpack.

It was about 7:30 by the time I woke up, and it took me several minutes to come to myself. I stared at my ceiling and let my brain remember who I was and what was happening in my life.

I pulled out my phone and saw I'd gotten a text from Emma. Thankfully it wasn't but twenty minutes old. I would have felt bad if she'd been waiting for a while for me to get back to her.

Hi, Hanna! I just checked with my mom, and she says the last name of the family was Sharp. I Googled their family and found a few articles about the disappearance and then finally they found her body a few years later. It's such a sad story!

She'd pasted a few links for me to read and one of them was the article I'd read already. The story was super sad, and I frowned for a minute, trying to figure out how this information could help me with both of the ghosts.

I thanked her and told her I would work on figuring out how this information could help and that we'd meet at her house after school the next day to try working with the ghost.

With a groan, I pulled out my backpack and moved to my desk where I could put in some serious homework time. I was behind from spending my evening yesterday chasing ghosts and now had the new homework from today.

The house was quiet, so I figured Mom was still out for the day, and Trina was inside her own room, maybe staring blankly at her homework books just like I was.

After a while, when my brain finally woke up and I was making some progress, I heard a light tapping on my window.

Sighing, I got up and opened the blinds knowing exactly who to expect. Sure enough, Caleb's white grin met me from the other side as he popped my screen off. I opened the window.

"You know you could just text me. This whole sneaking into my window thing is so last century." I stepped away from the window to let him climb in with his silent grace.

"But then I wouldn't get to see your pretty face. Plus, some things are too important to leave to a text." His teasing grin faded into a more somber look, his eyes taking on a more sincere urgency.

I sighed and gestured for him to take a seat at my desk. "What's up?"

"We really need to find out where Dion is," he said as he sat in my chair backward, facing me as I sat on the bed. "My queen is putting lots of pressure on me to do it this way before she starts to get violent. I've been reassuring her over and over that this is the easiest and safest way, but she has her doubts."

"Ugh, not sure if I should be upset or flattered that you had such confidence in me to assure the queen of a freaking vampire seethe that I could help her out." I took a deep breath, trying to steady myself.

Caleb put his long fingers into his hair and tugged at it. "I know, but I'm trying to save lives here. She's about to go postal on the city, and she isn't known for her sanity as it is. She doesn't care about human lives. The only reason she's been reigned in this long is by the pleadings of her council and my promises to get a Seer to help us."

"This begs the question of why do *you* care about human lives? You're probably the weird one in your vampire seethe, aren't you? You only drink blood from banks or willing volunteers. You don't like to kill people. You are going to high school even though you probably graduated several hundred years ago. What's wrong with you?"

The chuckle I had been going for surfaced to his lips for a second and then hid back away under his distress. "Yes, I'm the weird one. There are lots of reasons, but the ones that appeal to my seethe and make the most sense to them is survival. If we killed all the humans or even just some of them, we'd risk exposing ourselves. As weak as humans are—"

"Thank you."

"You're welcome. As weak as y'all are, if you get organized together, you could potentially do a lot of damage to us. There aren't many of us left, for various reasons usually having to do with inner politics, bored necromancers, or werewolves, so we need to be careful."

"Well, there's a twist I didn't see coming. I'm sorry I haven't been more helpful. I really don't know what I'm doing. I just recently decided that I should actually try to work with my powers but starting with a vampire and a poltergeist seems to be a bit out of my depth."

"I know. I'm sorry." He kept tugging at his hair. "That's why I was relieved to hear your grandma was still around. Do you think you could get her to help out more? She might be more helpful than your current partner, anyway. What does he even do?"

I laughed, despite myself and shook my head. "Sometimes I don't even know."

"Is he here right now?"

"No, we don't spend every second together. Thank you very much."

"Yet." Caleb's lips pulled up slightly on one side to give me a grin.

"Anyway, yes, I'll see if Gran can help, but I cannot do it tonight. First off, I can't keep sneaking out of my house so late. Second, I'm so exhausted I wanted to go to bed at seven. And third, I've just really got a lot of homework to do. You should have picked a Seer with nothing else to do but help ghosts all day."

"You're my only choice." His eyes focused on me with pleading intensity, and I actually started to feel bad. For a vampire.

"You saw what happened when we went in there, not knowing what to do. Who knows? This time the whole building could really collapse. Can you give me a day at least to get with Gran and figure out what she would do? I'll probably have to take her with me, and that will mean not sneaking out and leaving at a reasonable hour, which it is not right now."

Caleb stared at me for a second, and I could see him thinking, weighing the risks. Then he sighed and stood. "You have some valid points. Let's just hope that the queen will agree with you. She's losing her already fragile mind with having her niece missing. It's not going well. She's already killed three of Dion's followers, trying to get information from them, and that alone could start a war."

"Maybe Dion took the niece because he wanted to start a war. Did you think of that?" I may have bobbed my head a bit with some sass.

"Yes." His smile was slow but revealed his canines. "That's another reason why we don't want to go to war. That would be giving him what he wants."

"You know you're creepy sometimes, right?"

The predatory smile didn't leave his face as he climbed back out my window, put the screen in place, and gave me a little wave with his fingers.

I shook my head. "Ugh, vampires. Hey, Gran, are you there?"

Thinking about her blue form and her kind face, I tried to summon her like I did with Brandon. It took several more seconds while intensely focusing before she appeared in my bedroom.

Her eyes were wide as she looked around. "What? How did I get here?" Then she focused on me. "Did you do this?"

"Uhm, yes? Sorry. Were you in the middle of an important business meeting or something?"

"No, of course not. I was just keeping an eye on your mom as she worked retouching up some pictures she took today. There was an adorable baby girl there who kept spitting up every time your mom would take a shot. It was darling." Gran sat on my bed.

"Sounds lovely."

"It's just that I've never been able to summon a ghost like that away from their haunt." She shook her head and looked at me in wonder. "You can already do so many things that I couldn't do, and you're just starting. It's amazing."

I smiled awkwardly, unsure what to say. "Thank you? I don't know how I'm doing any of it, really. It's kinda like throwing spaghetti at the wall and trying to see what sticks."

"It looks like everything you're doing is sticking at this point."

I sat down next to her. "Not everything. That's why I wanted to talk to you. I need your help."

Chapter 12

It was late before I finally got to bed that night, and I still hadn't finished all of my homework. Gran and I talked and talked, trying to come up with a plan. She told me several stories of ghosts she had helped, but overall, she tended to keep away from those who had already lost much of themselves like the vampire's poltergeist had. The stories helped a little, and we came up with some things to try, but overall, I still wasn't feeling that great about it.

In P.E. class, after I'd finally dragged myself to school, Emma, Addy, and I jogged slowly around the gym. Since Addy was there, Emma and I weren't able to talk about weird things like ghosts, so we mostly chatted about the upcoming dance and other schoolish things.

I avoided Noah again in history class, sitting beside some other kids I didn't really know. Unfortunately, he came over to me after class let out.

"Hey, can we talk?"

I glared at my desk as I put my stuff away. "I guess."

"Look, I heard what happened between you and Andrea, and I feel really bad about it."

I stood and slung my bag over my shoulder. He was still taller than me by a foot or so, but I held my gaze steady and strong. "So bad that you had to text me immediately to check in on me and end your relationship with her right away?"

He wilted under my look, and his shoulders slumped.

"That's what I thought."

It would have been an excellent last line, but he grabbed my arm, not tight enough to leave a bruise but enough to keep me from walking away.

I turned and looked back at him with a frown.

"You don't get it. There are things going on here that I can't talk about, but you're important to me. I value our friendship."

"You mean you value my powers."

Stung, he dropped his hand from my arm. Despite being angry at him, I still couldn't help noticing how my skin tingled where his grip had been.

"That's the truth, isn't it? You've only been trying to be my friend this whole time because you suspected what I could do. Because you knew what my grandma could do."

"No, that's not it. I—"

"You're going to have to do better than that." I walked away from him and nodded once to Mr. Tyler who stood at his desk, trying not to appear as if he could hear us, but I was sure he could.

Although I felt like I didn't have any friends anymore, it honestly felt good to stand up for myself to Noah and Andrea. So what if I had to spend my lunches alone in the library? At least I wouldn't be as tempted to eat food, and I wouldn't have to put up with Andrea cheating off my math homework to have a table to sit at.

The cafeteria was overrated anyway.

The rest of the classes went by normally. I tried to focus on the lectures and what we were learning. It was hard with all that was on my mind, but I gave it a good go. At lunch, I did indeed spend it alone in the library, but I had extra homework I hadn't gotten to so there was plenty to keep me busy. In fact, it was nice to have the solitude for a moment.

I got a few text messages from Noah with more apology BS that I ignored. If he really meant it, he'd show me with actions. Words would only go so far.

When French class came around, Randi shot me a few sad glances, but I ignored her. As far as I was concerned, if she wanted to be my friend, she could approach me. She was making a stance by not making one.

Thankfully, being blocked by Andrea meant that she wasn't going to talk to me. So, aside from the tension while she made a pointed effort not to look at me, math class was smooth and ended without anything to distract me from the lecture. Well...except my own dizzying thoughts concentrating on the ghosts I was going to try and talk to after school.

Emma met me at my locker like she had two days before. Her brown hair was again piled in a messy bun on her head, but she was wearing less makeup and her eyes seemed less red. She greeted me with a smile.

"Hi, Hanna. How's your day been?"

"It's been a day. You?" I closed my locker and slung my bag over my shoulder.

She shrugged. "It's fine. I noticed you weren't around at lunch with your usual friends. Has something happened?"

It was my turn to shrug. "Nah. No big deal. Just been spending lunches in the library to get homework done or to research on people that aren't quite alive anymore."

I gave her a small grin.

She grinned back. "Ah, I see. Well, do you want a ride to my place? Are you ready to go?"

I nodded. "That would be great."

As we pulled up to her house, I glanced carefully at the neighbor's, noting there were still plenty of ghosts milling about. It was just as sad as it was terrifying.

Someone ought to help them out.

Emma's house was again quiet as we entered. I supposed she came home to an empty house nearly every day, which seemed kind of lonely. Sometimes Trina was a pain in my behind, but overall, I was glad to have a sister.

"She was quiet again last night. I think I heard a few cries, but mostly it was quiet," Emma said as she led me back up the stairs.

"That's good. I wouldn't say she was getting better, but maybe she is still worn out. The more sleep you can get, the better, right?"

"For sure."

"So, listen, this might be really weird, but I'm going to call for some help today."

Emma sat on her bed, and I stood near the doorway. She furrowed her eyebrows together. "Why would that be weird?"

"Because you won't be able to hear or see this kind of help." I pulled my lips up in an awkward smile. "It's kind of my dead grandma, and my other ghost friend who likes to help with these situations."

Emma stifled a giggle. "Hanna, it's fine. I'm the one who asked you for help with a ghost, remember? If you need other ghosts to help you with this one, who am I to judge?"

We shared another smile.

"Okay, just wanted to warn you, is all."

She waved it off with a hand. "It's all good. Do you what you gotta do. I just want to get some sleep, and after hearing that sad story, it would feel good to help this girl stop crying every night."

"Speaking of their sad family, I think I know where her sister is haunting."

Emma blinked a few times. "Her sister is a ghost, too? Are you sure it's her?"

"Not one hundred percent, but I should know by today."

"Do you need my help?" She scooted to the edge of her bed in eagerness, and it made me smile.

"No, not as far as I know. I'll go up there and call my gran and partner. You'll probably hear me talking to them. I promise they're real, as far as ghosts can be real."

Emma chuckled and shook her head. "Don't worry. After hearing this ghost for months and with what happened in the attic after you left the other day, you don't have to worry about me not believing."

"This might sound silly, Emma, but I have to admit it's nice to have someone who believes me and who I can talk about this with. It's been kind of lonely, apart from the several ghosts I see all the time, but yeah, lonely."

"I bet. Well, you can talk to me about it any time."

We shared another smile.

"Alright, let's do this."

Emma jumped up to help me with the attic ladder, and I climbed up the wobbly steps. The attic was in more disarray from the last time I'd been in there. Boxes had toppled over and many had spilled random contents onto the floor. We had made the ghost so upset, she'd done some decent damage to the room.

"Oh man, Emma. It's a mess up here. I'm sorry. Don't know how you'll explain that to your parents after this is over," I said, peering over my shoulder as I climbed into the attic.

Emma shrugged. "I'll worry about that later. Ghost hunting is messy business."

"Indeed."

As I stood on the wooden attic floorboards, I looked around the dim room for the young girl. There was a blue flicker or two, but I couldn't be sure. Mentally, I imagined Brandon and called to him first because it was easier with him.

"Brandon?"

The neck prickles skittered, and he appeared in front of me.

"Top o' the morning to ya, lassie!" he said in a funny accent, nowhere near the Irish one he was going for.

"It's afternoon, almost evening, but whatever. Grandma Carey?" I had prepared Emma for hearing me talk to myself, but I kept my voice quiet, not wanting to disturb the ghost if I could help it.

Brandon and I stood for a second, waiting for her to appear.

"Does it usually take me this long to show up?" Brandon peered around a heaped pile of boxes.

I shook my head and closed my eyes, focusing on Gran's image in my mind, calling to her mentally and verbally. "Grandma Carey, can you hear me?"

After a few more seconds of waiting, she flickered into view. In awe, she looked around. "Where are we?"

"Oh, Gran. So glad to see you. I was worried this wouldn't work. Remember what we talked about last night?"

She focused her ghostly blue eyes on me, and memories seemed to seep into her mind. "Oh, right. Is this the attic?"

I nodded. "And you remember Brandon, of course."

Gran smiled and bobbed her head in greeting. "Of course. He seems to be always around these days."

I gave her a warning look, and she gave me another sweet smile.

"So have you seen the girl yet?" Brandon asked, walking through the boxes, going further into the room. "Little girl? Are you here?"

"Do we know her name?" Gran asked, standing next to me.

"Yes. She was able to tell us last time. It's Riley," I said, also looking around the room for a ghost that I hadn't brought with me.

"Riley, dear? Are you here?" Gran's voice was soft as she looked, searching for any sign of the little girl.

I heard her sniffles before I saw her blue, transparent head pop up over the top of a box and look at us.

Brandon, Gran, and I all froze once we saw her, afraid to spook her. Ironic, isn't it? Us trying not to scare a ghost.

"Riley, is that you?" Gran asked.

I decided to let her take the lead as she had more experience.

"Who are you? Why are you all blue?" Riley's eyes grew wide. "Are you a ghost?"

Worried, I looked at Gran, unsure of what to say, but Gran smiled. "Yes, sweet child, I am a ghost, but don't worry, I'm the good kind of ghost. I'm here to help you."

Riley ducked down behind the box so only her eyes were visible, which seemed to be a good sign. She might have been scared, but she was curious enough to still want to see what was happening. "There are no such thing as good ghosts. Ghosts are just ghosts."

Gran took her time answering the question as she found a box and sat on it, still allowing Riley some space but trying to appear more relaxed and conversational. "Where do ghosts come from?"

"From dead people."

"And are all people bad? Or are all people good?"

Riley shook her head slowly. "No, but dead things are bad."

Gran kept smiling kindly and speaking softly. "But all things die. Does that mean even the kindest person you have ever known will be bad after they die?"

The girl thought about it for a moment. Brandon took the time to give me an appreciative nod, indicating he approved of Gran's logical and kind methods. I had to admit they seemed to be working better than whatever I had tried two days ago.

"No, my sister is not bad, and she is dead."

My heart went out to the little ghost. Little did she know, her sister had kind of become a bad ghost. Hopefully, we could fix her.

Gran nodded encouragingly. "Yes, so is it possible there are good ghosts?"

Riley copied Gran's nod, albeit more slowly. "I guess."

"I promise there are good ghosts, and I'm one of them and guess what?" Gran leaned in closer to the girl while still sitting.

"What?" she asked, rising a little more over the box she was hiding behind.

"You're a good ghost, too."

I winced, waiting for the girl to start whining and the boxes to rattle around us. Instead, the girl came out from around the boxes completely and took a step towards Gran.

Riley's eyes were round and sad. "Did I die?"

Gran nodded again. "What do you remember?"

"I don't know. Is he dead, too?" Riley pointed to Brandon who plastered a nervous, yet friendly smile on his face.

"Yeah, he's dead, too. He's also a good ghost, even if he doesn't know it." Gran's smile turned into a teasing grin that Riley reciprocated.

"And who is she?" Riley pointed at me.

I probably looked as nervous as Brandon had and I hoped my smile was as friendly and less awkward than it felt like.

"That's my granddaughter. She's alive, but let's not hold it against her, alright? She can't help it."

Riley giggled, and the knots in my chest started to loosen a bit. Perhaps we could get this to work.

"Do you want to know something really cool about my granddaughter?" Gran lowered her voice even more into a shared conspiracy whisper.

Riley took a few steps closer, making her way through the boxes instead of having to go around them. "What?"

"She can see and talk to ghosts while nobody else can. Isn't that cool?"

Riley's attention turned to me again, and I tried to keep the smile on my face. "Hi, Riley."

"You can see ghosts? Aren't you scared all the time?"

I nodded and kneeled on the wooden floorboards so I could connect better with her on eye level. "Sometimes I am scared, but I'm not scared right now. My grandma is teaching me about ghosts, and she's explained that almost all ghosts are confused spirits who used to be humans and need someone to help them finish some business before they can go on to the next place."

Riley glanced at Gran for a second but then looked back at me. "What's the next place?"

"I'm sorry, sweetie. I have no idea. I do firmly believe that as long as you were a good person in life, the next place is much better than a dark, smelly, old attic, though." I punctuated my sentence by widening my smile, hoping to keep her talking and her mind open.

"I've watched many ghosts cross over," Gran said from her perch on the box, "and I can tell you that most of them are happy when it happens to them. The next place *is* better than this place. It's even better than being alive on the best day of your life."

"Are you here to help me go to the next place?" Riley's wide eyes looked hopeful and nervous.

"If you'd like," I said, "but we were wondering if you could help us with something before you go. Do you think we could work to help each other?"

Glancing first at Gran, who smiled in encouragement, Riley slowly nodded. "Okay. How do I help?"

Later, after giving Emma a hopeful goodbye and reassuring her we were working on a plan, I met Caleb outside the church with Brandon and Gran in tow. I was beginning to feel like a celebrity or something with an entourage following me around all the time, but I needed both of them to help me with what we were about to do.

Pink and purple hues from the sunset bathed the stone building in bright colors. Long shadows stretched across the street warning of the darkness to come with the night. Cars passed by periodically, and a few people came and went while walking on the sidewalk.

"I really wish I could go in there with you. It doesn't seem right to stand out here while you're in there battling." Caleb frowned as we stood side-by-side in front of the gate and stared up at the formidable church.

"I'm sure it would be good to have the added protection, so that's why I invited another person to come along this time. Necromancers can enter churches, right?" I shot him a teasing grin.

"Say what?"

And right on cue, Noah drove up and parked his car across the street.

Scowling, Caleb turned around and watched my friend walk toward us. "You invited him?"

"I didn't want to, trust me," I said with a low voice, hoping Noah wouldn't hear. "But he's the only other alive person I could think of who could be helpful doing a weird task for a weird group of not-humans."

"Now we're a real party," Brandon muttered and shook his head. "But I can't argue that having someone who could help you in the physical world isn't a bad idea. Especially after last time."

"What happened last time?" Gran's eyebrows rose in concern.

"We'll have to tell you later," Brandon said with an apologetic smile my way.

"Hey, guys. Wow, nice place," Noah said as he jogged across the street.

"I'm only tolerating your presence because I can't go in there my-self," Caleb nearly growled.

Noah grinned. "Right. That's why."

Caleb scowled, and I stepped in between the two. "Alright, yes, we get it. You guys don't like each other. Fine. Let's focus on the task here. There's a ghost inside that we need to at least calm down. Ideally, it would be great to have a long chat with her and find out more about Dion for the vampires, but this is going to take time."

"Time we don't have. The queen is right on the edge. I don't know what she'll do next, but, if we don't get answers soon, she'll do something, and it won't be pretty." Caleb's eyebrows moved together in worry, and the confidence he usually had disappeared as he talked about his queen.

It was slightly unnerving.

"I know. I'm sorry. All I can say is we're doing the best we can. I've brought Gran along with me this time so she can help me do a better job."

Caleb pressed his lips together but didn't say anything else.

"Noah, I'm sorry to invite you here after I've been avoiding you, but you're the only one I could think of who could help."

"Thank you?" Noah's eyebrows drew together in confusion.

"You're welcome. Well, your job is to watch out for physical things that could happen to me. Like in case a hobo gets adventurous or a book comes flying out of the dark. Here's your chance to put those football skills to use."

Noah nodded eagerly, and I wasn't sure if he was excited to help with some ghost hunting or only glad to help me because we hadn't been on the best of terms lately. Since he was a boy, he probably didn't have any idea why I had been so angry with him. Boys didn't pick up on important things sometimes.

"Don't worry, sucker," Noah said to Caleb. "I'll make sure she's okay. Too bad you can't go in there, eh?"

Caleb didn't need to respond verbally since the anger rolled off of him in waves.

"Alright, great. We'll be back soon." I flashed a reassuring smile towards Caleb and squeezed my way past the gate.

Noah was too big to get in the gap, so he had to move it. Screeching in agony, it announced to anyone nearby that we were entering the property.

There must have been some structural damage to the building from the ghost's last tantrum because there was a notice posted on the doors stating that no one was allowed inside by statement of the city.

The sign made me pause for at least a half-second before I pulled on the door handle.

"Why am I surprised that it's locked?" I frowned staring at the double doors.

"Because it wasn't last time?" Brandon shrugged. "Too bad you're alive." He chuckled as he walked right through the thick wood.

Gran followed behind him but not before shooting me a worried look. "Maybe it would be best if you stayed outside. This place looks dangerous."

I sighed and turned to Noah. "Okay, any ideas?"

"Too bad you don't have a sucker," Caleb called from the sidewalk with a pointed look on his face. "One of those could just bust the door open."

Noah flipped a certain finger but that only made the vampire chuckle.

"I guess it wouldn't hurt to at least try. Maybe the lock is rusted and old?" Noah backed up a few paces, took a running hop, and slammed his shoulder into the door.

The only thing that happened was a thudding sound that echoed from inside the building.

Rubbing his shoulder and frowning, Noah said, "Well, that didn't work."

"Maybe there is another way in." I stepped down the stone stairs and began to circle the building, looking for a hole or a window or something that I could access.

"At least there aren't any other people milling about right now. Last time there were several in the building that got spooked by the ghost's wailing," I said to Noah as we looked around.

The courtyard around the church looked as one would expect from a church in disrepair. Gnarled bushes and vines grew through overgrown grass. I kept to the path, hoping that I wouldn't get any ticks or chiggers from the high plants. Darkness was seeping into the yard, and the overgrown plants added to the lack of visibility.

"Why don't you think the ghost is wailing right now?"

"Not sure. Maybe she's taking a break. I might be able to see and talk to ghosts, but I honestly know very little about them. Plus, I should mention the two ghosts with us have already gone inside. My gran might be talking to our new friend as we speak."

"That must be weird having your grandma be a ghost. Or sad. I guess it could be sad, too. Were you close to her before she died?"

Noah was walking behind me and seemed more intent on talking to me than actually finding a way in. I wouldn't have blamed him except I had a job to do. I have to admit, though, that his efforts to learn more about me were flattering. Too bad I was still mad at him for choosing Andrea for the dance, even though I had known it was going to happen.

"No. She died when I was little. It's been nice to have a second chance to spend time with her, even if I can't eat her famous good cooking."

He chuckled, and I found myself enjoying the sound before I shook my head and told myself to focus.

"Gran and Brandon will probably be fine in there, but I can't help feeling anxious that I'm not in there too. At the very least, I can lend them energy."

Noah was quiet for a moment as we picked our way around a broken statue that had fallen over the path.

"It must be so amazing to do what you can do. I mean, I'm not without some cool tricks but being able to talk to the spirits like that would be so cool."

"I've been meaning to ask you about what kinds of tricks you can pull." I gave him a look to which he returned a half-smile.

"Necromancers can talk to the dead too. It's just usually the kind that don't have any brains left. They aren't very good at conversation, frankly."

I giggled at the thought of trying to talk to a zombie. "I bet. How do you do it? Do you have to use weird things to cast a spell of some sort or do you stand there and put your arms out until a dead body climbs out of the dirt?"

Even though I was angry with him, I couldn't pass up a chance to get more information.

"Er, it's a bit more complicated than that. To be honest, I'm still just an apprentice. It takes a long time to learn all of that and get the skills. Pretty much I just run errands for the order and sit on the sidelines while they do the impressive stuff."

"Hmm. Guess you got to start somewhere," I said, stopping to stare at an odd tree with branches reaching towards the church.

"That looks climbable," Noah said, standing next to me. He was so close that our arms brushed lightly, and goosebumps skittered down my skin.

Both wanting and not wanting to get away from being so close to him, I approached the trunk and found footholds for my sneakers. Without me asking, Noah placed his hand on my back to help steady me should I fall or something. It wasn't super effective as I began to climb and was quickly out of his reach, but the thought was sweet. The night air was cold where his warm hand had been, and I thought about it the whole way up the tree.

Thankfully the tree was stout and sturdy instead of thin and tall. The branch held my weight as I crawled across it to the gaping dark window. The glass had already been broken and it was quite possible that someone else had used this as an entry point before.

Noah followed behind me, and we were both breathing heavily as we reached the window. The tree branch extended all the way to the stone, thankfully. I perched on it to peer inside. I was happy to see the drop from the window to the floor wasn't more than six feet.

"I'm going to go in backward so I can land on my feet," I said in hushed tones, unsure of who I didn't want to hear me.

Shaking, I turned around so my legs were going through the window first. Noah watched me with pinched eyebrows, worried that I would fall. We weren't too far off the ground, but it was far enough to be slightly scary.

Carefully, I backed my way through the window, grateful that the glass shards on the sill were long gone. With a soft thud, my shoes landed on the stones inside, and I backed up to allow Noah to come in after me.

He decided to crawl in frontwards and jump down from the sill with a much cooler entrance than I had done.

Feeling embarrassed at my clumsy self, wondering if Noah had thought that Andrea probably would have flipped through the window gracefully and landed like a gymnast star, I turned to see where we were.

It was darker inside than it had been in the waning twilight outside, and my eyes took several seconds to adjust. Heaps of clothes and garbage lined along the wall, and I realized we were in the hallway Brandon and I had discovered the last time we were there.

"Nice place," Noah said quietly as he stood next to me.

Before I could think about how close he stood again, a wailing howl echoed down the hallway, and the hairs on my neck started their ghostly dance.

Chapter 13

I ran down the hallway, trying not to trip on any piles of dirty clothes or other questionable objects. Noah kept pace behind me with the grace of someone who did a lot of running in life.

Slipping on the smooth stone, I skid around the corner into the large cathedral space. Instantly, I picked out Gran and Brandon's blue forms glowing strongly in the darkness. Then I noticed another blue form zipping and zooming among the rafters.

I put my hands over my ears as she screamed again.

"What did you do?" I hissed as loudly as I dared.

Brandon and Gran stopped watching the unstable ghost and came toward me, Gran more hurried than Brandon.

"I'm sorry, dear. This is a formidable poltergeist. I'm not sure there's much left inside of her at all," Gran said when she was close enough to talk quietly to me. It was still hard to hear her over the screaming of the poltergeist.

"I know! That's why I brought you to help."

"She was quietly singing to herself when we got here, and we talked for a few minutes. She didn't go crazy until I asked her a question though. It's not Gran's fault. Can I call you Gran, Gran?" Brandon said, joining our group.

"What's happening?" Noah kept his voice hushed, and his wide eyes looked around the room, searching for signs of movements he could see.

"We're dealing with a really angry ghost. Noah, I need you to stay hidden and quiet. The less overwhelmed she feels, the better. Brandon, you go sit next to Noah." I pointed to an overturned bench near the corner.

"What? You're literally benching me?" Brandon pouted.

Noah just nodded, understanding he was out of his element and that listening to me was the best way he could help.

"Listen, B. You're the one who just made her mad. Let me try to calm her down. The less out-numbered she feels, the better, okay?" I said, urging him with my eyes to listen.

Frowning, he huffed and crossed his arms over his chest. "Okay, but if Noah starts trying to put the moves on me, I'm out of there."

I would have chuckled if not for an old boot that came hurtling through the darkness. I saw it just in time to duck.

Noah and Brandon scurried behind the bench, and Gran moved between me and the ghost as if she could protect me in some way.

"Clara!" I yelled, trying to at least get her attention. If she could recognize her name, it would be a good step in the right direction.

The girl screamed again and blew through a pile of clothes, sending up dirty fabrics into the air.

"Clara! What would Riley think?!" I yelled into the rafters, hearing my voice echo through the empty space.

The wailing stopped abruptly, and the silence that descended was both startling and a relief.

I didn't dare breathe in case doing that would set Clara off again. The others must have felt the same way because none of us moved or said a single word.

"Riley?" Clara's voice came from everywhere, but it was still somehow hushed.

A blue flickering appeared on the stage, and, when she fully formed, I was struck again by how small she was. After having spent more time with Riley, I could see that, even though Clara was the oldest, Riley had died older. They were both still just little girls.

Slowly, I took a few steps up the aisle towards the stage. "Clara? Can you hear me?"

She sniffed and wiped at a few ghostly tears.

I took it as a good sign and walked closer. "Do you remember who you are?"

Hiccupping, she took a deep breath. It probably wasn't because her lungs actually needed oxygen, but rather because it's what a human did when they were sad. "Of course I do."

I'm sure Brandon at that point wanted to tell her how lost she was, but thankfully, he was wise enough to keep quiet.

"Of course. What's your favorite color, Clara?" I was halfway down the aisle, and I paused for a moment to give her more space.

Ironically, Caleb needed this information fast, so I needed to take my time or else we'd probably upset her so badly we'd have to come back another day. If there was any building left to come back to.

"P—purple?"

The way she formed it as a question made me smile empathetically. Being a ghost must have been hard.

"Purple is an awesome color. How about your favorite animal?"

Several moments of silence went by as she sat and stared at the worn red carpet of the aisle.

"Clara? Do you remember your favorite animal?" I tried again.

She sniffed some more. "Why do you keep calling me Clara?"

My heart broke for her then, and all I wanted to do was gather her into a hug and rock her until she remembered who she was.

"Clara is your name. Do you remember?"

"Not really, but when you talk to me there's something different. Are you different?"

I nodded and continued to walk slowly. "Yes, I'm different. What can you feel?"

She scrunched up her nose as she looked at me. "It's like you feel...like a rock. Like I could stand on you or sit on you and you wouldn't move."

I smiled at the metaphor. "Okay. I'll take it. You're right. You can count on me. You became quiet when I mentioned Riley. Do you remember Riley?"

"Riley?" She brought her eyebrows together in thought. "That name feels important."

"It is important. Maybe I can help you remember."

I stopped walking at four or so paces away. It was close enough to talk quietly but far enough to still give her space. It was hard work trying not to spook a ghost. I closed my eyes and pictured the other lost little girl I knew. I brought to memory her unicorn t-shirt and the leggings she wore and sent a call out to her.

"What are you doing?" Clara asked after a few seconds of silence.

I kept my eyes closed and held up my palm to tell her that I needed a few more seconds.

When the hairs on my neck wavered, and I knew there was another ghost nearby, I opened my eyes, happy to see a confused-looking Riley ghost standing next to me.

"Hanna? Did I do it right?" she asked, her voice smaller than even her sister's.

I kneeled so we were eye-level. "You did great. Remember what I said? Just act like she's bumped her head and can't remember very much and go slow, or you might scare her."

Riley nodded and turned towards her sister who was still sitting on the stage, her legs dangling off the edge, but had her head tilted to the side in curiosity.

"Who is this?" Clara asked.

Riley took a deep breath. Again, it was probably not to breathe but to steel herself, and she took a few steps toward Clara, putting them in touching distance. "My name is Riley. Do you remember me?"

Their questions and interactions with each other were so sad, I had to take my own deep breaths to remain composed. The last thing they needed was to be distracted by a Seer who was sobbing into her jacket.

Clara stared at her sister for a moment and then her eyes drifted towards the shirt she was wearing. "I remember that shirt. I was wearing it the day Dad took me... us? Took me and someone else to the fair. We got cotton candy and rode the giant Ferris wheel."

Riley nodded enthusiastically. "Yes! Then when I was big enough, Mom gave the shirt to me, although..."

Riley trailed off and looked back at me as if asking how much she should reveal about Clara's life.

Honestly, I didn't know how open she would be to hearing other details but, then again, we didn't have all night. I shrugged and gave her an encouraging smile, hoping to convey that I trusted she knew what was best for her sister.

Turning back, Riley continued, "Mom was always sad when she looked at your old clothes because she missed you. We all missed you."

Clara frowned. "I remember Mom. She has brown hair and always smelled good."

"Yes! Do you...do you remember living with us?"

"We shared a bedroom with Minnie Mouse on the walls."

"Yes! Do you remember the night you didn't live with us anymore?"

A garbage pile somewhere to my left rustled as Clara shifted uncomfortably, her eyes darting about the room in agitation.

Riley glanced around but kept pushing, trying to get an answer to the question that had haunted her and her family for years. "Where did you go? Who took you?"

Some of the benches started rattling, and I heard a muffled curse come from behind me, probably Noah, unaccustomed to the unseen ghostly occurrences. Of course, *I* still felt like I was unaccustomed to it.

"I don't know. It hurt, and it was dark, and I was always, always cold." Clara wrapped her arms around herself and hugged tightly as if to try and gather all the body warmth she could even though she had no body.

Riley reached her hand out to Clara's knee, proving that ghosts could touch each other. "That sounds scary."

"I was scared. I am scared." Clara shivered at the memories she had probably worked very hard to forget.

"Just tell me who did this. I have to know why you left. Our family has been sad ever since."

The more Clara shivered, the more the benches next to me shook. It took a lot of self-discipline not to go running for cover. I was looking for errant books that might fly into my leg or something worse, like the stone collapsing around us.

"They called him Dion," Clara said, her voice icy and tone short.

Chaos erupted as Clara jumped off the stage with a wail and began zooming around the room. I'd never seen a ghost fly but perhaps something about being a poltergeist lent her the ability. Everywhere she went damage followed. Dust rained down from the rafters, wood cracked as she flew through it, benches jumped into the air to fall in different places, and dirty clothes, plastic wrappers, and all kinds of nameless garbage flew all over the place.

Unsure where to go that would be safe, I ducked behind the nearest pillar. The stone was cold to the touch and groaned with the effort of keeping the roof up. Worried, I kept glancing at the rafters, praying that they wouldn't all come down on us.

Riley, the poor girl, was still standing where she'd been and was watching her sister zoom around the room with wide eyes. "Clara! It's okay! No one can hurt you anymore!"

Her words went unheeded as more trash exploded onto the stage.

"We should leave," Noah said, suddenly next to me and grabbing my hand. "Now!"

"Wait! We've got to fix this! It's only going to get worse. I can't leave it like this!" I said, tears finally perching on my eyelashes. "They need closure!"

Noah winced as another rafter cracked, and we both looked up to make sure one wasn't going to smash down right on top of us. "You're as stubborn as the ghost!"

Gran had come up to stand next to Riley and took her hand. "It's okay. We won't give up."

Riley looked up at my grandma and something changed on her face. "Of course we won't. My mom and dad never gave up looking for her. Now that I've finally found her, we're going to be a happy family again!"

Gran's eyebrows rose at the spunk in the little girl. I smiled, ducking behind the pillar to avoid a stiff pair of jeans while Noah caught a rock flying on the other side of us.

"Clara! Stop worrying about only yourself. I know what you went through must have been terrible, but you can't let this Dion guy win! You have to be stronger than him! Haven't you wondered why I'm a ghost too?!" Riley screamed the last part out with as much force as she could.

Clara wailed again, but this wail was different. It was full of heartache and pain for someone else instead of for herself. She kept crying and screaming, but, even though she was loud, the rafters cracking and snapping above my head were even louder.

"We're leaving, now!" Noah scooped me into his arms, giving me no time to protest.

I wrapped my arms around his neck and peered over his shoulder, ignoring my fluttering heart and the intoxicating smell of his cologne and skin. Gran and Brandon stood next to Riley while she cried, although a lot less violently than her sister. Stones and wood fell from the ceiling, leaving a poignant picture in my memory I would never forget as those three ghosts stood still amid the chaos.

My ride in Noah's arms was anything but smooth as he wove in and out of danger and jumped over broken wood and stone. Finally, he reared back and kicked the door open. Cool night air bathed over us as he made it out.

"I'm not a sack of potatoes!" I shoved myself out of his arms, and he struggled to put me down without dropping me on the stone walkway.

The church groaned and moaned as several parts of the roof caved in. Clara was still yelling, but the screams weren't as continuous as they had been, as if she was running out of energy. It probably helped that I was further away, and she couldn't use me as a battery anymore.

The dust settled around us as we stood, still inside the gate, and watched the church shudder into a pained, lopsided ruin of its once beautiful walls.

"What did you guys do?" Caleb asked, watching the whole thing from the sidewalk.

I gave him an awkward smile. "We're trying to talk to a poltergeist."

Noah looked me over to make sure I was all in one piece and then walked back out through the gate and confronted the vampire. "You could have gotten her killed, you know!"

Caleb smirked and folded his arms across his chest. "Are you more concerned for your friend's life or the fact that you'll have to go find another Seer to schmooze?"

Noah's hands curled into fists, and, for a second, I was worried he'd hit him. Then I remembered Caleb was a vampire, and I was probably worried for the wrong person.

"How dare you—"

I left the boys to their bickering and turned back to the church. Clara's wails were dying out, her energy spurting, and I wondered if my ghost team was inside still trying to get her to talk to them until the three of them wandered out, looking quite dazed.

"Wait, are you guys okay? Did she hit you or something?" I took a step closer.

Brandon shivered. "That was weird."

"None of us haunt this place, remember?" Gran said with a kind smile while still holding Riley's hand. "You got too far away, and we either were going to pop back to our places, or we had to make it back to you. It's so odd to have so much freedom as a ghost. I'm impressed by your powers more and more every day, m'dear."

"Thank you, Gran." I flashed her a grateful and slightly embarrassed smile.

Riley was still crying while clutching my grandma's hand tightly. "What's wrong with my sister?"

I kneeled in front of her again so we could talk eye-to-eye. "Remember when I told you she had been a ghost for a while, and she was scared and used up a lot of her energy?"

Riley sniffed and nodded.

"That's what happens to ghosts when they do that. If you use your energy to interact with the physical world, you start to lose pieces of who you are. Promise me you won't try to do anything like that, okay?"

Riley nodded again. "But we can't just leave her like that." She turned around to glance at the crumbling church. "We've got to do something. We've got to help her."

"Yes, we do. Unfortunately," I stood and looked at Gran and Brandon, "I have no idea how or what to try next."

They nodded their agreement, Brandon's pinched eyebrows look-ing lost and frustrated while Gran's sad eyes thoughtfully peered down at the small girl still holding her hand.

"I can't believe you put up with him," Noah said, coming to stand next to me. "He's impossible."

I glanced behind us to see Caleb pacing back and forth on the sidewalk, the fumes of anger radiating from him almost visible. "Yeah, but he's not the only stubborn one around here. At this point, I don't care at all about the vampire's issues. I just need to help Clara. Both of these girls deserve closure."

Noah pressed his lips in a sympathetic, thoughtful look. "I can't see anything that's been going on, but you know I've got your back."

Caleb scoffed from the sidewalk.

"I appreciate that. At least someone is making sure I'm safe," I said the last part loudly for Caleb's benefit.

Noah grinned and Caleb scoffed again.

Brandon frowned and put his hands into his pockets. "I could help out more, too, if you'd let me."

I knew he was referring to using more of my energy to manipulate the physical world. I was too unsure about what the effects could be on me or him to rely on that too much, which Brandon already knew, so I didn't bother restating it for him.

"We need to regroup and decide what to do next," I said, turning from the trio of ghosts, leaving the church grounds, walking past the squeaking gate, and standing next to Caleb. I watched for a second as he kept pacing, the rest of my entourage following behind. "We got her to remember some things about her life with Riley's help."

Caleb paused and looked at me. "Who's Riley?"

"Her sister. She's also a ghost I found earlier this week in quite a set of coincidental events."

"Everything happens for a reason," Gran said behind me.

"Did she say anything about Dion?" Caleb pressed, allowing some hope to enter his eyes.

I gave a pointed look towards the church and then back to Caleb. "That's when *that* happened."

Caleb grumbled something unintelligible and went back to pacing.

"You know, you're being very ungrateful about this whole thing. You weren't in there to see how hard Hanna was working and how dangerous it got. She could have been killed, and all you can think about is getting information for your stupid queen! That's what I hate most about vampires. They're so selfish!" Noah turned to me at the last bit of his statement.

His words made Caleb stop in his tracks, turn towards Noah, and lift a menacing finger to point in my friend's face. "You think you're so good and righteous just because you don't need blood to survive, but you honestly have no idea about real life. You're so young, it's almost sickening that I'm stooping to explain myself to you. Do you know how old I am?"

Noah shrugged nonchalantly, and I wasn't sure if it was because he wasn't scared of the vampire or too dumb to realize he should have been. "Too old to be playing as a high school student. You're sure not to sleep with anyone under eighteen, right?"

Rage flickered across Caleb's face, and, before he could strangle Noah's neck, I stepped in between them. This meant I was super close to both of them. My shoulders brushed against Noah's chest, and I had to bat away Caleb's accusing finger so I could have space for my head.

"Listen. This is not helping. We need to think about how to calm that ghost down inside and to get her comfortable enough to answer questions. Not be out here bragging about how old we are."

Caleb's eyes darted to me once but mostly kept staring at Noah.

I could feel Noah's chest moving with his angry breathing, but a small part of me noted that he hadn't tried to back away from me. Was it possible that he wanted to be as close to me as I wanted to be to him?

No, he had clearly chosen Andrea, and it was absurd to be thinking about anything like this while we were trying to help these two girls.

"Ah, yes. This is the Caleb I remember," Gran said, adding a chuckle. "Such a temper. His bark is worse than his bite, so to speak."

I smiled at her words and that caught Caleb's attention. "Gran says you've always had such a temper. Are you prepared to put your bite where your bark is?"

"Ugh!" The vampire flung his arms into the air and turned away from me. "Only because you humans are so frustrating!"

"If he's not a human, what is he?" Riley asked Gran with big eyes.

"Oh, not to worry, dear. He's one of my oldest friends, both because he's old and because we were friends for over fifty years." Gran pat the outside of Riley's hand with the one she wasn't holding. "He's good people. Well, not people, but you know what I mean."

As she explained Caleb's status, the vampire in question was roaming around the street, muttering to himself and walking in circles. I was grateful it was later in the evening and the street wasn't busy. If a car did happen to drive by, I wasn't sure which one of them would turn out worse for the meeting.

"Alright," I turned around, facing Noah and the three ghosts. "I need time to think things over. We're not going to solve this tonight. Riley? I know you're scared and worried about your sister, but we need more time to save her. Can you go back home and wait patiently? Maybe you can be trying to remember lots of good times you had together so we can remind her about them?"

Riley glanced up at Gran who smiled and nodded encouragement. Then she looked back at me. "Okay."

The smallness of her voice broke my heart.

"Thank you for being so brave. I'll check in with you soon."

Riley gave me a shaky smile through her drying tears and disappeared, presumably to go back to her haunt.

"Gran, I'll see you back at home. Brandon, I'll check in with you soon too."

Gran smiled and disappeared.

Brandon, still with his hands in his pockets, spared one more look in Noah's direction. "Right. Remember to be safe."

He popped out before I could refute his insinuations, and it was a relief that Noah hadn't been able to hear what he'd said.

"Ugh, ghosts! Am I right?" I said to Noah, giving him an awkward smile. "These whole one-sided conversations you're seeing have got to be so weird to watch. Sorry about that."

Noah smiled, and his hair slid slowly down his forehead and into his eyes like I liked. "No worries. This is the most fun I've had in ages, even if I had no idea what's going on."

"Arguing with vampires is fun?"

He laughed, and the sound lifted my heart from some of the night's sadness. "Something like that."

"Thank you so much for your help. I'll talk with you tomorrow if I come up with any more ideas." I smiled, forcing my arms to stay by my side instead of folding into him for a secure-feeling hug.

"Any time. Seriously, don't hesitate to ask." Noah gave me another heart-melting smile and strode off towards his car across the street.

Once I was alone, Caleb finally came back, still muttering to himself quietly. "We don't have another day, Hanna. This isn't good."

I took a deep breath to steady myself. "I know. I'm sorry. I've done everything I could think of. I would do more if I just knew *what* to do. I told you, talking to ghosts like this takes time. Just like us stubborn humans, they need time to process stuff. They're unstable and don't adapt to change. I'm doing the best I can."

My rambling explanation gave him pause, and he looked at me for the first time that night. It felt like he finally *saw* me, paying attention to how I was feeling and where I was coming from.

He took a pause and shook out his arms. "I'm sorry, Hanna. I know you are. I'm just feeling a lot of stress here. You don't understand what my queen is capable of."

I frowned and shook my head. "No, I don't, but I do have an imagination. As terrible as I feel suggesting this, why don't you bring her with you the next time we confront Clara so she can see how difficult it is?"

Caleb studied me for a moment before answering. "She doesn't leave the seethe house, but I appreciate your trying to help, I mean, more than you already are, that is."

"Oh, well, surely she'll believe you when you tell her what's happened?"

He looked out into the night, his gaze and thoughts moving far from here. "Maybe."

"We'll try again tomorrow, okay? I'll think of something by then, I promise. I'm sorry." I turned to walk back to his car so he could take me home, but he caught my arm and pulled me into a tight hug.

At first, I was tense, wondering if I should be trying to fight him off or that I would feel sharp teeth sinking into my neck at any second, but when he just kept holding me, his arms firm and unwavering, I allowed myself to relax slightly. Even if it wasn't from the person I wanted it to be from, the long hug felt nice. It told me more than words could, and I wrapped my arms around Caleb's muscular back and put my head on his chest, listening to the silence where a heartbeat should have been.

Chapter 14

There were two days left of school and then the homecoming football game on Friday night and the dance on Saturday night. I was already too much past exhausted to be excited. Not to mention, I still didn't have a date, and a night of watching Andrea and Noah be all over each other didn't sound super fun.

After all the ghost business, I felt like I could use a whole day just to sleep and rest.

On Thursday morning, I pulled myself out of bed and got ready for school like a robot on autopilot.

When I was in the kitchen grabbing my soda, Gran fazed in. "Have you thought more about how to help that poor girl yet?"

I sighed and frowned, closing the fridge. "It's basically all I can think about, but I can't come up with anything. I was hoping you would be able to give me some more sage advice from when you had a situation like this."

She shook her head slowly. "I, too, am at a loss. I tried to avoid poltergeists, focusing on helping the ghosts that were easier and more open to my help. Not to mention that, since using ghost energy and the inner-self isn't really an exact step-by-step science, all poltergeists are different. They have their own triggers and whatever will help them get out of it is different too…if anything will help. We may have to face the possibility that she's too far gone."

Riley's sad eyes came to my thoughts as I considered her words. "I can't just leave them like this. I have to keep trying to help."

Gran smiled kindly and nodded her head. "I know you'll do the right thing. I wanted to tell you I was really impressed with you yesterday. You may feel like you failed, but I hope you don't. You came up with the idea to see if her sister could help, and the way you talked to that poor girl, it felt like you knew what you were doing."

A piece of weight broke off from my chest and floated into the air at her words. I hadn't realized I had been carrying around that weighted feeling of worry until she said that.

I returned Gran's small smile. "Thank you. I'm overwhelmed with all of this, but it's nice to hear that I can maybe handle at least some of it, or that I'm at least going in the right direction."

Mom bustled into the kitchen then and went straight for the coffee pot.

"You're welcome," Gran said. "You've got this. Just keep trying."

School was secondary in my head that day. P.E. was the same as Emma and I couldn't talk much ghost talk with Addy around. We did manage a quick conversation before our friend arrived, but all I learned was that Riley had been quiet, hopefully heeding my advice about not using energy to make contact with the human world.

Noah flashed me some friendly smiles during history, but he kept up his good-school-boy persona while at school nearly all the time. It was like he was a different person than the vampire-accosting necromancer that I knew.

I spent lunch in the library, again, trying to catch up on homework and avoid the fact that I didn't seem to have many friends. I thought about trying to find Emma and sit with her, but, since I didn't want to eat anything but diet soda and breath mints, I figured it was pointless to try and hang out with anyone in the cafeteria anyway.

Randi held simple small talk with me through French while Andrea pointedly sat on the other side of the room during math. I was totally fine with that.

Even though I thought about Clara the whole day, I couldn't come up with any other ideas of how to help her. Calling in Riley to talk to her had been my best hope, and while it had gone well at first, the church building's falling roof was physical evidence that it hadn't ended well.

Thursday night I holed up in my room and did homework. I expected to hear a tapping on my window all evening. Caleb had been so concerned about getting the information quickly. I figured he'd want to try again that night, even though I was clueless about what to do, but he never texted or showed up at my window. Perhaps he had finally started listening to me when I had told him this was going to take some time.

Friday's school day was much the same as the day before. Things were falling into more of a routine there, and I was glad for the stability.

One oddity was that I didn't see Caleb at school either day. I had planned on trying to avoid him if I had seen him, but he wasn't around. It was possible that we'd just missed each other in the halls, and since I avoided the cafeteria, it was clear that I wouldn't have seen him there. Mostly, I was glad I didn't have to answer any more questions about how to help Clara or the vampires.

On Saturday morning, I slept in until eleven o'clock. Sunshine poured into my room, and I curled my toes as I stretched like a purring cat.

"I needed that," I said to no one, hoping a ghost didn't pop up to comment on my talking to myself.

Thankfully, none did.

I'd stayed up late the night before because, after sitting with Emma during the football game, she invited me to her house for hot cocoa. I met her mom and dad and, overall, had a very nice no-ghosts-involved time.

We did chat about Riley and Clara some during the loudness of the crowded game, but there wasn't a lot of new developments there, so we found ourselves easily chatting about simpler things like what boy she liked and about some of her other friends.

It had been nice to feel normal for an evening.

I checked my phone and was again surprised to see I didn't have any messages from Caleb. A tickle of dread formed in the back of my mind, and I wondered if something bad had happened to him. But he was a vampire, super strong, and powerful and stuff. He was probably fine.

Trina and I spent the afternoon getting ready for the dance. She helped me with my hair and makeup again, and instead of having a confrontation with my history teacher on our lawn after dressing up, maybe I'd get to show off my look to more than to the neighbors.

"Can I tell you something?" Trina asked as she secured a bobby pin into my hair.

"Obviously." I watched Trina's deft fingers from the mirror, wondering if I could learn to do hair as well as she could someday.

"I'm impressed with how brave you are, going to the dance by yourself. Does that make me sound stupid?"

I smiled. "No. Honestly, I'm nervous. It may seem brave, but it's probably closer to being stubborn and petty. I can't let Andrea win. She has to see me with friends, even if they are your friends."

We both chuckled.

"Well, you're always welcome to come hang out with us, just as long as you stop giving Caleb googly-eyes."

"Hey, you can't blame a girl for looking. He's hard *not* to look at, but don't worry. I find almost everything else about him to be annoying."

We shared a grin in the mirror. I was glad she took my answer as truth, and I mean, most of it was the truth, but it wasn't the complete truth. I had to go to the dance because it was part of the bargain Caleb made when he'd given me money for Trina's dress, and, even though I wasn't always smart, I was smart enough not to mention that to Trina.

After we finished with our hair and makeup, we went to our separate rooms to get dressed. My stomach felt hollow and my legs weak, but, as I looked at myself in the mirror, I decided all my hard work of not eating was paying off.

The dress was midnight blue with small silver beads sewn in it, reminding me of a twinkling sky on a clear night. It had sleeves that puffed out, but they were off the shoulder, giving the top of my dress a straight line. It narrowed at the waist and flared out into a puffy skirt that ended just above the knees. We'd found some silver shoes to pair with it, and I couldn't help but do a twirl, smiling as I looked like the princess I had dreamed of becoming since I was a little girl.

And then, so I could have someone to show it off to, I mentally summoned Brandon. Yes, I know how shallow that sounds, but I couldn't help it.

"What? I thought I wasn't—Woah! I don't know what to say. You look amazing!"

I smiled and twirled for him. Lame, I know.

He gave me a soundless clap and nodded appreciatively. "You clean up good, kid."

"Thank you." I curtsied. "It's fun to dress up sometimes, even if I don't have a date."

Brandon frowned and sat in his usual chair next to my desk. "I wish I could be your date. I haven't wished I was alive this badly in a long time."

"Way to bring things down." I sighed. "I'm kind of tempted to let you take energy from me all night and be my date. How fun would that be?"

We shared a wistful smile. "It would be really fun."

"Maybe we can share just one dance?"

He nodded. "I would love that."

Trina pounded on my door, interrupting our sad, yet somehow thrilling, conversation. "Are you dressed yet?"

"Yes!" I flung open the door, and Brandon followed behind, always the invisible companion.

Trina's dress was a deep-green mermaid-cut gown with a halter top. It accentuated her silky chestnut brown hair and womanly curves. She looked even better in it with her hair and makeup done than she had when she'd tried it on a few days ago.

Mom was working on her website in the kitchen as we both came down the hallway wearing our gowns. Gran was seated at the table next to her, looking almost bored.

"Wow!" Mom set down her glasses and stood up. "You girls look so amazing! I wish your fath—"

She stopped talking as a pained expression crossed her face.

Gran had stood as well with an admiring smile, but at Mom's comment, she shook her head and sighed.

"We don't need him, Mom. He can see the pictures online. I'm sure he'll be fine," Trina said shortly and handed Mom her phone.

Mom nodded and took a breath. "Yes. Exactly. Okay, let's get some inside and outside."

"You girls look lovely," Gran said and then nodded towards Brandon. "I bet even the lost ghost puppy agrees."

"I do, indeed," Brandon nodded regally.

After Mom used Trina's phone for a few poses, she pulled out her fancy camera to take some shots for herself. I was content to let Trina tag me in the pictures, so I didn't feel the need to get any for myself.

Towards the end of the photography session, Trina kept checking her phone and frowning.

"Did he say he'd come pick you up?" I asked as we stood in front of a bush outside and linked elbows while Mom took more pictures, and Brandon pretended to take pictures, using his fingers to make a square.

"Work it. Move it. Smile. Stick out that butt," Brandon said, pretending to be a professional.

Trina frowned. "Yes. It's not like him to be late. He's usually early to things."

I frowned too and chewed on my lip. That trickle of dread was growing.

"Hey," Mom said and peeked up over her camera. "What's with all the frowning? You're supposed to be looking happy in these pictures, not like someone just stomped on your toes."

"Caleb should be here by now." Trina looked at her phone again.

"Oh, maybe he's just stuck in traffic? I think we've got enough pictures. Although, if you ask me, there are never enough. I can't believe how old you girls are. You've grown up so fast." Mom stared at us fondly.

"Aw, we're still your little girls. We'll always be here for you," I said as we all joined into a hug.

Gran beamed at our love, and even though no one could feel it, she put her arms around us anyway.

Brandon puckered out a pouty lip. "You guys are just the cutest."

I rolled my eyes at him behind my mom's back.

We pulled apart, and Trina checked her phone again. "He's really late."

"Maybe we should go without him. He could have gotten confused and thought we were supposed to meet at the dance. I mean, he is like super old. Old people forget stuff all the time."

Gran and I shared a knowing smile.

Trina didn't waste energy trying to figure out what my joke was. "I guess we could go. Mom, you'll let us know if he shows up here?"

"Of course."

We stuffed ourselves into Trina's car and waved to Mom and Gran as we pulled out of the driveway. Brandon hesitated to follow, unsure what to do, but I gave him a subtle head bob to tell him he might as well come along.

It wasn't like he'd be crashing my date or anything.

The gym was transformed and sparkled as we walked into the side doors. A balloon arch bobbed above us, and lights danced and twinkled all around.

"Who knew the gym had a disco ball?" I said, staring up in awe.

"Yeah, they bust it out for dances. Not sure why they hide it the rest of the time. It would really spruce up a basketball game."

We both laughed at Trina's joke, but I knew she was using it to hide the pain and worry. Had Caleb stood her up? He'd said over and over again that he didn't want to go to dances. After I found out his truth, I could understand why, but we had made a deal. Surely he wouldn't have dashed Trina's hopes so easily.

The dread in my mind grew.

"Ah, the classic 'Night Under The Stars' theme." Brandon nodded his head in appreciation as he walked into the gym behind us. "I feel very underdressed. It would be nice to change my clothes once in a while."

I agreed but didn't say it aloud.

Music thudded around the room as streamers danced in the air currents above us. Students stood in groups, nodding their heads to the music and holding drinks, while adult chaperones walked around the edges of the room, trying not to look too bored.

Mr. Tyler gave me a wave as he saw my gaze. I gave him a friendly smile and nodded.

Andrea and Noah stood in a circle with our other friends. I had to admit she looked gorgeous, but I wasn't surprised. She wore a light purple dress with no sleeves, showing off her ample assets, that narrowed at the waist and flowed down in soft ripples to her ankles, giving her figure a long, lean look. A high slit ran up the length, enabling her toned and tanned leg to peek out and hint at the rest of her underneath.

Noah was dapper in a suit with a purple bowtie that matched Andrea's dress. His hair was styled neatly to the side, but a few strands still fell into his eyes once in a while. As I was watching, he laughed and pushed the strands back, reminding me of how attractive he was.

As if I could have forgotten.

"I mean, I guess he is good-looking, but do you really want to date someone who raises the dead for a living?" Brandon stood next to me with his arms folded over his chest, having noticed who I was staring at.

I kept my voice low. "At least he has a real body to raise the dead with instead of just being dead."

"Rude."

I smiled and then stopped when I saw Trina stepping into the gym ahead of me, searching through the crowds for a vampire who probably wanted to be anywhere but at a high school dance.

"Where do you think he is?" Brandon asked, once again noticing what I was looking at.

I shrugged and followed her through the crowd until I caught up and linked my arm with hers. "If he's not here, I know he has a very good reason." I had to talk loudly over the music and the crowd.

She swallowed thickly and kept looking around as if she was trying to hold back tears.

Brandon followed us, walking through the students instead of having to push through them. He grinned every time someone shivered as he passed through, and I decided he was having way too much fun.

A few of Trina's friends approached, crooning at her dress and giving me polite smiles. She vaguely acknowledged their presence, her eyes still searching the crowd.

"Have you guys seen Caleb?"

They all frowned and shook their heads. We left them after they agreed to also look for him, but, as we made it to the other side where the refreshment table was, we both knew Caleb hadn't come.

We stood in a corner, and Trina pulled out her phone for the hundredth time. I pulled mine out too, just in case.

"Maybe he's out on the town, drunk on some blonde girl's blood, and enjoying his evil ways," Brandon suggested.

"Caleb is a good guy," I said for both Brandon and Trina. "If he's not here, there's a good reason."

Trina sighed and put her phone inside her clutch purse. "If he's not here, there's no reason for me to be either."

"Wait a minute." I grabbed her arms before she ran off like Cinderella. "Didn't you just tell me how brave you thought I was that I was going to the dance alone? Look at you! You're being brave too. Your other friends are here, I'm here, and you don't need a stinky vam—er, guy to make your night a memorable one. Then later when we see Caleb again, we can give him a cold shoulder and a smoldering eye, so he knows he's in big trouble."

She pressed her lips together tightly, trying to keep herself calm. "I'm going to get a drink and a cupcake."

"If she starts crying, I'm going vampire hunting," I muttered to Brandon.

"Me too. The turd."

I stood for a moment, watching my peers dance and chat and laugh. Andrea and Noah had moved to the middle of the dance floor and were dancing with each other. Noah was doing the usual cool-guy shuffle, not wanting to bust into anything crazy, while Andrea's moves were a little riskier, causing me to raise an eyebrow.

"So, this is a high school dance. Lovely. Maybe Trina's right, and we should just go home," I said, not bothering to lower my voice since it was clear no one was paying attention to me over the music and chatting.

"They can be fun if you're with the right people. Look at those kids. They're having a good time." Brandon gestured to a small group of students, the very same ones that spent lunch in the library playing cards. They did indeed look like they were having fun even though they weren't wearing the most expensive clothes or hair in the most fashionable ways. Even their dancing was terrible, but none of it seemed to matter.

"Maybe I should go hang out with them, my new library friends." I was only half kidding.

Trina came back with a half-eaten cupcake and was talking with two of her girlfriends. Her hand still trembled, but there was a smile on her face, and they all laughed together after making a joke at Caleb's expense.

"I think she's going to be okay," Brandon said, feeling the need to whisper into my ear for some reason.

Chills hopped down my skin as I remembered the feel of his lips, and a yearning welled up inside of me, bypassing all the mental walls I'd kept up to prevent myself from feeling. It was fun to joke around with Brandon, but it wasn't as fun to feel the reality of what we wanted and what we couldn't have.

"I'm going to go talk to my friend," I said to Trina. "I'll catch you guys later."

She nodded, still smiling from their joke, and I headed towards Emma who I had glimpsed for a moment passing through the crowd.

Before I could spot her again, a dark form stepped in front of me, blocking my path.

"Excuse me," I said and looked up to find the most gorgeous man I'd ever seen, even more gorgeous than Noah and Caleb put together. If Caleb was a Greek god, this guy was an angel. His blond hair was long and wavy, flowing down to his shoulders, and, even though that wasn't a look I usually enjoyed, for some reason it worked for this dude. I found myself staring into his brilliant blue eyes, being dazzled by a smile that made me wonder what his lips tasted like.

"Oh, no. Excuse me. I've been admiring your beauty from across the room, and I just had to ask you to dance," the stranger said with a soulful, rumbling deep voice.

As if on cue, the current fast-paced song ended, and a slow song started. It also happened to be one of my favorite songs that played on the radio, and the music beckoned me into his arms.

Nodding, while feeling slightly dizzy and entranced, I gave him my hand and let him lead me into the heart of the dance floor.

"Hanna? Who is this guy? Do you know him?" Brandon tried to get my attention, but his voice sounded far away and fuzzy.

Once, a few years ago, my mom had made me and Trina sit down and watch one of her favorite movies. In the movie, there was a scene where the girl, all dressed in white with pearls in her hair, danced with the goblin king. It was a dizzying and beautiful moment where the girl had only eyes for the handsome king, and he only had eyes for her. At the time, I'd been too busy making fun of the movie with Trina, much to my mom's annoyance, but when I began to dance with the stranger, I felt exactly like the girl in the movie had.

It took me several moments before I thought to ask, "What's your name? Who are you?"

The world spun behind him and faded into darkness. It didn't matter what else was happening in the room. Even if it crumbled all around us, I would only have eyes for him.

"I'm N—er, Nathan."

I blinked, my confusion lasting for only a few seconds before feeling entranced again. "Nathan. I've never seen you here before. Are you a new student?"

He leaned in so close, his cheek brushed against mine. The words he whispered tickled my ear and neck, sending shivers down my body. "Something like that. I've watched you for years, you know, wondering what I would say when I was free to say what I wanted."

"What?"

"There's always something stopping me from saying what I want and how I truly feel, but, right now, it's just you and me. I can say whatever I want."

His soft mouth breathed into my ear as he talked, and sometimes his lips brushed against the sensitive skin of my earlobe. My heart was beating rapidly in my chest, and my whole body was attuned to his next move, hoping it would bring more thrills.

"What do you want to say?"

"Hanna, you're more beautiful than you realize. I wish you could see yourself through my eyes. There's no wonder a ghost guy follows you around all the time. He's as probably in love with you as much as I am. Too bad for him that he can't do this, though." Nathan's hand that was resting on the small of my back suddenly pulled me in closer so our bodies lined up. With a deft movement, he dipped me backward and our eyes locked. Feeling completely secure in his grip, knowing I'd fall if he let me, I relaxed and prayed he'd cross the last inch between us so I could finally experience what those lips tasted and felt like.

"Hanna? What's going on? Who is this?" Trina's voice threaded into my conscience from somewhere.

With an easy spin, Nathan brought me upright, and I found myself disappointed that his lips weren't pressing onto mine.

"Hanna? Can you hear me?"

She was easy to ignore until she touched my shoulder. Something washed over me, and the room came crashing back into reality. We weren't in a grand ballroom inside a giant castle in the Swiss Alps. We were in a high school gym that had been jazzed up a bit to host a dance. I wasn't dancing with my one true love, but actually a stranger I'd never met before.

"Trina? What's going on?"

Trina's hands were on her hips as she looked back and forth between Nathan and me. "That's what I want to know. Who is this? Are you really going to have your first kiss with this guy? Someone you don't even know?"

I couldn't tell her that I'd already had my first kiss, and even though most people might not have counted it as a real thing, kissing Brandon had felt real enough to me. Remembering Brandon had been here, I looked around, trying to spot his ghostly hue.

Nathan frowned as he assessed Trina. "It was just a dance. Nothing to be so worried about."

"That looked like way more than just a dance."

While Trina and Nathan debated, I found Brandon standing right behind us, a worried crinkle between his eyebrows. "Hanna? Can you hear me?"

I backed up, letting go of Nathan, and tried shaking my head to clear it. "I feel so dizzy."

Nathan's and Trina's attention moved to me.

"Maybe you should sit down," Trina said, glancing back towards the wall where a few chairs were lined up.

Nathan grabbed my elbow and put his hand on my back again. "Here. I've got you."

As we walked towards the chairs, three more people seeped out of the crowd and blocked our path, reminding me of how I had met Nathan a few minutes ago.

"Talon, what are you doing?"

I looked up to see the speaker. The three of them were older adults, two men and a woman, and, while they were dressed in dress clothes, they were definitely not students.

Perhaps chaperones?

"Who are you guys?" Trina said, putting herself between them and me.

My smile at her bravery turned into a scream as the second man pushed my sweet sister aside, causing her to fall into a heap on the waxed wooden floor. I tried to pull away from Nathan to go to Trina, but he held my arm so tight it was like being trapped halfway inside a marble statue.

"Why are you messing around, Talon? Just grab her already! You weren't sent here to relive your human life and dance," the female vampire said

Nathan shook his head as if coming out of a trance as well and then spoke, answering their questions and making me think he'd lied about what his name was. "There's a necromancer here. He possessed me and made me dance."

Instantly the three others went rigid, their eyes darting around, looking for the danger.

"What an odd thing for a necromancer to do," the woman said, looking more curious than the men.

"Let's get out of here," the first male said. "Grab the girl."

Nathan/Talon looked into my eyes again, and the world narrowed into a pinprick. He was the only one that mattered, and I was going to follow him into any place and do anything should he desire it.

We marched past the other students who started to stare but their faces were blurry. None of them mattered.

Chapter 15

In a classic technique they probably stole from movies, they shoved a black pillowcase over my head and stuffed me into the back of a sedan. Someone pushed me over and grabbed my hands to tie them behind my back. The four piled into the car, based on the number of doors that slammed. It was tight in the back seat next to the two big males with broad shoulders. I probably couldn't have caused any trouble even if my hands hadn't been tied.

After the bag had been shoved over my head, and I lost contact with Nathan/Talon, reality slammed back into me.

"What's going on? Where are you taking me? Who are you guys?!" I struggled with my bonds, rocking my shoulders into the guy next to me who felt like a brick wall.

No one answered, not that I had expected them to divulge all the information or anything, but it would have been nice to have some answers. The car turned on and sped out of the parking lot and onto the road.

"This is a cozy ride," Brandon said, and relief washed over me.

At least I wasn't alone.

I was dying to ask where Brandon was since he had to have been sitting on someone's lap to be fitting inside the cozy car. The image made my lips perk up for a second, even though I was still trembling from fear.

"I'm pretending we're in a spy movie. These guys are secret agents, and we're going to be meeting their evil overlord soon who will go into a long tirade about his secret plans to take over the world. At the last moment, we'll escape in a clever and amazing way." Brandon kept talking, and I wasn't sure if it was to help me focus on his voice and feel comforted, or if he was rambling to assuage his own nerves.

"Hey, is no one going to put a seatbelt on me? It's rude to tie someone up before they can put their seatbelt on. It's the law, haven't you heard?" I asked, my voice muffled by the pillowcase.

None of them spoke the whole ride. Brandon prattled on about the things he saw as we drove, helping to put a type of map inside my mind about where they might have been taking us. As I listened to him and tried to mentally keep track of where we were, my mind also raced, trying to figure out what was happening.

Who were these people? Why had they kidnapped me? What had they been talking about with a necromancer and possession? Were they zombies sent to do some master's bidding?

They certainly seemed more intelligent than I would imagine a zombie to be, but that didn't mean much. The only things I knew about zombies came from horror movies, and I wasn't sure I could trust them as a source for the real-world creatures I was quickly learning were not as made-up as regular humans liked to believe.

And the question looming over it all pounded inside of my skull—where was Caleb?

After what I could guess to be about thirty minutes, Brandon said, "Oh, and here we are. We appear to be turning into a driveway with a formidable iron gate and a towering stone wall."

I heard clattering as the car paused and the gate was moved aside.

"For this next part of the tour, ladies and gentlemen, I will direct your attention to the immaculate grounds. You may notice the taste of the residence's is classic whereas yours truly would have chosen the more outrageous topiaries to display throughout my gardens. Ah, and here is the house. It is more like a mansion than a house, looming over the curated lawns and carefully constructed gardens. I count...twenty-seven windows just on this side and more chimneys than I know how to count to. This is definitely a place where somebody hoity-toity lives," Brandon said, his voice taking on a decent British accent towards the end.

As stupid and silly as his commentary was, I had to admit it was working to help me focus on something else besides my scary predicament. At least I could be assured they weren't out to kill me just yet. Obviously, they needed something from me first, and maybe I could hold out on that so I could put off my death as long as possible.

Gravel crunched as the car slowed to a stop. The strangers climbed out, and one of them opened my door, hauling me out by my elbow.

Brandon stayed nearby still narrating what he saw. By this point, it was clear that none of the others could see or hear him, and I had never been more grateful for my gift.

"Wow, someone has a lot of money. There is art all over the walls and sitting on expensive tables and stuff. It looks like art from all over the world and from many different time periods. Maybe we're getting kidnapped by a time traveler. Wouldn't that be super cool?" Brandon said, his voice coming from nearby my left shoulder.

The carpet did feel soft and squishy beneath my silver heels.

"What's happening?" I asked again, not expecting an answer, but feeling like I shouldn't just keep going along quietly with the whole thing. They might get the impression that I wasn't upset at being kidnapped and that I maybe even liked it. Then who knows what would have happened? People might start kidnapping me all the time under the mistaken assumption that it was something I found fun.

We passed down a hallway, made several turns, then started down a winding staircase.

"Seriously, I want to know who is responsible for all this money and what their job is so I can grow up and do that thing. This place is amazing. We're going down a set of stairs now, and, even though they appear to be heading into a basement, they are actually quite wide and finely carpeted. Can you feel that spring beneath your feet? Only expensive carpets give you that."

My legs were burning and wobbly when we finally finished our descent, and the man who was escorting me had to hold me up.

"Okay, now this is just gaudy. We're going into a room with giant double doors coated in what I assume can only be real gold. How vain is this person?"

Hushed whispers greeted us as we entered the room, and I felt that we were not alone. It also helped that Brandon confirmed it.

"Holy crap. Who are these people? Wait. Is that—"

He cut off, and I would have gone crazy with curiosity except someone whipped off the pillowcase, and I could see.

The room was large, like almost ballroom large. Candles on giant chandeliers and free-standing candelabras cast the room in a warm and pulsing light. Several groups of people were looking at me, and I couldn't help but stare back.

Most of them stood in groups of three or four, but some of them sat on opulent wooden chairs embossed in gold. Every single one of them was gorgeous—men, woman, and even the children, of which there were only a few. Although, upon closer inspection, the children seemed very unchildlike. They were all wearing clothes that fit in perfectly with the house—all from different time periods and eras. Several of the women wore corsets and dresses with laced bodices and giant fluffy skirts. The men wore finery from all over, including fluffy-collared shirts or intricately embroidered robes. There were many different beautiful people to look at, but none compared to the one sitting at the other end of the room.

Despite being dressed in dance formal, I almost felt underdressed. It was an odd juxtaposition.

The crowd had revealed a path to the other side of the room where a woman sat. She was so beautiful and regal, she could have only been described as a queen. Her dark hair was as black as midnight and flowed in ringlets down her shoulders. She wore a small tiara that sparkled in the light when she moved, which was not often. Her dress was something I could imagine Queen Elizabeth would have worn. It was white with pearls dancing around the seams and hems. Each had to have been hand-sewn, and the threaded embroidery on the gown had probably taken months to create.

"Ah, here she is. The elusive Seer," the queen said, steepling her fingers under her chin.

As she named me, I knew her. This is who Caleb had been trying to warn me about. This was his queen.

But there was still no Caleb.

The queen's chest didn't bother to move like she was breathing, and I guessed the other vampires might do that only to put humans at ease. Indeed, she was so still I could have mistaken her for a painting.

"What do you want from me?" I pulled my arm out of Talon's grip. He let me go that time, rightfully assuming I wasn't going to be able to escape this room full of creatures.

Brandon had finally been shocked speechless, and he gaped at the queen with an open mouth. If ghost-drool had slid down his chin at that point, I wouldn't have been surprised.

"From the way he talks about you, I would have figured you were smarter than that." She stood as she spoke, her movements stiff and precise.

Once, Caleb had mentioned how his queen didn't go outside, and I could see that perhaps part of the reason was she would have had an awfully hard time blending in with the humans.

Everything about her screamed "other" and predator. My human instincts were both screaming for me to run and demanding that I get in closer, lured by her supernatural beauty and probably some skill vampires used to catch their human prey.

"Where is he?" I asked, finding that I could stand on my own feet, even if my knees felt weak.

She laughed, and the sound sent goosebumps down my arms. "Don't worry about him, dear. He's getting what he deserves. Now," she took several steps toward me that looked almost robotic, "we've wasted enough time. Let's get to why you're here."

"Surely you're not so old you've forgotten your manners. How about we start with introductions? Where am I? Who are you?" Apparently, I was sassy enough to challenge a vampire queen, even when very nervous. What can I say? I was sick of people telling me who or what I should be afraid of.

I also probably knew the answers to my questions, but I didn't need her to know that.

"Oh, girl. You better be careful or we'll *both* be ghosts." Brandon's eyes were wide as he stood next to me.

Her eyes narrowed as she stopped walking, only three feet away from me. I was sure that was close enough for a vampire to murder me before I even figured out what was happening, but, if she wanted me dead, I would have been dead.

"You know what Caleb is. He must have told you about me." She gestured to herself with long, spindly fingers tipped with blood-red nails.

"Maybe you aren't as important as you think you are."

Titters and coughs sounded from the others around us, whom I assumed were all vampires as well.

Still as stone, she stared at me, and I looked at her expectantly, waiting for her to respond.

"Were you this insolent towards Caleb? If so, I cannot imagine why he's been protecting you. Your flippant attitude is going to get you killed," she finally said.

"He's been protecting me? What are you talking about? I haven't seen him in days. In fact, he stood up my sister tonight, and I worked very hard to set up that date." I matched the queen's stare.

"Interesting. A date with a human. Of course you haven't seen him around. He's been busy." She grinned and shared knowing looks with the others around her.

"Busy?"

"Oh, yes. Entertainment is so hard to come by these days, and I don't get to torture my own people very often. Lucky for me, Caleb has been bad, very bad." She pouted her lip as she spoke while her eyes sparkled mischievously.

Brandon tapped his lip with a finger. "That explains why he's been missing. Torture implies that she wanted something from him. What could that be?"

"You've been torturing him?" I asked, fear pressing down on my chest. "Is he okay? Why would you do that to someone in your own seethe?"

She tilted her head back and forth a few times as if listening to music only she could hear, or perhaps it was screams. "He was a bad boy. He was keeping you from me, and the more he resisted telling me who and where you were, the more I wanted to meet you. Also, I was impressed with him and grateful he is in my seethe. His resistance to torture is quite extensive."

"But then he finally broke, and you kidnapped me from my first high school dance?" I would have continued with a sassier remark, but concern for my friend had chased away some of the attitude.

"Since I can't do much to help you out here, I'm going to go see if I can find Caleb or whatever other horrors are around here," Brandon said and blew me a kiss. "Try not to piss her off anymore."

The only response I gave him was the barest tilt of my chin and a blink. Apparently, that was enough, and he walked away to explore what else the queen hid in her lair.

"Caleb did tell me he explained to you several times the importance of time here. I think you'll survive missing out on a few dances in a musty gym." She twitched her mouth into a small smile. "Maybe. And no, he didn't break. We only figured out who you are because we caught Caleb's car running a red light. One of my seethe members is a cop and happened to see your face in the traffic camera. There was only one person you could be, so we tracked you down at the dance. Does that make you feel better about your sweet, twisted friendship?"

I scoffed. "Whatever. He did tell me your niece is missing, that you need help to find some guy named Dion, and this one ghost was supposed to know where he is. We tried, we really did, but talking to a poltergeist takes time. Surely, you've been around long enough to know that by now. Even when we did get her to talk to us, her memories are missing. I'm not even sure she knows what you expect her to know. Now everyone keeps telling me how we need to get this information quickly, but all I see are a bunch of weirdly dressed vampires trying to relive their glory days, and a dead chick who fancies herself a queen trying to intimidate a nearly sixteen-year-old girl. Maybe we should bypass all this crap and get to figuring out where your niece is, yes?"

Silence descended upon the room so thick, I worried I'd choke on it, being the only one there who needed to breathe. The others didn't even dare titter or cough at my words and judging by their wide-eyed stares towards their queen, they were simply waiting for her to stab me through the heart with her pointy nails.

Instead, the queen kept still for so long I'd wondered if she'd finally truly died, leaving a motionless corpse behind.

No such luck.

After at least two minutes, she seemed to make a decision. Clapping her hands, she turned to the vampires who had escorted me, including Talon, and nodded her head.

"She's right. Let's go. We're going to talk to this ghost and get what we need." Her eyes slid down towards mine again while a mocking smile spread across her lips. "And you are going to help because you wouldn't want anything more to happen to your dear friend. He's merely hanging on by a thread as we speak. Poor creature."

Anger welled up inside of me and threatened to spill out of my eyes in the shape of shameful tears, but I pushed it back, refusing to give the queen any of that kind of satisfaction. "You don't have to threaten me. I'm willing to help anyway. Something tells me her unfinished business has to do with this vampire nonsense, and I want to help her pass on."

"How noble." She gestured to the vampire goons who put the pillowcase back over my head and forcefully escorted me out of the room and back up the stairs.

Brandon appeared next to me as we left the house and got back into the car. "I couldn't get too far away from you, but I did find Caleb. He's pretty broken up...literally his body looks like they broke several of his bones and let them heal back incorrectly. My guess is they'll have to break them again for him to be able to walk or look any kind of normal."

I held in a pinched cry as Talon, or someone, shoved me into my seat and slammed the door. Since the pillowcase was hiding my face, I did allow a few tears to escape.

Everyone piled back into the car. Whoever sat next to me had large shoulders that took up more than his fair share of space.

"But listen," Brandon kept talking, his voice coming from right in front of me, probably sitting partially through the passenger side seat and facing my direction. "He's still in good spirits. He was even humming some old sea shanty while still chained to a wall with dried blood caked onto his face. I don't know what he's made of, but it's something sturdy. Oh, there's another car following us out of the mansion. It's one of those black Cadillacs. Do you think the queen is in there? Wait. Didn't Caleb say she never left her lair? Hmm. Interesting."

I felt the car start up and turn back down the driveway. Gravel crunched beneath the tires, and the squeaking gate opened before us.

"So where do you think we're going? Are they taking you back to that church? I don't think we're going to get much progress there. Poor Clara is just too upset. I mean, it's been a few days since we were there, and maybe she's calmed down, but I'm betting that once you bring up Dion again, she'll flip out and probably collapse the entire building this time. And you don't even have a strong, sexy necromancer to protect you. These wussy vampires can't even put a foot on the holy ground. What are they expecting to get done, exactly? Ugh. I hate it when people don't think through their plans."

His rambling words got me thinking. As I awkwardly used the pillowcase and my shoulder to wipe up my tears, I realized where we needed to go. Unfortunately, that was going to put some other people in danger, and I really didn't want to do that.

Caleb's warning words from a few nights ago floated through my mind. He'd said something like we needed to fix this situation or else a vampire war would break out.

Telling myself a vampire war was worse than what we were about to do, I said, "We shouldn't go back to the church. Clara needs a happy, familiar place to help her with her memories. The church there holds nothing but pain for her. If we go there again and try to get more information, we're just going to freak her out, and that will probably cause the church to completely collapse and kill me inside with it. The queen sure would be sad not to have a Seer to help her out."

"Okay, I see you," Brandon said with an appreciative nod.

The others in the car were silent. I began to wonder if they'd heard me at all, or if I would have to yell all of that again so their old-person ears could pick it up when I heard the button chime of a cellphone, and the woman started talking.

"The Seer says we need to go to a different location. She thinks there's a better chance of the ghost recovering the memories and less chance of the church collapsing on top of her. I'm sure the queen would not want the Seer to die."

Whoever was talking on the other end of the phone mumbled quietly enough that I couldn't make out the words.

"Seer, where do we go?" The woman asked after a few seconds.

I gave her the address and sent a prayer to whatever god was listening that I wasn't about to bring in more innocent humans to this mess of a night.

Chapter 16

"**A**re you sure this is a good idea? What if her parents are home?" Brandon asked as I was dragged out of the car again.

We'd stopped, and, although I couldn't see, I could feel a horde of ghosts nearby and figured they had gotten to the right place.

Indeed, when the pillowcase was ripped off my face and the zip tie was cut from around my wrists, I saw we were parked in front of Emma's house. There were a few lights on inside, and my heart sank. I'd seen Emma at the dance, so I figured she was probably still there, but her parents, or whoever was home, was about to get caught in some vampire drama.

"You better behave yourself or we'll break your lover for good this time," Talon's voice whispered harshly in my ear as he freed my hands.

I winced, not at his words, but at his tone. He sounded so different than he had while we were dancing. It was like he was another person entirely.

"Huh. Look at how they're reacting to the vampires," Brandon said, gesturing to the house next door.

Instead of playing or talking or walking as they'd done before, the ghosts retreated, eyeing my four companions, and going inside the house to hide somewhere. Weirdly, it was a relief to see that yard empty and the ghosts gone, but it was also chilling to see them react in such a way.

I hadn't even known ghosts could fear something.

We waited outside as the second car pulled up behind ours. It must have gotten held back in traffic or something. Three other vampires stepped out, and one opened the passenger side door to reveal the queen.

Her dark eyes traveled around the scene and looked at the house before us with a sneer. "The human world has certainly changed. Why must there be advertisements on everything? Ugh. We need to go back to the dark ages. The darkness is so much better than scalding neon colors."

Several of the vampires in her group mumbled their agreement while I rolled my eyes.

"Boo-hoo. If you're that upset about it, maybe you should have died in your time instead of becoming an immortal bloodsucker. I feel like the world would be a better place," I said, finding some of my attitude again.

If Caleb could hum sea shanties while being held captive by the people who were supposed to be his own family, I could serve the queen a sharp insult or two.

The queen was suddenly in my face, and I saw the rage in her eyes that hadn't been there before, even though this hadn't been my first sassy remark. Being out in the world must have put her more on edge.

She was only an inch taller than me, but it felt like more as she snarled her lip and revealed a sharp canine on one side. "You'll learn to hold your tongue, or I'll rip off your leg. I might need a Seer alive, but that doesn't mean you need to keep your limbs."

"I think she's serious. You better be nicer, Hanna. Although, I do enjoy watching her get angry. I'm not sure she's ever been talked to like that in her life, her long, long life." Brandon grinned, and I had to force my features not to share it.

Instead, I nodded and let my eyes convey the fear. I mean, I wasn't totally stupid. She did scare me.

She backed up slightly and stared at me in her statue way for at least three seconds, which felt like a long time when staring into the gaze of a vampire queen.

Perhaps finding whatever she was looking for in my face, she turned to the house again. "So, you think bringing Clara here will help her regain some of her memories somehow? I've never heard of a Seer being able to summon a ghost to a different location. If I weren't so desperate, and if Caleb hadn't told me the disasters you've had at the church, I wouldn't have bothered to come here. For all I know, this is the house of someone who is strong enough to protect you from all of us. Unlikely, but possible, I suppose."

The vampires around us stood stiffly, but that didn't fool me. Their alert eyes told me they were ready for anything that might come at them. Lucky for them and unfortunate for me, there wasn't anything but a couple of middle-aged humans inside.

As she spoke, I realized that going somewhere I could have gotten help would have been a much better idea. Too bad I didn't know anyone who could take down several vampires.

"I hadn't lied when I said I wanted to help Clara. This is where she grew up. Her family doesn't own the house anymore, but Clara's sister, Riley, haunts the upstairs attic. When I brought Riley to the church, she seemed to help clear Clara's head some, and I'm hoping that if I bring Clara to the attic, it'll help even more. Just promise me that no one gets hurt. The humans living inside are innocents and have nothing to do with this mess. I won't take another step towards helping you if you can't promise me that."

The queen's stiff neck rotated her head until she was looking at me again. "You must think badly of us vampires. If we went around killing needlessly, we wouldn't have survived this long. We have other abilities than just sucking blood, being gorgeous, and living long lives."

"Promise or I won't do it."

She sighed loudly and looked up at the sky to show her exasperation, not to pull in needed oxygen. "We promise no innocent human will be harmed."

"For some reason, I don't think a vampire promise is really worth anything. It's not like they can't lie. But," Brandon shrugged, "I guess it's the best we can hope for."

I nodded, took a few steps towards the house, and then remembered. "Oh, and Caleb gets to go free if I do this, right?"

"That's vampire business. Don't worry about him. He's survived much worse."

The queen walked past me and gestured for one of her goons to knock on the door before I could protest anymore.

I shared a look with Brandon who shrugged again. "I'm sure he'll be okay," he said.

Hoping he was right, I walked to the door, still flanked by Talon and the three other guards. Maybe I should have been flattered they thought I needed a total of four vampires to escort me around, but mostly I was annoyed.

Emma's mom, I assumed, open the door. At first, she looked confused and slightly alarmed to see so many oddly dressed strangers, but one of the goons in a frilly shirt stepped up and spoke to her. Instantly, her eyes were riveted on the vampire's face, and she stepped back to let us in.

Another vampire did the same when Emma's dad walked into the room. With a few barked commands, both of her parents were sitting rigidly on the couch and staring at the wall across from them.

It was late, but it appeared that Emma was still out at the dance or with friends somewhere. I prayed she didn't come back home during the middle of all of this.

The queen turned to me with her lips pressed together and eyebrows up in a haughty expression. "Good enough for you?"

Chills skittered down my back as I knew firsthand what kind of entrancing power a vampire had. I was nearly certain Talon, who had called himself Nathan for some reason, had used it on me to dance with him. It had been disorienting, and while he hadn't made me do anything against my will directly, the aftereffects had left an unpleasant taste in my mouth.

"Why didn't you just do that to me? It'd be so much easier to get the answers you need instead of having to put up with my sassy mouth." I asked the queen, still staring at Emma's parents as we all entered their home and shut the door behind us.

"Oh, I guess you don't know everything. How sad for you." The queen gave me a mocking smile. "If you entrance a Seer, they are unable to see ghosts, which would be the opposite of what we're trying to accomplish here."

"Right. That makes sense." I remembered how I'd lost sight of Brandon while dancing with Nathan/Talon, and for the first time since being with the vampires, I looked directly at the ghost who happened to be my best friend.

He smiled. "It's okay. I forgive you. I'm just glad you got out of that. It was scary."

Another thought occurred to me, and I turned back to the queen. "How do I know you aren't going to kill me or keep me captive once I do this job for you?"

She smiled that predatory smile that Caleb had given me a few times, showing off her canines and sending my human fear instincts into screaming overdrive. "Guess you'll just have to see." She said the last part with an emphasis that implied she was making some kind of Seer joke.

I didn't laugh. Instead, I frowned and hesitated to go up the stairs. What was I doing? How had I gotten mixed up in all of this? Again, I was way over my head.

"Let's go. If we don't finish this tonight, I'm going to burn the city until I find Dion's corpse," the queen said.

Talon gave me a shove towards the stairs. I began to ascend them automatically, my brain racing with ideas of how to escape the vampires once I'd given them what they wanted, or even if I didn't. They'd probably kill me if I failed since my only valuable skill was being a Seer, and, if I couldn't use my powers to get what they needed, what value was I?

As we reached the attic door, and I pointed upwards, one of the goons pulled open the ladder door and stepped back. It clattered down loudly. Numbly, I climbed up, trying to get my mind to figure out how to help Clara instead of wondering what kind of method the queen would use to murder me. Would it be fast or slow?

I probably should have been nicer to her.

Riley's small head looked up as Brandon and I came through the floor door with the queen stiffly following behind us. It had probably been several hundred years since the queen had needed to climb a ladder. The fact that she'd come on this expedition herself spoke to how important this was to her, even if her insistence of urgency had not.

Riley smiled in hope as she saw me and then melted some when she saw the queen.

"Hanna, I'm glad to see you! Have you figured out how to help my sister? Who did you bring with you this time?"

I didn't bother to explain to the queen what I was doing or who I was talking to. I figured she was smart enough to figure it out. It was, after all, the whole reason we were here.

"Riley," I sat down on the wooden floorboards, trying to appear as less intimidating as possible. "Remember how I said we needed to learn some things from your sister? This is the... lady who needs to know the information. Her niece is lost and only Clara knows where to find her."

"Okay, but why are you here? Shouldn't you be taking me back to the church where Clara is?"

I glanced at Brandon who gave me a smile and a small nod of encouragement.

"I'm thinking maybe we bring her here? Seeing the familiar might help her get more memories back. Be more stable."

Riley jumped up in excitement. "Yes! That's a great idea!"

"Let's just hope she doesn't get mad and take the house down with her," Brandon said, his mouth tilted to the side.

"Ugh, great. One more thing to worry about." I sighed. "Maybe this wasn't such a good idea."

"What's happening?" The queen asked, trying to follow by listening to only my side of the conversation. She was still standing by the exit, having too much queenly dignity to sit on a dirty attic floor like I was.

"We're just telling Clara's sister our idea. She's very excited to see her sister again, but I'm worried that Clara's anger might be dangerous to the house like it was to the church. I'm not sure if Caleb told you, but we almost got the whole building to collapse because she was so angry."

The queen nodded. "Yes, he tells me everything, except where to find you, apparently. At any rate, it's worth the risk. If the house begins to collapse, we'll easily be able to grab you and escape without harm."

"And the humans downstairs too." I gave her a stern look.

She waved her hand in the air at my concern. "Yes, yes. Of course."

I turned back to Riley. "Are you ready?"

She nodded eagerly.

Thinking about Clara, I closed my eyes and tried to summon her to the attic. I focused on what her smile looked like when Riley had appeared in the church. I focused on the sound of her voice when she wasn't angry or wailing like a banshee.

It took several seconds, and I felt something waver along our connection. Perhaps she was fighting my call.

When I called Brandon, he usually popped up with a mere thought in his direction. It was so easy; I was scared I'd do it accidentally sometimes.

With any other ghost I'd tried summoning so far, it took a lot more effort, but I kept at it.

"What are you doing? Are you taking a nap?" The queen's scornful tone almost broke my concentration.

"Shush!" I sliced my hand through the air in her direction.

She sniffed angrily at my rudeness but didn't interrupt again.

Finally, my awareness of Clara moved closer and the hairs on my neck rolled in a wave.

"Where—where am I?" Clara asked, her voice small and timid.

I opened my eyes with a triumphant smile, and Riley jumped up and down next to her sister. It was still odd to see them next to each other knowing that Clara had been the older sister, but, since she'd died first, Riley looked older.

"You're in my attic!" Riley threw her arms around Clara's shoulders while Clara looked around the room in confusion.

"How did I get here?" Her eyes finally found me, and they focused on my face. "It's you again," she looked at Brandon and frowned slightly, "and the pushy guy."

Brandon had the decency to look awkwardly apologetic by pulling his lips into a grimace and darting his eyes around. "Right. Sorry about all that."

"Clara," I still sat on the floor, but I scooted towards the sisters a few inches, "I wanted to bring you here to help restore some of your memories. Do you recognize this place?"

She looked around, taking in the boxes and old furniture, and then finding the queen who was standing so still she could have been mistaken for one of those sewing dress dummies. "Not really. Who is she?"

I glanced to where Clara was pointing and back to her. "Oh, don't worry about that lady. She's just here to make sure we're all safe. Even though she doesn't look like it, she's very strong."

"Okay. This is weird. What's going on? Why am I not in the church? I haven't been able to leave since... since I—"

A few papers rattled nearby, and I began to get worried she'd lose her composure so quickly. After that happened, we'd be lucky to get out of the attic unhurt while getting any more information from her would be impossible until she calmed down.

Thankfully, Riley was learning more about ghosts and how to handle them right along with me.

"Hey, sis. Look at me."

After Clara's eyes found Riley's in the dark, the younger sister smiled. "We're in my attic. This is where I live as a ghost. Isn't it neat?"

Clara kept looking around, but she nodded slowly to answer Riley.

"The neatest thing about it is we're in the house that we grew up in. Here, come look over here." Riley grabbed Clara's hand and pulled her towards the front of the house where a small circular window looked out onto the neighborhood.

Carefully, I got up and followed. I worked slowly around the boxes and disheveled piles of unnamed forgotten items hoping I didn't spook either ghost.

The queen and Brandon followed behind me, both so quiet they almost didn't exist.

"Look at this!" Riley proudly pointed to the corner of the room.

I craned my neck and saw a little girl's hideout. A few pink blankets had been hung from the ceiling and positioned so they covered the corner, draped across each other. Beneath the blankets was a little table, complete with a slightly disturbed tea set mostly covered in dust. Pillows and cushions surrounded the table, and there was even an old forgotten teddy bear peeking out from underneath a blanket.

Clara gasped and put her hand over her mouth. "I remember this!"

Riley beamed as she pulled her sister towards their spot and gestured for her to take a seat. "I was so glad when the new owners of the house didn't change this. They talked about it for a few minutes and said they'd get to it eventually, but, so far, it's still here. Isn't it great? I love this place. We had so many great memories here of having secret tea parties and sneaking snacks we weren't supposed to eat."

"Yes! I loved those biscuits grandma brought over that one time. We snuck the whole tin up here, and Mom was confused for days."

The girls shared giggles as they sat down on the pillows across from each other.

I kept my distance and was afraid to breathe or call attention to myself for fear of breaking their happy spell. Brandon and the queen must have felt the same because they silently stood next to me.

At first, it didn't seem to bother them that they couldn't interact with the teacups or the kettle. They were just happy to have found another moment together, but, when Clara went to pick up the teddy bear, she frowned.

"Riley?"

Her sister looked up from the table where she'd been staring at a dusty sugar spoon. "Yes?"

"We're really dead, aren't we?"

Silence descended around us, and my heart went out to her. I probably would have leaked a few tears, except I was too eager for her mind to keep progressing. It might have been sad to watch the sisters who had both been robbed of growing old and creating families, but I was also glad to see we might be able to get more help from Clara. Perhaps those weren't quite a righteous mixture of emotions, but the queen's presence reminded me that my own life and of others was on the line here.

"It's not so bad, though. At least we're together now?" Riley flashed a kind smile.

"Only because that creepy girl is here," Clara glanced at me with a pointed look, "and her friends."

Riley shrugged. "She brought her grandma to help me talk to you that one time. She was really nice."

"Riley, I'm sorry I didn't ask this before. How did you die? What happened?"

The younger sister who looked older plucked at a piece of lint on her leggings. "After you... disappeared, life wasn't the same. I didn't have anyone to play with, and Mom and Dad were so sad all the time. It was just like life was hollow, empty. There seemed no point to it."

Clara frowned. "I'm sorry. I didn't mean to leave. It wasn't really my choice. Some man came in the middle of the night, sneaking into my room through the windows as silent as a ghost. I made the mistake of looking into his eyes, and, after that, I can't remember much for a while."

"That sounds scary. What did the man want with you?" Riley leaned in closer over the table.

Clara shrugged, but her eyebrows pulled together in pain from her memories, and the teacup closest to her started to tremble. "Blood, mostly."

Riley sat back and frowned. "What? Blood?"

The teacup shook faster, the clattering sound bouncing around the quiet attic. Clara glanced at her sister and back down at the floor. "Do you believe in vampires?"

"Vampires?" If Riley's face hadn't already been pale, it would have been at that moment.

Clara nodded. "But anyway, yeah. It's okay, though. You never finished your story about how you died."

Part of me wanted to urge Clara to keep talking about her experience, hoping that we'd get the information of where Dion was hiding, but a stronger part said to wait and not force it. We'd pushed Clara too far at least twice and that hadn't ended well for any of us.

At least the teacup stopped shaking.

"Oh, right. So, I just got real sad, and one day I decided it wasn't worth living life without you. When Mom wasn't looking, I ran away. I knew she'd try to find me so I went where I figured she wouldn't look, but, before I could get there, I had to cross a street. It was wet and raining, and the ground was slippery. There were horns honking, some bright lights, and a thunking sound before I woke up here, in the attic, by myself."

This time the emotions overcame my eagerness to find the truth, and I sat back down on the wooden attic floor and felt a few tears drip down my face.

Brandon sat down next to me and frowned at his shoes. We were both too worried about breaking the spell on the two sisters, so we didn't say anything, but he put a ghostly hand on my knee. Even though I couldn't feel it, he left it there.

The queen kept standing and continued her silent vigil.

"Oh, Riley," Clara said, and got up from the table to sit next to her sister. She put an arm around Riley's shoulders and pulled her in tight. "I'm so sorry. You must have been hurting."

Riley hugged her sister back. "You must have been so scared."

We let them sit there as long as they needed, crying and comforting each other. My butt grew numb from sitting on the hard floor, but I didn't care. I was too preoccupied wondering how much it would hurt to be hit by a car or to be used as a human blood bank over and over again.

"Hanna has told me that we're ghosts now because we still have some unfinished things we need to do," Riley said after their crying had quieted some. "What do you think your business is?"

"Probably not to terrorize an old church full of homeless people," Clara said somberly.

Riley giggled, causing Clara to look at her in surprise before she also burst into giggles. "You really are a scary church ghost. Why do you think that is where you ended up living as a ghost? I think I'm here in the attic because this is where we had the best memories."

Clara puckered her lips in thought for a second. "I think because it was the first place I felt safe after I was taken by that guy. At some point—months or maybe years, I don't know—after I was taken, someone came to rescue me. I don't know who he was or why, but he tricked the others into letting him take me, and then we ended up at the church shelter. He told me not to leave the grounds since vampires can't step foot in there. For a while, I listened and lived there. The people who own the shelter gave me clothes, food, and kept a watch over me. But even though I felt mostly safe there and the vampires couldn't come get me, I also knew I couldn't find my family staying there. One night I left. It was dark, and I couldn't see, and I fell into the river. It was cold and scary, and then I...well, you know I was never a good swimmer."

Riley's eyebrows perked up in surprise. "You mean you didn't get killed by the vampire, or whatever, who took you? You died from drowning?"

Clara shrugged again. "I guess?"

Pieces of the puzzle were coming together in my mind, painting a clearer picture about what had happened to these poor girls, but I still had so many questions.

"Clara, Riley, I'm so sorry for all the terror you girls have gone through. I can't imagine having to experience things like that while being so young."

As I spoke, both girls whipped their heads towards me as if I'd surprised them, as if they'd forgotten we were there.

"Now that you've come to terms with your deaths, I can try and help you move on to a better place. You aren't meant to stay here as ghosts forever. There is more beyond, and if there is any justice in the world, you two will go to the highest heaven there is to offer."

They looked at each other and thought things over.

"And, I'll do my best to help you both so you can go together." I added an encouraging smile for good measure.

"Actually," Riley looked out beyond us, past me into a space I couldn't see. "Something feels different. There's a weight off of my chest. I think I just needed to find out what had happened to Clara, and now I can go be free."

Clara scrunched up her eyebrows and looked in the direction Riley was looking. "I don't feel different...maybe less angry, and I have more memories than I did before, but I don't feel free. I still feel heavy and dark."

"Is this what a ghost feels like when they cross over?" Brandon glanced at me in concern. "Didn't you say you'd help them go together?"

"Hey, I'm trying my best here! How was I supposed to know that knowing where Clara went was enough for Riley?" I said while looking at Brandon and then turned back to Clara. "What do you think we can help you with? Is there anything you wanted to get done in life that you didn't get to do? Is there... perhaps some revenge you're wanting to get?"

I held my breath, waiting for her to start screaming and a teacup to beam me in the head. Instead, she watched Riley's transfixed gaze into the nothing and turned to me.

"Yes, but you have to promise me you won't go yourself. Get some of your weirdo strong friends to help you, okay?"

I nodded and glanced to the queen who was still stiffly standing there, waiting for me. I had a feeling that if she'd been more human, she wouldn't have had so much patience. As it was, she was probably used to being still and merely existing.

"I promise. I'm not going anywhere near a vampire if I can help it."

"The evil vampire guy kept me there." She pointed out the window and to the side. "Do you think you guys can kill him? It? He's a monster."

She wrapped her arms around her chest and shuddered while Riley woke up from her trance long enough to give her a hug, and the rest of us crowded into the window to see where she had been pointing.

"Wait," I backed up. The queen, curiosity peaked, bustled her giant skirts past me and peered out of the window.

I turned back to Clara. "Are you saying he kept you *next door*?"

"I told you there was a vampire there!" Brandon moved to smack my arm, but his hand went through me.

"No, you said there was a serial killer."

"Same thing."

"Clara, the whole time you were gone you were next door?" Riley's eyes filled with tears, and she hugged her sister even tighter. "How come we couldn't find you? How come we didn't know?"

Emotion waved through me. I focused on breathing evenly while it welled up inside. For some reason, knowing that Clara had been that close the whole time made the experience that much more horrible. Had they been able to hear their little girl's cries if they'd just gotten closer to the house? Or gone outside during the night?

The queen moved stiffly away from the window and looked at me. "I gather that the lair is next door. Thank you for the information. We'll go ascertain the accuracy and see if he still occupies it, or if we can get more leads from the building. Tell your ghost that Dion will never see the light of another day."

I blinked and she had disappeared, presumably to go assemble her vampire warriors and infiltrate the house next door.

"Did you hear that, Clara? She's going to take care of him and all his monster friends who helped him hurt you. He won't hurt anyone else ever again," I said, kneeling on one of the pillows next to the girls.

Riley's body had started fading and giving off small sparkles like dust. Her gaze kept looking out into nothing, but she was working hard to stay with her sister as long as possible. I could tell because she kept shaking her head and turning back to Clara to give her another tight squeeze.

Clara looked out the window for a second and then back to me and nodded. "Yes, good. I hope he feels pain and suffers."

"I'm sure that he will." I shared a meaningful look with Brandon. Even though it was a dark thought coming from such a little girl, I was sure that anyone who had experienced what she'd been through would think even worse things.

"My chest feels lighter too." Clara's face lit up with excitement, and she looked to where Riley had kept looking. "I think it worked!"

Relief flooded through me. Thank goodness it had been enough just to set his demise in action. I don't know what I would have done if she had needed to physically watch Dion's murder go down. That might have been too much for me to stand.

Brandon and I shared grins, and, I had to admit, helping these ghosts felt pretty good. Maybe that's why my gran had done it so often and for so long. It was hard work, especially with these two little girls, but they deserved to move on to a bright and happy place where they could frolic with puppies in the daisy fields.

All right, so I didn't really know what it was like after they crossed over, but I chose to think of it as heaven, and, if anyone deserved to go to heaven, it was these girls.

Riley faded first, but Clara wasn't far behind her. Their transition looked so much different than what Rose had done to capture the other ghosts. If I had seen a real transition before working with Rose, I would have known immediately that what she was doing wasn't helping the ghosts at all.

The familiar shame and guilt washed over me, overshadowing the relief and hope I had been feeling.

Then Brandon and I were alone in the attic. The pillows and tea set sat in the dust like the girls hadn't been there in years. Which, I supposed, they hadn't.

I stood and dusted off my butt. "Well, I guess that's what a ghost crossing over looks like."

Brandon pursed his lips thoughtfully. "Doesn't look too bad, does it? Well, at least when they are going to the good place anyway."

"Could feel the same no matter where you're going." I headed towards the door in the floor to descend the ladder. "There's only one way to find out."

"You'd miss me too much," he said with a teasing grin, but I found myself staring at his face before I climbed down the ladder.

"Yes, I would miss you." I wanted to kiss him again and feel the soft chill of his lips, but I was too embarrassed to ask him to materialize for a moment. Plus, I kept needing to remind myself that we had no idea what kinds of weird side effects we might invoke by using my powers like that.

So I decided to laugh off the moment and turn it into a joke.

"But I'll never admit it to you because that would make your big head swell even more." I grinned and started climbing down the ladder.

"Yes, no one likes a cocky ghost." He jumped down into the hole and was standing triumphantly next to me as I stepped off the ladder.

Shaking my head but still wearing a smile, I pushed the creaky ladder upwards, and, while it took me a few tries and a couple of unladylike grunts, I managed to put it back in place.

"Emma will be glad to hear we've gotten rid of her ghost. Hopefully, she'll be able to sleep better after this," I said as we walked down the stairs, more to chase away the quiet between us that kept making me think of stolen kisses.

"Unless the several many ghosts next door decide to start acting up. Who knows what will change with Caleb's seethe rushing into the place?"

He had a point, and I was frowning as we rounded the stairs and walked into the front room. Emma's parents were still sitting on the couch and staring at the opposite wall, but I was surprised to see there were still three vampires standing in there with them.

Talon was among them, and he turned to me as we walked into the room.

"There you are. Took your time getting down here, did you?" I was reminded again how different he was from before.

"Right, sorry. Human body, human legs. Kind of slow and all that. Alright, pleasure doing business with you guys. See you later!" I headed towards the door, but, before I could take two steps, all three of the vampires were standing between me and it.

"Did you think we were just hanging out in here for fun? Thanks to you, I've had to miss out on all the action in Dion's lair. Even now, I can hear his tortured screams." Talon looked off into the distance as if he really could hear something. And what did I know? He was a vampire. Maybe he could hear the screams. I just hoped they were smart enough to keep it quiet so the neighboring humans couldn't hear them.

"What does he mean 'because of you'?" Brandon's question brought me back to the moment.

"Right. So even though I helped the queen, she's not going to let me go, is she? That seems rude." I pouted, trying to show off an unconcerned attitude instead of the hammering fear in my chest.

Talon's mouth morphed that predatory smile I was beginning to associate with vampires and their pointy canines. "And let our personal Seer free to get snatched up by another seethe, or even worse, an order of necromancers? The queen is too smart for that."

I frowned and made the mistake of looking into his eyes, trying to appear braver than I felt. Immediately, the world around me turned to fuzz, and all I could see were Talon's brilliant blue eyes.

Chapter 17

The next few hours were a haze. I wasn't unconscious, but I was there and kind of wasn't there. I couldn't act on my own and had to follow the directions of Talon. They must have ditched my phone somewhere because I couldn't find it on my person or inside the room.

I do remember seeing the queen at one point. They'd taken me back to their lavish lair, down into that basement that was like no basement I'd ever seen with its high ceilings and gilded doors, and finally into my own little room.

It wasn't bad, as far as prisons go. I had a four-post king-size bed with a thick quilt and at least five pillows. I didn't let myself think about who else had slept in that bed and what might have happened in it.

There were giant pieces of art hanging on all my walls, and, while I knew little about the art world, I was grateful to have something interesting to look at while I spent hours in the room by myself. Besides the bed, there was a wardrobe full of old-styled dresses that I prayed no one would expect me to wear, and a matching bedside table. The whole thing kind of reminded me of Belle's room from *The Beauty and The Beast*.

I finally understood why Belle was so ungrateful about the whole being captured thing, even though she was inside somewhere quite fancy. It didn't matter where you were if you weren't able to be your-self.

Aside from the inanimate furniture, there was also a vampire in my room with me at all times. At first, it was Talon, but then he was switched out for someone else. Before they did the switch, Talon forced me to look into the other vampire's eyes long enough for him to entrance me.

Thankfully, that was the worst they had done so far. Neither had tried to suck my blood or kiss me or any other creepy things. However, a small part of my mind knew that if they had wanted to do any of those things, they would have been able to force me to easily, and then, probably just as easily, make me forget.

When the queen came to see me, I was surprised by the personal visit. She was dressed in a different dress, a cream-colored gown in a similar style with a tight bodice and a large skirt. The fabric looked every bit as expensive as the other one had, and I wondered how much money she'd been able to make being a vampire queen over several hundred years.

"I would apologize for keeping you in here, but I don't feel bad at all. Maybe it would have been different if you'd had better manners and known how to treat a queen, but as it is," she sighed dramatically and waved her gloved hand in the air vaguely, "alas, here we are."

"Did you find your niece?" I asked, ignoring her insults, glad I could speak my own words when the vampire controlling me let me have a little room on his tight leash. I only knew that because I was constantly forcing my will against his, and it only came through when he let me.

The grip of a vampire's trance was impressive, I had to admit. And also, super scary. He could literally make me do anything. The only drawbacks I could see was that it appeared he had to be in the same room as me, and he couldn't hold it longer than a few hours, if I could take any indication for Talon needing to switch out.

"We did. In some ways, that is good for you. Thanks to your help, we were able to sink our teeth into Dion, and rescue my poor niece who was in rough shape. She needed some of her fellow vampire's blood to heal properly. Your help also prevented me from searching through every human house until I found what I was looking for. The human city owes you a medal or something. Too bad they'll never find out."

"Right. I don't care about getting a medal. I'm just glad I kept others from getting hurt. Now, when do I get to go home?"

Her lips pursed into a smug smile. "Consider this your new home. You were so helpful, there is no way I can let a Seer go free. We must keep track of our best assets, and Seers are too rare. Who knows what would happen to you or who would try to kidnap you?"

I wasn't surprised, but I also wasn't thrilled.

"Okay, but why keep me entranced all this time? I'm a mere human. How am I supposed to fight my way out of a giant house populated with tons of vampires? Surely I'm relatively safe down here."

The queen waggled her finger at me. "Tut tut. Don't act like I'm stupid. I saw how you kept looking in weird directions. I know you have more than one ghost friend hanging about. After watching you summon another ghost into the same haunt as that first ghost, well, I know you have extra special powers that I can't let out of my sight and definitely cannot let you use to save yourself. Keeping you entranced prevents you from trying to contact your ghost friends who might try to rescue you, as foolish as that would be."

The bit of hope I had been holding onto sank with her words. It hadn't really hit me that I was trapped yet, but the fact that she knew enough about Seers to keep me from my ghosts helped the gloom settle in more.

I was just a regular human. How was I supposed to get out of there? I was no match against even one vampire, let alone the several that lived and lounged all over this mansion.

I was seriously stuck.

"But what about my family? Are they going to think I just disappeared? Your people who kidnapped me weren't wearing disguises, and there are cameras at school. Surely the police will trace them back to you and figure out where I am."

The queen laughed. "None of that matters when you own the police. Remember how I said we'd found you in the first place? Believe me, even if some of the human police get involved, none of them will trace your disappearance to me. Give me credit. I've been avoiding human authorities for a long time."

I sat slowly onto the bed. "But my mom and my sister and all my friends will be so worried. Why can't you just let me live my life while I promise to help you talk to ghosts or whatever whenever you need it? Wouldn't it be better to have a happy Seer working for you rather than a crushed, depressed, trapped Seer working for you? What if I get so sad that I can't even access my powers? I'll be useless."

She stared at me, unmoving for a few seconds. I wasn't sure if she wanted me to think she was considering my words or had just forgotten she was undead, and thus alive, kind of, for a second and needed to respond. Whatever it was, her gaze was suffocating.

"Or maybe let me at least talk to my mom and sister one last time so they know I'm not dead? That might help give us some peace of mind." I kept talking, trying to search for something she would grant me. There was no way I was accepting this as my future.

Finally, she shook her head. "Listen, I'm sorry it has to be this way, but this is the only way I can keep you safe. If I let you live your life as a regular human, it's only a matter of time before someone else captures you to use you for their own needs. I'll think about letting you write a letter to your family for their peace of mind, but only if you're on your best behavior."

And with that, she flounced out of the room, leaving me to cry while a stoic vampire I didn't know stood watching over me. At least he didn't stop me from crying. It would have felt like some kind of torture to be denied the ability to express the sadness sinking into my bones.

Why hadn't I listened to Noah and avoided Caleb? Turns out, he'd been right the whole time.

Vampires were nothing to mess around with.

Chapter 18

I'm not sure how much time passed before they brought me some food. Honestly, I was surprised that they fed me at all. But of course, they wanted to keep their new pet human healthy. It wouldn't do to have me waste away and then not be able to use my powers.

A vampire I didn't recognize wheeled in a cart of food. She was taller than the average woman, and she added more height by wearing fierce black heels. Her dress was long, formfitting, and silver. She had dark hair that flowed down her back like a waterfall, and, if I hadn't seen a room full of gorgeous vampires only a few hours before, I would have sworn she was the most beautiful woman I'd ever seen.

"Hello, dearie. Your room service has arrived. I think you'll find we still know how to cook even though we don't need to eat anything anymore. Some of us still like to have lavish dinners just to feel that decadent spirit again, you know? We might be dead, but we still remember how it felt to be a human. Some of us haven't even been dead that long. Plus, Pierre was a fancy French chef many years ago, and he's just been *dying* to cook again for someone who would appreciate it."

She chattered as she pulled the cart into the room and started taking off the lids of various items she'd brought. I had honestly never seen a vampire talk so much, and her friendly attitude confused me for several seconds.

I did have to admit, though, that the food smelled and looked amazing. It had been a long time since I'd eaten much, having kept my mind distracted most of the day with getting ready for the dance, then the dance, and then some weird ghost crap. Plus, I'd officially been a vampire prisoner for three hours.

My life felt as crazy as it sounds.

"Personally, I'd start with the side salad here. There is some good nutrition, and it would be better to get full on the healthy food before diving into the other stuff, but you have to keep room for this amazing duck. Have you eaten duck before? This orange glaze is amazing. Honestly, I'd never had duck until I came here. I wish I had been able to taste it while I was alive. I'm sure it would have tasted all the better. Come here and check this out. Don't be shy. I won't bite."

Her genuine smile, relaxed attitude, and my hopelessness at being a captive kept me from being scared of her.

I sat at the table on the far side of the room as she piled the food onto the smooth surface. It really did look incredible, and my stomach grumbled. The thought flitted across my mind that since I was trapped and the only people I was going to see for the rest of my life were vampires, it wouldn't matter if I got fat. Maybe I could find some small happiness in life by indulging in fantastic foods. It was the least I could do for myself as escaping was not much of an option.

Then the vampire did something weird and leaned in closer and continued talking but abruptly changed the subject. "You'll also want to make sure you try the rolls. We've used homemade honey butter, and we're coming for you. Don't lose hope. We know that you're entranced and can't talk or call your ghost friends. Brandon made contact with Trina, so we know where you are. We're making plans to come get you. Vampires never have been and never will be a match for necromancers."

Then she stood and wheeled the tray to the side of the room as if nothing odd had happened. "I'll just leave this here and you can pile your empty dishes on it. I'll be back for it later. Ta!"

She flicked her hand in a flippant goodbye and left me staring at the door she had closed behind her.

There was still the other vampire who was keeping me entranced standing guard next to the door. I guess my staring didn't bother him even though it took me several seconds to look back down at my food.

It seemed he hadn't heard what the woman had said to me which was odd because it felt like it had been loud enough for a vampire to pick up with their sharp hearing. Perhaps he'd been distracted by keeping me entranced. Perhaps her chattering had lulled him into boredom, and he tuned her out early. Perhaps he didn't care, knowing that I was stuck under his influence and could do nothing about it.

Luckily, he'd given me enough control over myself that I could eat. My mind whirled as I tasted and savored the feast before me. It was astonishing that vampires could cook so well since they didn't need to eat at all.

How had Brandon made contact with Trina? How had Trina known about necromancers? Was this connected to Noah somehow?

I remembered how the vampires had seemed uneasy at the dance once Talon mentioned that there was a necromancer around. It seemed like they feared them, but why?

More memories of the dance flitted through my head as I chewed on a tender and juicy bit of duck meat. I'd never had duck before, and I decided I wouldn't mind having it again.

Talon had called himself Nathan when we had danced. No, wait, he'd started saying an "N" name and then backtracked to Nathan. What if he had been about to say Noah?

My heart started beating quicker in my chest as I considered the possibilities. I certainly didn't know much about necromancers, but was it possible that they were somehow able to control vampires? I knew from video games and stories that they usually raised dead people and those were usually mindless zombies. What did that mean regarding vampires? On some level, it made sense that they could have power over them. They were certainly undead.

I sat back in my chair and took a deep breath.

Had that been Noah I was dancing with through the body of a vampire? Talon certainly seemed like a different person during and after the dance. He was friendly, charming, and seemed to know me personally.

Holy cow. The implications of necromancers being able to do that to vampires were awe-inspiring.

It didn't take long before my stomach felt so full, I was worried I'd throw up all that I had eaten. As good as it had been on the way down, I didn't want to try it on the way up. Plus, I had a feeling I would need my strength to handle whatever was coming next. In fact, after eating, my arms felt less like noodles and more like arms. My head was clearer despite still being entranced and unable to use my ghost powers, but, overall, I felt better.

Then I looked at the grease cooling on the platter next to the duck and felt ashamed. I'd eaten that and taken some into my body. It could take forever to burn off that fat, and it would probably go right to my thighs.

I frowned, staring at the food and rethinking the throwing-up plan. Maybe I should go to the bathroom while it was easier to get rid of the fat I'd just eaten without having to run several miles.

Before I could get up, a voice sounded in my head that was very familiar.

"Hanna? Can you hear me?"

I blinked and looked around the room. It was the same fancy place with only one other person inside, that stoic vampire who was content just to keep me entranced while staring at the wall, apparently.

He didn't react when I looked at him, so I knew it wasn't he who had said anything. Plus, I recognized that voice.

"It's me, Caleb. Can you hear me?"

I furrowed my eyebrows and wondered how to respond to him. If I started talking aloud, my guard could hear me. Should I just try to project my thoughts to him somehow?

Maybe I was finally going crazy. After the vampires had taken the ghosts away, it had left room for other voices to come inside my brain and try to convince me to do bad things.

"Uhm, hello?" I gave a voice to my thoughts inside my head, kind of like praying without speaking, if that makes sense.

Apparently, it worked. *"Hanna! Oh, I'm so sorry! I don't know how they finally found you, and I tried so hard to keep you a secret, but they must have figured it out somehow. I've been... indisposed for a few days or I would have contacted you earlier to warn you. Now I can feel that you're nearby, and my heart sings in sorrow that they've captured you."*

Another glance at my guard told me that he didn't suspect anything. Slowly, I stood and started placing the dishes back onto the cart. Not because I wanted to give my vampire captors less work, but more because I wanted to do something with my hands before I either freaked out and either ran to the bathroom or ran around in circles pulling at my hair like the crazy person I clearly was.

"How are you talking to me? Am I finally hearing crazy voices?" I projected to what felt like a warm kind of presence inside my mind. I hadn't realized it was there until it had started talking with Caleb's voice, but once it had, I'd realized it had been there for at least a few days.

"Right. So, remember when I helped you heal from that wound? I didn't tell you then because I didn't want to freak you out, but, as long as you still have my blood inside of you, we're bonded. If you kept feeding from me, even in small amounts, you would become attached and somewhat of a human slave."

"What?! And you didn't feel like that might be important for me to know?"

"Not while you were dying. Plus, I didn't think I'd need to use it, so it wasn't a big deal. I figured once my blood passed from your system, there would be no issues."

"Well, there certainly are issues!" I threw up my hands in frustration then realized Caleb couldn't see me, but the guard could.

I glanced back at the vampire, but he still didn't move. If I hadn't seen him walk into the room with my own eyes, I would have sworn he was just a well-made manikin or something.

"I know, Hanna. I'm so sorry. I was really worried Kieran would do something drastic, and she didn't disappoint. Are you okay? Have they hurt you at all?"

"No, I'm fine. I'm entranced so I can't see my ghosts. Why didn't you warn me that vampires can entrance people like this? Who is Kieran?"

"You've probably met her by now if you're in her house. That's the queen of our seethe. Also, how would you have reacted if I'd told you about that? There are lots of dangerous things vampires can do, Hanna. I kept trying to warn you to be careful."

All the dishes were cleared and put on the cart. My stomach twisted as I looked at the food when before I'd been eager to eat it all. Weird how much hunger impacted the body.

Trying to pretend like nothing important was happening, I sauntered around the room for a bit and ended up sitting on the side of the bed. I stared ahead at the opposite wall which displayed a painting of a delicate bouquet of lilies.

"So far, you've been full of warnings, but you also keep trying to reassure me that you'll protect me. How has that worked out for you so far?"

Our connection was odd, and I didn't know how much he could hear and feel from inside my head, but I could feel faint parts of him. An echo of regret bounced around from the warm place in my mind that I had decided was his influence.

Maybe I had been too tough on him. The queen, or Kieran, had mentioned how they had tortured Caleb, and he'd held out from telling them who or where I was. I remembered Brandon had said he'd looked broken up and then forced to heal that way, so he'd have to break again to be able to function.

"I really am sorry." His voice sounded sad in my head, and I was impressed with the whole ability to exchange thoughts and feelings through the mind somehow.

"I know. I'm sorry. I shouldn't have been so rude. Kieran told me that they tortured you. Are you okay? Are they keeping you prisoner too?"

"In a way. I'll be fine. I just need time to recover. That's kind of why I couldn't talk to you for a while, but I'm on the mend already. That was my first clue that they found you. They stopped trying to get information from me. Did she say how they found you?"

I didn't know how much my vampire guard was watching me or how much I should act bored, but I sighed and flopped down onto the bed and stared at the ceiling. The plaster marks were in swirls, and I followed the patterns with my eyes while talking to the new voice inside my head.

"She said something about a traffic camera snapping a picture while we were driving together."

Caleb cursed. *"Of course. I should have been more careful."*

"It's okay. In case you've forgotten, they're vampires. They probably would have figured it out eventually."

"That's truer than you know. I figured they would find out, but it wasn't going to be because I spilled it."

"I do appreciate that even though now you're in a rough state, whereas, if you'd told them, you might have been healthy enough to come rescue me like a knight in shining armor."

There were a few seconds of silence where tiredness seeped into my eyes. I had no idea what time it was, but they'd kidnapped me around eight o'clock, and I hadn't slept yet, so it was probably pretty late at night, maybe the next morning already.

"I hadn't thought of that. I can sense that you're tired. Maybe you should try and get some sleep so you'll be at your full strength in case there's a chance you might escape, somehow."

"Oh, right. About that. A woman vampire came in here earlier and gave me food. She kept chatting away and then quickly whispered to me something about getting me out and necromancers."

Caleb cursed again, and it was the last word I remembered before drifting to sleep.

Chapter 19

I awoke to a confusing disturbance, and it took my brain several seconds to catch up before I could figure out what was happening. By that time, my vampire guard was face down on the carpet, and two bright blue ghosts appeared standing next to Noah, Trina, and my mom.

Yes, very confusing.

"This is a weird dream. It's like the setup for a weird joke or something. My friend, my sister, my mom, and two ghosts walk into a room..."

Mom was the first to move, and she rushed over to my bed and wrapped me into her arms. "Oh, sweetie! It's not a dream. I'm so glad you're okay!"

I breathed in her warm scent and relished feeling free from the vampire's entrancement at the same time. It was nice to be able to do what I wanted again, even though they had given me some free reign. Mostly, it was just nice not to have a strange vampire, besides Caleb, inside my head and to be able to see my ghosts again.

Yeah, I never thought I'd say that. Stupid ghosts being friends and loved ones.

We parted from our embrace, and Trina and Noah walked up beside my mom while Gran trailed behind them, and Brandon jumped right into bed next to me.

"Nice digs! They might be vampires, but they sure know how to lock a person up!" Brandon said as he jumped a few more times on the bed.

Of course, the bed didn't move with his presence, but Trina's eyes followed his movements, and she stifled a smile.

"Wait. What's going on? Why are you all here? Trina, can you *see* him?"

Blushing, Trina turned her eyes back to me. "So, I can see ghosts, too. Surprise?"

"It's been kind of fun having another person who can see me, but boy we got lucky that they went to the skatepark to look for you," Brandon helped add to the answers.

"That's why Gran was freaking out so much when she found out I could see ghosts. That's why she said there weren't supposed to be two of us. Gran? There are two of us?"

Gran smiled and nodded. "I'm sorry I couldn't tell you before. It wasn't my secret to tell. The necklace she always wears keeps her from being able to use her powers. That's also why I didn't have it to give it to you. I never thought there would be two Seers born into our family."

"Right." I peered at Mom who was smiling at me and stroking my hair as if to make sure I was still there. "And Mom knows too?"

Noah glanced towards the door and back to our little reunion party. "I'm sorry to break things up, and I'm sure you have a billion questions, but we really shouldn't stay here. The blessing won't hurt us once it's finished, but a crazed vampire could come find us any second."

"Wait, wait, wait. What blessing? Will it hurt the vampires?"

"We've got a lot to explain, but can we do it when we're outside and safe again?" Noah added a tenuous smile.

"Not before we get Caleb out too." I hopped off the bed and ran into the hallway.

"Caleb?" Trina followed behind me, and I finally noticed she was still wearing her homecoming dress. We probably looked silly running around dressed up so much, but, then again, we'd fit right in if we ran into any vampires.

Which would be bad.

"Yes, they tortured him for days. That's why he wasn't at school or the dance. He wasn't avoiding you, Trina!" I turned around and grabbed her hands in excitement. "Isn't that great?"

"Wait a minute. Your date was with a vampire?" Mom's furrowed eyebrows would have normally scared me, but there were too many other things going on to get worried about that.

"But he's a good vampire! He held out against torture for days to keep my identity hidden. Unfortunately, they found out anyway," I said, giving Trina's fingers a quick squeeze, and then followed Caleb's presence by somehow using his connection in my head.

"Caleb! My family and Noah came for me and got me out! We're coming to you right now. Noah said something about a blessing and hurting the vampires, so we have to hurry."

"What? That's a lot to take in."

"I know! I'm still very confused myself."

"Where are we going?" Noah's voice brought me back to the hall-way I was half-running down, trying to figure out which room Caleb was in. "I could probably take one vampire if we ran into one, but any more than that and we might have trouble. Unless you guys are hiding any superpowers that I don't know about yet?"

"He's just up here. I can feel him."

Trina was behind me with Mom behind her. Noah took up the rear, although he didn't realize two ghosts flanked his sides. Brandon kept disappearing through the walls to check in the other rooms. Sometimes he commented on a "nice rug" or "sick statue" when he came back into the hallway with us, but for the most part, I ignored him.

"You can feel him?" Trina asked.

"What does that mean?" My mom echoed her thoughts.

Gran groaned. "Oh, great. That's just great."

"Feel? Oh no. You didn't let him feed off of you, did you?" Noah's voice sounded the most alarmed. "That is not a good idea."

"Ew. Vampire kisses." Brandon made a retching sound. "Did he taste like a dead body?"

"No more than you did," I said, unable to help from making the joke even though it confused Mom and Noah and made Trina and Gran look at me sharply in concern.

Brandon just cackled. "Oh, burn!"

Finally, it felt like Caleb was close, and we'd still not run into any vampires. Whatever the blessing thing was that Noah had mentioned, it was doing a good job keeping them distracted.

"In here!" I turned a golden doorknob on the room to my left and pushed with my shoulder.

It was locked, and I frowned at the pain from trying to shove it open.

Brandon walked through the door, and I could hear him from the other side. "Oh, man. You look rough, boy."

"Here. Let me," Noah said.

I backed up and gave him space as he kicked the door a few times until the doorframe splintered.

"I hope no one could hear that," Mom said, glancing behind us. "I'm not sure I like being in here."

"No one said you had to come. In fact, you should have stayed in the car. This whole situation isn't a place for a mom to hang out in," Trina pointed out right as Noah gave his last kick.

"I was not going to let you come in here by yourself!"

Noah pushed open the door, and we all piled into the room.

Brandon had been right. Caleb looked rough.

He was on his knees, his wrists and ankles bound in wooden shackles. There was blood all over. I mean, like all over—the floor, the walls, his clothes, his skin. It looked like someone had taken buckets of blood, dumped them, and splattered them everywhere. One of his legs looked oddly bent, and I realized that's what a broken bone looked like. I made sure to advert my eyes as the sight made my stomach do flips.

"Caleb?" Trina went to him and kneeled onto the floor, apparently uncaring about getting her dress bloody. She hesitated before touching him, drawing her fingers back for a second, but then made a decision and tried to wipe some of the drying blood off his face. It came off in flakes, making me cringe. "What happened? Are you *okay*?"

Mom stood next to me and cursed in a way I hadn't heard from her before, but her reaction was nothing compared to Gran's.

"Caleb!" Gran also kneeled next to the beat-up vampire, but, unlike Trina, she couldn't touch him. I swore I could see ghostly tears drip onto her cheeks. "How could you let them do this to you? What did you go through to protect my granddaughter?"

That was when I realized I really could trust Caleb. He'd been through hell to protect me, and, whether it was because I was just a Seer or because he felt something for Gran and our family, I didn't know. What I did know was that he hadn't had to endure any of it if it weren't for love and loyalty.

"We really need to get out of here. Either they'll finish the blessing and Caleb will be incinerated, or the vampires will win and come back down here to finish us," Noah said as he went straight to the shackles around Caleb's arms and pulled on them, testing how well they were connected to the wall.

"Don't you think I've tried that already, amigo?" Caleb said with a teasing smile, despite the blood that crackled. "Thank you for coming to save me, but that was stupid. You all should get out of here. If she catches you…"

"That's what I keep telling them, but Hanna insisted we had to save you. If it were up to me, I'd let you rot down here until you burst into flames after the order finishes the prayer and turns this whole property into holy ground." Noah inspected the wooden shackles some more but couldn't seem to find any weakness to exploit.

"He doesn't mean that." I shot Noah a glare. "We wouldn't let that happen to you. Not after everything you've done for me."

"You mean 'not after we shared that super romantic kiss and I somehow made a mental connection with a vampire'?" Brandon said while using a high-pitched voice that was apparently supposed to be an impression of mine.

"We did not kiss! He just gave me some blood so I could heal, is all. You were there! Stop trying to make Trina think we made out." I gave Brandon a scalding look.

Sometimes he really did make me mad.

Trina frowned and inspected the shackle on Caleb's other wrist, opposite from Noah. "How do we get these off? Aren't... I can't believe I'm saying any of this... aren't vampires super strong? Can't you just break them?"

Caleb's response time was slower than I wanted it to be, but so was everything else. I felt antsy standing inside the room while a vampire could come in at any second and take out our whole mortal group. I had seen Noah do something to the vampire guard in my room, but I didn't know how many he could take at once, or if he could even do it again, and it was pretty clear that Caleb wasn't going to be any help. We also certainly couldn't rely on the two ghosts with us or the two mortal women, unless my mom had some secret martial arts training hiding just like she'd hidden some kind of knowledge about ghosts. She was going to have a lot of explaining to do.

"Usually, yes. It would be painful because the wood splinters would lodge into my skin and bring poison to my heart, but, at full strength, I could handle these." He frowned and looked down at the puddle of blood seeping into Noah's and Trina's clothes. "But right now, I'm drained."

"Uh oh, I have a feeling I know where this is going. Maybe we should cut the dramatics and get on with it so we can get out of here. Hanna, just offer him your neck." Brandon said while crossing his arms over his chest and studying the kneeling vampire.

"Don't you dare!" Gran glared at Brandon.

Trina looked up at their exchange and then looked at me. "Maybe we can help you get back some strength, hopefully at least enough to break these shackles. Then we can get out of here, and you can go hide somewhere to rest."

Caleb frowned and furrowed his brow. "Logically, I know I wouldn't let that happen, no matter how much danger I was in, but this might be the thirst talking and the knowledge that if I'm able to help defend you against other vampires, it will be worth it. I'll agree to taking blood from one of you as long as it's not Hanna. She still has my blood in her system. If we exchange, there could be weird consequences. It takes more than that to make a vampire, but not much."

Gran huffed and frowned while my mom kept looking back and forth between the distressed vampire and her daughters. Noah stood and scrubbed at any blood he'd gotten on his hands.

"Whatever we do, we need to do it faster than this." Noah glanced towards the door again, and my quickly beating heart agreed with his urgency.

"I know I don't get a vote here, but I have to admit seeing a vampire Hanna would be pretty cool," Brandon said while tapping a lip with his finger in thought.

"I'll do it," Trina said while turning her head to the side. "Don't argue with me and just get it over with so we can get out of here."

Caleb looked at my mom first, and while we all knew that if Trina wanted to do this, it would be hard for my mom to stop her, but it was nice that he was giving her a chance to offer permission or not.

Crashing sounds from somewhere upstairs made all of us look toward the door in fear of being caught.

Mom turned back to Trina. "Are you sure you want to do this? Will there be any lingering effects?"

Trina nodded. "Yes, it's fine. He won't take too much, right?"

Caleb nodded, his eyes still on my mom. "I won't take enough for anything but strength for the next few minutes. She'll have no lasting effects. It's not nearly as dangerous for the human if I don't take much as it would be if she were to drink my blood."

My cheeks colored as a few people looked at me, Gran included.

"Oh," Gran shook her head and clutched at her heart, "I should have never gotten you all mixed up in this."

Mom did spare me a glance, but another crashing sound pushed her into motion. "Alright. Don't take a lot and don't cause her pain."

Noah grimaced. "I'm going to go scout out our path. I'll be right back."

"Be careful!" I said as he left. He flashed me a grateful smile as he passed, his brown hair falling into his face for a second before he brushed it back.

"Could you be any more obvious?" Brandon shook his head, and, for once, I did feel a bit bad. It's not like we were dating or anything, but we had shared some intimate moments the last week.

Gran had been right. Being friends with a ghost was complicated.

Trina moved in closer to Caleb and tipped her head to expose her neck to him. My heart rate quickened as I could only imagine the trepidation and also excitement Trina must have been feeling.

"I'm sorry if this hurts," Caleb said and leaned in, his canines growing as we watched.

"Ugh, I can't watch this," Gran said and left the room.

"It is pretty gross." Brandon nodded his agreement but didn't follow Gran through the wall.

Thankfully, Caleb was able to drink quietly without any squelching or gulping sounds. That would have made the situation even worse. Trina did hiss when his mouth made contact, but then her shoulders relaxed.

It was a bit too much for me, I admit, so I gave Mom a hesitant smile and also dipped out of the room. Mom stayed behind to ensure he didn't take too much, I assumed, and I looked around the hallway while I waited. There was even more art hung all up and down the hall, and, while there were overhead lights using electricity, there were several sconces hanging on the walls with long candles. With the electric lights off and all the candles lit, this place would have been exactly what I would have pictured for a vampire lair.

I didn't see Noah, so he must have taken a turn somewhere. The hallway was long, stretching in both directions for several paces until one side ended with a room that had double doors while the other was where we had come from. I knew there was a staircase somewhere in the backwards direction, but I wasn't certain enough to go wandering off on my own.

"What? Didn't like the look of one of your boyfriends biting your sister's neck?" Brandon said as he walked through the wall to join me.

He wore a teasing smile on his face, but there was an undercurrent of bitterness to his tone.

It didn't take long before I heard a guttural snarl and wood snapping. Mom, Trina, Gran, and Caleb came out into the hallway. Caleb was still covered in blood, but more had dried and flaked off during his movements. At least he was standing. Both of his legs looked normal, and I supposed the infusion of blood had helped restore his quick vampire healing.

I wouldn't have enjoyed being addicted to blood for survival, but there certainly were many benefits of being a vampire, superhuman strength and rapid healing among them.

"Do you know your way around here? What's the best way out?" I asked as they came out of the room.

Trina did look paler than before, and her eyes were somewhat unfocused and foggy. There were two red puncture wounds on her neck, and I made sure not to keep looking at them. Gran was still frowning, looking between Caleb and Trina, back and forth several times. Mom's eyebrows were pinched in worry, but her gaze was focused and looking for a way out.

"Yes. There is only one set of stairs upwards, but then we can sneak to the back of the house and get out that way, hopefully," Caleb said, nodding his head in the direction we'd come from.

I was happy to note he was able to talk quicker, and his reaction speed was more of what I'd expect in an emergency situation like this one.

Caleb took the lead and we jogged down the hallway. Just as we neared the corner, Noah zipped around and almost collided with the vampire.

"Oh, good. It's a mess up there." Noah was breathing heavily, but his words tumbled out in a rush. "The order is holding its own, but they aren't able to continue with the blessing quite yet. The vampires are giving us more of a fight than we expected, so we don't have to worry too much about Caleb bursting into flames yet. However, we do have to worry about running into angry groups of vampires and trying to stand against them. Caleb, are you with us, or are you going to turn on us when we run into your seethe members?"

There was a challenge in Noah's eyes that echoed a fear in my heart I didn't know I'd been nursing. Yes, he had withstood torture for several days to protect me, but that was different from physically standing against his entire seethe, essentially his family. Was he willing to engage in that level of betrayal?

We all looked at Caleb, except for Trina who seemed to be staring at a spiderweb in the corner.

He held Noah's gaze steadily. "I will not betray you. I will help you escape and see that everyone here gets to safety, even if that means I have to hurt someone from my seethe."

Noah waited only for another second, perhaps debating on if he could trust the vampire, but then probably came to the same conclusion I had—it was worth the risk. We needed his help to get out.

Nodding, Noah's eyes assessed each of us, stopping for a longer second on Trina who was still staring off oddly and humming to herself.

If I had to guess, I'd say that being drained by a vampire, even just a little bit, was somewhat like being high.

But at least she was standing and would follow us around. That was good enough right then.

"Okay, let's go," Noah said and ran back the way he had come.

We followed after him, and, while we probably should have worried about trying to sneak down the hallway quietly instead of thundering down it in loud clacking high heels as we ran, we favored speed for stealth.

Again, we didn't run into any vampires as we jogged through the hallway and up the stairs, following Noah and Caleb. I was beginning to think we either had very good luck or very bad luck and they were going to all descend upon us at once.

As we reached the top, Noah turned back to us abruptly. Caleb's reflexes were recovered enough that he was able to stop in time and catch Trina before she stumbled. Mom was in front of me, and we bumped into each other, but it wasn't enough to push anyone back down the stairs.

"I should add," Noah said, glancing out into the open area before us, "if you see a zombie don't be scared. They're the good guys, so please don't try to attack it. They're hard enough to keep together as it is. We found a lot on the property, unsurprisingly so from a vampire seethe, but most of them aren't in great shape."

"Wait, what?" I only had time to say before we were moving again.

Brandon giggled from beside me. "This is so cool."

Gran had stuck close to the back of the group, and her face was still pinched in worry. It made me wonder how much adventure she'd had in her life of being a Seer. How much of the underground occult stuff did she know about? Had she battled vampires before? She certainly seemed to understand the dangers of them at least. Of course, she'd spent some time with Caleb. Who knows what kind of stuff they had gotten into before I was born?

With images of a younger version of my Gran fighting off vampires in my mind, I followed Noah into a large kitchen and dining area. We didn't immediately see anything dangerous, but several of the windows around the dining room table had been broken, and glass was scattered all over the place. The sounds coming from the outside were hard to describe, and, if I hadn't been afraid for my life before then, I certainly was now.

Snarls, grunts, angry shouts, thwacks, smacks, and more crashing and crunching sounds had me wincing and craning my neck for sudden attackers. Everything was coming from either outside or the front of the house, but we were near the back and, so far, seemed to have gone undetected.

"This is too easy," Noah muttered as we made our way to the back door.

Caleb was walking backward, his attention on the dining room in case anything charged through the windows or down the hall. "I agree. Kieran would have kept guards on Hanna."

"We were able to sneak inside this way without being seen. Perhaps everyone is just too busy making sure the ground doesn't get blessed," Mom said, keeping her hand on Trina's back so she would keep up with us.

"A Seer is too valuable." Gran shook her head.

Noah opened the back door and stuck his head out, checking for danger. I couldn't see much over Trina and Mom's heads, let alone into the dark night. He must have been satisfied with what he didn't see, because he stepped outside and motioned us to continue.

Caleb took up the spot in the back, still facing backward, his legs slightly bent, and his eyes roaming for any movement.

Gran paused as she walked by him and stroked his cheek. The tenderness in her eyes was moving, and I don't think she cared that he didn't know she was there. "I'm glad you're okay. Thank you for protecting my granddaughter. A lesser person would have given in."

He didn't look in her direction, but his head did tilt to the side as if he was sensing something was happening.

I figured I'd tell him later what she'd said.

The backyard was huge, and beyond the deck was darkness, potentially full of angry vampires. The battle was louder now that we were outside, and, as undignified as it was, I grabbed Trina's arm and huddled with her and my mom who had grabbed her other side. Noah's pace was slower than it had been inside as he stopped and listened carefully before taking a few steps at a time. His eyes roamed around in the darkness, and I wondered if necromancers had better vision than regular humans or if there was another sense he was working with.

Caleb shut the door behind us and turned his attention to the grass and darkness that stretched before us. Several trees and bushes provided plenty of places for nasty creatures to jump out from, but Caleb's face didn't reveal any concern. He probably was gifted with better sight at night than us weak humans, so I watched him carefully in case I needed to dive under a lawn chair or something.

My feet were killing me in the heels I'd worn for way longer than heels were meant to be worn. I wondered if I had bloody blisters, and if it would just be better to take them off completely and brave bare feet. We made it as far as off the deck and a few steps onto a stone path before anything confronted us.

Noah had been right. Our escape had been too easy because appearing to seep out of the darkness itself, Queen Kieran blocked our path with a sneer on her face. Her once immaculate dress was in tatters. There were blood stains and other unnamable dark substances on the cream fabric, but, despite the ruined state of her gown, her hair was still done up neatly in a firm twist.

"Traitor!" The queen yelled and slashed her hand out towards Caleb.

Unable to even say a word, he collapsed into a heap as if he'd been a puppet and she'd cut his strings.

"So much for our strong vampire protector," Brandon frowned and looked down at his body.

Noah cursed and tried to stand between her and the three of us. "Give it up, Kieran. You're outpowered here! You should run away and hide like you usually do, although we would really prefer that you'd stay on the ground until the blessing is complete, and you crumble into a pile of ashes."

I couldn't see Noah's face, but hearing his voice be commanding and taunting was impressive. I'd never seen that side of him, and it didn't help to ease my crush on him any. It took guts to stand against an enraged vampire queen.

Kieran's anger at seeing Caleb helping us escape receded as she studied the necromancer and the three human females before her. "You didn't think I'd let you escape, did you? How nice of your mom and your boyfriend to come pick you up. Too bad you'll never make it back to the car."

"You forgot to mention her ghost friends," Brandon said, putting his hands on his hips and bobbing his head with attitude.

"Maybe you should have brought some backup. I have a feeling you'll let us do exactly as we want." Noah put his arm out towards the queen, and his fingers arched as if he were trying to attack her with a power I didn't understand.

The queen only laughed as Noah groaned, his fingers arching even more. "They really should have sent someone stronger, but, even then, one necromancer is no contest against a vampire queen. I'll even let you touch me."

She extended a slender pale arm while her porcelain features appeared bored.

Physical contact must have helped strengthen his powers because he reached out to her, grasping onto her wrist with his curling fingers. I was sure that if the contact didn't help, he wouldn't have wanted to get so close to her.

Noah growled, and his upper arm started shaking with the effort.

"Okay. I'm bored." Quicker than I could see, the queen rotated her wrist, gripped Noah's forearm, and thrust him to the side.

He yelled as he flew into the air and landed with a grunt several paces away.

"Noah!" I tried to go towards him, but Trina must have woken up from her daze because she clamped her arm to her side and trapped my own against her body.

"Don't leave me." Trina's eyes were wide, and her body was trembling.

"I've never seen a queen so powerful," Gran said as she rushed to Noah's side where I could not. She bent to check his breathing and stood to look back at me. "He's alive! Probably broke some bones, but at least he's alive."

I turned an angry glare towards the queen, careful not to look her in the eyes. In a matter of minutes, she'd taken out our strongest protectors and some of my best friends. Her sights were now on my mom and sister, and my heart pounded hard in my chest with the resolution that she wouldn't hurt them.

The problem was that I had no idea how I would stop her.

Chapter 20

If there was one thing I had learned from hanging out with vampires against my will is that it was not a good idea to look them in the eye. At least not with the vampires you didn't trust, which for the average person was probably all vampires. Hopefully, despite how strong she was, the queen wouldn't be able to entrance me without eye contact.

"Leave us alone! You won't get away with this! The police will find out and maybe even the FBI." My mom kept a tight hold on Trina's arm, and bless her heart, was not too afraid to yell at a vampire queen.

"Wait! Don't look her in the eyes!" I yelled too late as Mom's shoulders went slack, and her eyes stared blankly ahead.

The queen and my mom laughed as one. It was super creepy, and goosebumps skittered down my arms.

"Maybe I should take some energy and try to stab her with some wood? Where's a stake when you need one?" Brandon whirled in a circle, looking for something he could pick up.

"Search Noah's pockets!" I remembered the stake Noah had pulled on Caleb. He had named the thing, so it was probably something he'd carried with him most of the time, especially to raid a vampire's seethe.

The queen narrowed her eyes and looked back at Noah's crumpled body in the grass. There was no one physically alive beside him, so it was clear I was talking to someone she couldn't see. With a snarl, she closed the distance between us quicker than I could blink.

My mom let go of Trina, who yelped in fear. Mom grabbed my head from behind. She was stronger than I had realized, and she forced my face in the queen's direction.

Despite being face-to-face with her, I squeezed my eyes shut. It was better not to see anything than to be entranced, unable to even breathe on my own without the queen's permission.

"Look at me!" The queen screamed in my face. I could feel the air she'd needed to take in so she could talk, and my stomach twisted thinking about that oxygen coming from inside her corpse of a body. Caleb had always felt more alive than the queen ever did. Even the queen's movements were stiff like she'd been a corpse for a long time and had forgotten what it was like to be human.

"No!" I screamed back at her, still keeping my eyes tight.

Gran's calm presence was suddenly by my side. I didn't need my sight to feel her there. As she spoke, her voice was calm and soft, so out of odds with the situation that I immediately listened. "Keep it up, Hanna. You're doing great. You can do this. Brandon is searching through Noah's pockets. If he can find the stake, he'll take enough energy from you to carry it over and put it into your hand. Hopefully, the queen will not see it."

I felt cold fingers grab my chin, and the queen shook my head. "Open your eyes, girl! I'll kill your sister if you don't. Then you can have another ghost friend to hang out with. Wouldn't that be nice?"

Trina's fingers dug into my arm. "You wouldn't dare kill another Seer. We're too valuable, remember?"

The queen was quiet, and, even though I couldn't see her face, I imagined her eyes sliding over to Trina and studying her.

"That's right. There are two of us, and clearly your kind is afraid of us. There must be something we can do against you that you don't like. Now, I wonder what that could be. Let's see. We can talk to ghosts and that's pretty cool. I probably don't have to mention that your house is haunted. Like *very* haunted. The ghosts tend to avoid the vampires when they see them, but I keep glancing at them milling about when they think it is safe. Isn't it interesting that ghosts pay attention to where vampires are and avoid them? Unlike humans who ghosts usually ignore. I wonder what that's about."

While she was talking, the queen slowly let go of my jaw. I was proud of my sister for bravely exposing herself and continuing to talk, hoping to buy Brandon enough time to get the stake to me.

I forced myself not to sigh in relief as her talking paid off, and I felt something heavy slide into my fingers that were hidden behind my fluffy skirt.

"There are never two Seers in one generation of a family. You're lying to me," the queen's voice was directed to my side, but I still didn't dare to open my eyes.

I felt Trina's shoulders shrug against my own. "But you wouldn't dare kill me just in case that was true, would you? Besides, it's easy enough to prove. I ran into your niece outside as we got out of the car. She warned me about you and then told us to kill you and your whole seethe. It seemed like she was really mad at you for some reason. What did you do to her?"

Risking a peek, I saw the queen's jaw clench in anger, and her eyes were the most alive I'd seen them since I'd met her. Luckily, Trina had been wise enough to keep her eyes closed when the queen's gaze bore down on her.

"Nothing she didn't deserve!" The queen snarled.

"Do it, now—while she's distracted!" Gran urged.

Tightening my fingers around the smooth wood so I had as good a grip as I could get, I swung my arm around and stabbed the stake into Queen Kieran's chest, or I would have if she hadn't stopped me.

My human speed was no match for her vampire reflexes. Her fingers were like a ring of searing cold metal around my wrist, and her smile was as if pure evil itself had been given a body. Her fangs glistened in the lights from the deck behind me, and her eyes stared right into my soul.

That's when I realized I'd made a bigger mistake than just trying to kill her and maybe incurring her wrath. I had looked into her eyes.

The now-familiar feeling of being entranced came over me, and Gran and Brandon's presence slowly faded from my awareness. Except, just as she disappeared from my sight, I heard Gran growl and somehow push her way *into* the queen.

Ghosts fazed in and out of walls, trees, and people all the time, but the way Gran had done it looked different. It was like she was going *inside* the queen instead of only going *through* the queen.

I watched as the Kieran's eyes went from an evil angry into a confused determination. Elation soared into my heart as I felt the release from her mind. I was myself again and the queen was...my grandma?

But the struggle wasn't over yet. I could see the queen fighting my grandma's presence. Her expression kept changing, cluing me in who was in charge at any given moment.

Mom's clenching fingers relaxed from off my head, and we all took a step back, confusion written onto all our faces. It looked like the queen couldn't keep control of my mom or me while she was busy fighting a ghost who was trying to take over her body.

"What's going *on*? I didn't know ghosts could do that! So cool!" Brandon watched the queen's struggle with fascination.

At one point, Gran found control over the queen's mouth while her hands pulled wildly at her hair, finally giving it the messy look to match her tattered dress. "She's fighting me! You girls can both give me a boost. Focus your energies on me and give me strength!"

The queen's angry gaze flashed back to us, and she snarled in rage.

Trina and I locked eyes and nodded to each other before mentally pouring as much energy as we could into my grandma's soul. It was an odd feeling as I'd never tried it before. Usually, Brandon or the ghost took the energy from me without me having to do anything. This time, I pictured Gran as a cup and me as a pitcher pouring into her until she was overflowing.

I wasn't sure if I could have given her enough power on my own, but, with Trina's help, Gran was finally able to take full control of the queen. It was obvious when it happened because her stiff body stopped writhing and merely stood straight and calm as if waiting in the line at the DMV.

Gran's kind eyes looked out from the queen's pale face. "Phew! I wasn't sure that would work. Good job, girls!"

I did feel drained in a way that reminded me of when Mr. Tyler had siphoned ghostly energy from me a week or so ago, but it was only slight compared to that incident. It had probably helped that I'd eaten recently and that I hadn't given Gran as much energy as Mr. Tyler had taken.

Trina and I shared a triumphant grin.

"It's not so bad being able to use your powers now, is it?" I said.

My sister shook her head in amusement. "Maybe sometimes. At least it's nice to see who you've been talking to all this time."

I scoffed. "Hey, it's hard to ignore them. I mean, have you heard the comments Brandon makes sometimes?"

Trina looked over at Brandon who was beaming with a bright smile. "Yes, I don't know how you put up with him."

Mom stepped up to the queen and looked back and forth between her and us. "What's going on? Why isn't she inside my mind anymore?"

I took a deep breath. "I'm not sure how to tell you this, and I have no idea how you got involved and aren't freaking out about learning both your girls can talk to ghosts, but here's another fun fact. You've been haunted by Gran since she died, and, right now, she's inside that queen and stopping her from attacking us."

Mom's face was exactly as confused as one who had just learned such news might have been. "Wait. What?"

Noah stirred with a groan and echoing sounds from the battle out front brought us back to the situation at hand.

"Okay, so we've got control of the queen. Now, what do we do?" I turned to Queen Gran.

Gran's eyes flickered from her daughter's disturbed face and back towards the house. "We end this battle. Evacuate the vampires and then...kill the queen?"

"Anyone up for vampire murder?" Brandon rubbed his hands together like an evil mastermind planning something diabolical.

Gran closed her eyes, and, I assumed, was contacting the vampires left fighting in the queen's seethe.

Confused shouts and grunts still echoed from the surrounding property, but the sounds of battle died down.

"It must be working," I said and looked around into the darkness, wondering if I would catch a glimpse of fleeing vampires.

Noah groaned again and sat up.

Deciding that the queen wasn't dangerous to my sister and Mom anymore, I jogged the few paces to Noah's side and kneeled in the dewy grass. "Noah! Are you okay?"

He was rubbing his head and squinting as he looked around. "I guess. I don't know—Ah! The queen is still here! Wait, why aren't we scared, and why is she just standing there calmly?"

"I'm not sure how to say this except to just say it. That's my Gran. She's taken over the queen's body."

Trina had run over to Caleb's side and was checking him over. I wasn't sure what vital signs you could check on a vampire since a heartbeat and breathing were probably not something they did while unconscious, but I was glad she was at least trying to help him.

"She what? Can ghosts do that?" Noah asked and gathered his legs underneath himself.

I helped Noah stand while trying not to think about the warmth of his arm or how all I had to do was lean over a little more and we'd be close enough to kiss.

"Apparently, a Seer ghost with the help of two more Seers can." I helped Noah join our group again.

He eyed the queen warily, but my gran merely smiled at him. It was unnerving to see a friendly smile on the queen's face with her sharp canines sticking out, but it was also kind of cute in a way.

"I'm sorry for throwing you," Gran said, still smiling.

"Right. It's okay. I guess. Wait, I don't hear the battle. What happened to the vampires? I'd ask if they'd completed the blessing but neither the queen nor Caleb have gone up in smoke and ashes, so I'll assume they haven't."

"I told all the vampires that were left to run away and go be better creatures. I gave them strict orders not to feed from humans anymore and figure out the blood situation without violence." Gran looked proud of herself and that expression coming from the queen made me giggle.

"What a kindly and considerate queen," Brandon said, grinning.

"Okay, so the vampires are no longer fighting my order? That means they're going to get back to blessing the ground." Noah glanced back at Caleb's form still on the grass while Trina kneeled nearby with a worried press to her lips. "We've got to get him off the property before they finish it."

"On it!" Queen Gran zipped over to our friend's body, scooped him up, and zipped away.

Her movements were too fast for me to follow, but the glimpse of her small, lithe frame picking up the much-larger Caleb was almost comical.

Trina blinked and stood, looking off to where Gran had gone.

Mom jogged over to my sister and grabbed her hand. "Let's go make sure she doesn't do anything else while wearing a vampire queen's body." She glanced back towards me. "Are you coming?"

"I will be right behind you. I'm going to help Noah and make sure he's okay."

My mom hesitated, and I could see she wasn't keen on the idea, but she took a look at Noah and nodded. "Be careful."

They jogged towards the front of the house, hopelessly way too slow to stop Gran from doing anything.

"Can you walk?" I asked, keeping my gaze steady into Noah's eyes even though we were only inches apart.

"I think so." He nodded but didn't pull away.

Brandon rolled his eyes and huffed. "I'm never going to be able to leave you two alone, am I?"

His tone was a teasing sarcasm, but there was an undercurrent of pain that made me feel bad. What was I doing, anyway? I blame it all on stupid teenage hormones.

I stepped away from Noah and retrieved the stake that had fallen into the grass. "We stole this from you hoping to kill the queen. I'm sorry but Stabarella or whatever her name is, didn't even get close enough to scratch her."

Noah laughed then groaned sharply and grabbed his side. "Oh, no jokes allowed. I've at least bruised a rib."

"We'll try not to tickle your funny bone then," Brandon said but without the usual grin he used when making such terrible jokes.

"I'm sorry. That fall did look brutal, but I have to say it could have been a lot worse." I handed him the stake, and we started walking.

"The night isn't over yet," Noah said with a half-joking glance my way.

Brandon followed us as we walked down the garden paths and around the imposing mansion, but he was quiet instead of his usual commentary on all the things that were happening around us.

Most of the ground-floor windows of the mansion had been bashed out, I assumed from vampires fleeing the house when the necromancers had started their blessing. The lights spilled out onto the grass and reflected off the glass in unpredictable ways as we passed by.

There was enough light to see by and, unfortunately, enough to see the bodies in the grass. When we came upon the first one, Noah advised me that it was best not to look, but I've never been great at taking advice.

The first we came upon was definitely a zombie. I'd never seen one before except in movies or pictures, but it looked pretty much like that, except maybe more dried out. The clothes were tattered, and the skin had shrunk, so it was mostly leathery bones. There was stringy hair for sure, but the eyes were gone, the empty holes staring out into the starry sky. It was still twitching as if trying to obey the necromancer's call, but his head had been severed from its body and was likely unable to issue any commands to the emaciated limbs.

"Wow. That's gross." Brandon stopped to stare at the body for a minute while we walked on.

"So, necromancers can really raise and control the dead?" I asked quietly. Even though I knew Gran had commanded all the vampires to leave, I still couldn't shake the feeling of danger while walking among dead and deader bodies.

Noah was breathing heavily while holding onto his side. He was still upright, which I took as a good sign, but he was obviously in pain, and the going was slow. "We can. The strongest among us can raise several zombies at once and command them to do all different things. There is a cost, though, so we don't often go around raising zombies just to do the dishes or something."

Laughing, Brandon said, "Oh, hey, Edgar. Be a dear and go grab my dry cleaning. If that lady tries to overcharge you again, just savagely attack her so we can have another zombie to play Monopoly with, which, since I control everyone, means I win no matter who wins. Huzzah!"

"I've been wondering why a necromancer may need a zombie in this modern age. It's not like we live on a battlefield or that you could send your zombie to grab an order of groceries or... dry cleaning, I guess."

We came upon a fleshier corpse that I was surprised to learn was a vampire. A stake had been shoved into his chest, and his head had also been relieved of his body. Decapitating seemed like a common theme. It was probably the best way to stop the undead creatures, and I logged it away inside my mind in case I needed it later.

I really didn't want to need it later.

"Right. We save it for times like this which may happen more than you'd think. The vampires and necromancers seem to always have some kind of situation going on."

"That's good. Well, not really, but I was feeling guilty for starting a battle. I didn't mean for all of you to get involved. I'm grateful, for sure, but I still feel indebted to you guys." I eyed another desiccated zombie corpse as we passed by. "And your zombie friends."

There was a stone bench along the garden path. Without asking Noah, I brushed the glass off using some leaves and sat down, allowing him a rest. His breathing had gotten worse, and his rib must have hurt every time he inhaled because he kept wincing. Plus, it was a perfect time to get answers. Caleb and Queen Gran were off the grounds, and the necromancers were either done with the blessing or had to have been close to completing it. Despite the dead bodies and broken glass laying around, this was probably one of the safest places to be.

Oh, also, my feet were killing me. I wanted to take off my heels, but, with the amount of glass crunching beneath them, I knew it would have been worse to have cut up feet rather than split-open blisters.

Noah flashed me a grateful smile and eased himself onto the bench. "You're worth it. Besides, we couldn't let the vampires have a pet Seer, no matter who it is. That just wouldn't be fair to us or the werewolves or the witches. Honestly, it was just a matter of time before someone else came in there and stole you away. It might as well have been us."

Brandon sat down on a bush next to the bench and kept looking around us, probably to spy more corpses. Were all ghosts so morbid or just this kid from the 90s?

"Oh, you know how to make a girl feel special."

He laughed, then winced and groaned. "No more jokes. It hurts to laugh. You are special, Hanna."

We probably would have shared a semi-romantic moment (as one could get with zombie and vampire bodies lying around), but Brandon sighed dramatically and reminded me that we weren't alone. It was probably the polite thing to warn Noah before he started kissing me or whatever.

Not that I wanted him to kiss me.

Right.

"Brandon thinks the zombie corpses are cool," I said, pointing to the bush beside us. "He wants to know if you could teach him to raise one too. Really, Brandon? How are you going to keep him bathed without his skin falling off?"

Noah grinned and glanced at the bush. "Sorry, mate. Only alive necromancers can control the dead."

Brandon rolled his eyes and shook his head. "It's just not as fun when the other people around know I'm here. It seems harder to make fun of them."

"Poor baby." I gave Brandon a pouty look and turned back to Noah. "What's the cost for a necromancer to raise the dead?"

"You're about to see for yourself," Noah said, raising his head and looking down the garden path.

There were indeed crunching sounds as a group of people, zombies, or people and zombies headed our way. I took a deep breath, trying to brace myself for meeting Noah's order and possibly some disgusting zombies who had helped earned my freedom.

"Noah! Where are you?"

"Noah!"

Several of the people were calling out, and I used my best detective skills to deduce that they had finished their blessing and were now coming after the whole reason for this debacle.

Me.

"Why do I feel nervous like I'm meeting your parents or something? Are your parents in the order?" I asked and debated on whether I should stand up to greet them or stay by Noah who probably didn't want to stand up at all.

"I hope they bring the zombies!" Brandon jumped off the bush and tried to peer around the trees.

"I'm over here!" Noah called out, but it wasn't super loud. "No, just my uncle. Don't worry. You're not meeting my parents yet. We'll have to go on a proper date before we do that."

He grinned, but his face was pale, and his mouth wobbled slightly.

"Yuck." Brandon stopped his search for zombies long enough to shoot me a disgusted look.

I couldn't help the smile, and so I was sitting on a bench with Noah and grinning like a dork when I first met the leaders of his necromantic order.

Chapter 21

"Noah! Oh, are you okay? Is this her?" One man saw us first and rushed over to check Noah's vital signs.

Noah nodded and patted his side. "I think I've got some broken ribs, but I think that's not too bad having gone up against a vampire queen."

The man's bushy eyebrows raised in surprise. I took a second to study him and had trouble placing his age. There were a few wrinkles around his eyes and bits of gray dusted throughout his hair, but he seemed younger than middle-aged. The way he talked and carried himself made me want to think he was in his young thirties. "You ran into the queen?"

"I was wondering where that old bat had flown off to," another man said as he hobbled toward the bench. "You look younger than I expected."

"And you look *way* older than we expected," Brandon said, peering into the old man's face.

"You're one to talk about how old people look," Noah said with a grin.

The old man gave Noah a flat stare. His head was nearly bald with a few wispy strands of grey hair that waved in the cool night breeze.

Light from the house shined on the bald patch. There were so many wrinkles on his face that would have taken quite a while to count. Age spots peppered his hands and disappeared under the sleeves of his high-end suit. His shoulders were stooped, and his milky eyes seemed to see more than they should have.

Most of the other necromancers laughed at Noah's joke. There were seven of them, one of them a woman, and they were all dressed in various styles of clothes. One of the men was even wearing a classic set of striped pajamas.

"I presume you are Hanna," the old man said and extended his hand. I found it surprisingly steady and strong when I shook it.

"I'm so sorry to cause such a mess. I can't tell you how grateful I am that you guys risked so much to come save me."

"How in the world did seven necromancers take out an entire seethe of vampires?" Brandon put his hands on his hips and surveyed the group. "Especially all these old folks? What? Did they raid a retirement home on their way here?"

Most of them did look much older than I'd expected. I started to realize that maybe it had something to do with being a necromancer.

"No, no, no. It was our pleasure. Please don't be sorry. We enjoy any excuse to kick some vampire butt. In fact, we should be thanking you for sending a ghost to tell us where this vampire seethe was. It's been years since I've been able to take out an entire seethe." The old man smiled at me and then turned to his companions who all nodded in agreement. Some even grinned like he did.

"Okay, you're welcome?"

A few chuckled at my weak joke.

"I'm not sure you took out the whole seethe, though." I glanced at Noah to confirm my story. He nodded for me to continue. "The queen got away, but, before she left, she commanded all the other vampires to flee. I have no idea how many were here to begin with or how many survived to meet up somewhere else. You may be facing some dangerous reciprocation."

The old man shrugged. "Probably. They're not the only ones with secrets, though. We'll be able to handle it. Plus, it's worth it to save the life of a young lady."

"Are you really a Seer?" one of the other men asked, and it kind of creeped me out to see so much hope and fascination in his eyes.

"Back off, Grady. Don't you think we're creepy enough by showing up with zombies?" Noah said after looking at my face.

"Marcus, will you examine Noah?" The old man gestured to my friend and then turned to me. "Are you hurt, Hanna? Did they do anything to you?"

"They wouldn't dare hurt a Seer," the woman said as she stood off to the side in jeans and a t-shirt.

I nodded in agreement. "She's right. In fact, they made sure I was well-fed and had a lovely place to sleep. If I hadn't been entranced by a vampire and unable to even go to the bathroom unless they allowed it, then it might not have been so bad."

The old man nodded. "At least the bloodsuckers can understand the value of a Seer."

As we waited for Marcus, a man who appeared about sixty with spry fingers and who was wearing scrubs to appraise Noah's condition, I debated on what to do.

I glanced at Brandon, and he voiced my thoughts. "So, did you just get rescued from vampires to become the property of necromancers instead? We should go find your family and see if Caleb is okay. Perhaps the queen will make us a lovely batch of cookies and sing us a bedtime song before tucking us snug in our blankets."

We shared an amused smile before I turned back to the older man who seemed to be in charge. "I'm super grateful for all you have done for me, but I'm sure my mom and sister are worried."

"They drove here so they're probably waiting by the car wondering where you are by now," Brandon said while looking back down the garden path. "They might even come looking for you again."

Noah hissed as Marcus prodded his ribs. The old man looked back and forth between me and Noah, his mind obviously thinking about what to do next and how he was going to keep me for the order to use when they needed but also let me go and not break any laws or let me get kidnapped by another group who wanted to use my help.

"Thank you all again, especially you, Noah. I'd give you a hug, but it looks like that would do more harm than help at this point." I gave him a smile and stood up, waiting for someone to stop me at any moment.

Noah smiled at me and then winced again. "It's okay. You can hug me later."

"Oh, I'm sure she can." Brandon huffed.

"Right. So, my mom is waiting just outside. Thank you!" I started to walk away, wondering how hard I would fight these guys who had just rescued me if I needed to.

"Wait!" the old man said.

I was tempted to run away and hope they wouldn't catch me somehow, but I did the polite thing and turn around. "Yes?"

"Alberto," the old man nodded his head towards the first middle-aged guy who had approached us. "Escort her to her mother's car, would you? We wouldn't want anything to happen to Hanna after we've worked so hard to free her."

Alberto nodded and stood next to me.

"Oh, thank you." I didn't dare protest in case it made them want to go even further to protect me.

We walked in silence as we made our way around the rest of the mansion, again passing several bodies, mostly zombies.

Brandon kept pace with us, although he'd stop occasionally to check out a particularly gruesome corpse.

The silence felt heavy on my shoulders, so I took a chance to learn more about necromancers and what they could do.

"What will you guys do with this property now that you've blessed it and the vampires can't come back?"

Alberto shrugged. "Just because we've blessed it, doesn't mean it's ours. It belongs to whoever owns the deed, and the vampires can work out if they want to sell it or whatever. We'll be nice, though, and rebury their dead we borrowed for a time."

I returned his amused smile. "I can't believe just the seven of you were able to take on so many vampires. They're so fast and strong, and as far as I can see, necromancers seem to be regular humans."

"I wouldn't exactly say we are 'regular humans', but it's true that we aren't blessed with the supernatural speed and strength that vampires possess. Instead, we have our own set of gifts which include being able to put bodies between the vampires and us which does slow them down some. The other thing is that vampires desperately want to avoid touching us." Alberto held up his fingers and rubbed them together.

"Since vampires don't have a soul, we're able to possess them in a way that forces them to do our bidding."

"Kind of like when a vampire entrances someone?"

"A lot like that, actually. The cool thing about it is when we've got control of a vampire, we're able to use their powers and turn them against their own kind. So, in a way, we've got what they have too."

He grinned again.

"That is pretty cool. What else would you use a vampire for? Do you think anyone would use a vampire to...I don't know, dance, maybe, at a school dance?"

Alberto laughed and shook his head. "Oh no. I'm not sure what the point of that would be. Why would someone want to use a vampire to dance?"

Brandon gave me a look. "Yes, why would someone want to do that?"

"Okay, that was a silly question." We were rounding the side of the building and would be approaching the front yard soon. "Noah had said something about necromancer powers requiring a cost of some sort. Does it have something to do with making your bodies age quicker?"

Alberto nodded. "You've got good observation skills. Perhaps that's why they call you a Seer?"

We shared a chuckle even though I was reminded of my dad and his jokes.

"Yes. When we use our powers, our physical bodies tend to age quicker. The oldest necromancers have virtually no use of their bodies and sit inside the temple while controlling others in order to go about their business."

"Wow. That's kind of intense."

"Necromancer monks. How crazy. Well, guess you have that to look forward to when you marry Noah. I can see it now—his old, wrinkly body next to your young twenty-something self. Although...he could possess a new hot vampire, and you could have a new boyfriend all the time! Sounds kinky."

"Ugh, that's gross." I glared at Brandon who only grinned back.

"Yes, sorry about the zombies. We arm them with stakes, and they're actually decent against vampires because they can't be entranced. Also, it's harder to kill them since they're already dead, you know? So, your mom is just waiting outside? Is that weird that she drove to a vampire seethe at the same time we're here and just happens to be ready to pick you up?"

I didn't correct him about what I had been saying was gross because the zombies were also really gross, so it was fine. We'd finally gotten to the driveway, and I could see a ring of zombies that had fallen protecting something inside. It must have been where the necromancers had made their stand and where most of the fighting had happened.

The smells finally hit me as the zombies were more congested, and we had to get fairly close to pass by and head down the driveway. I had always known dead bodies didn't smell good but knowing it and actually experiencing it were two different things.

"Yes." I may have gagged. "Oh, this reeks! How can you guys stand it?"

Alberto eyed the pile of corpses. "Honestly? I try to breathe through my mouth and not smell them, but I'm still not used to it. I'm not sure that's a smell anyone can get used to."

Brandon must have been satisfied with his inspection of corpses for the night because he didn't go closer to the carnage. "For once, I'm glad I don't have a nose I can smell with."

"It's disgusting!"

"Oh, yeah, and then when Noah comes home from a hard day's work smelling like zombies. Oh baby, sexy. It's on." Brandon waggled his eyebrows.

I gagged again. "Sorry. I didn't know I had such a weak stomach."

Alberto waved it off. "Don't apologize. I get it."

After a few more minutes of walking, we made it to the gate. The metal rails were bent inwards as if someone had madly driven into them. "You guys must have made a pretty bold entrance."

"I'd hate to see the car after that," Brandon said, eyeing the mangled gate.

Alberto shrugged with another grin. "We were in a hurry."

Mom and Trina came running towards us as we walked off of the driveway and onto the street. I was relieved to see there were fields surrounding the property instead of it being in the heart of a neighborhood full of humans. I suppose that's why we hadn't gotten attention from the cops. It was probably one of the reasons the vampires settled down out here. This couldn't have been the first time there had been such commotion at the mansion. No way a house full of vampires wouldn't cause drama and chaos.

"Hanna! We were wondering if we'd have to go back in there again." Trina's bare feet slapped on the pavement. She'd ditched her heels somewhere, probably in my mom's car that was parked a few paces down the street.

"Oh, thank goodness." Mom grabbed my shoulders and planted a kiss on my forehead. "I don't think my nerves can take much more of this."

"I'm sorry, Mom." I decided Trina's idea was a good one and there was less likely to be glass out here than there was by a dozen smashed windows. Relief washed through my feet as I took off my heels, and, even though they stung from raw blisters and small rocks poking me from the road, it was still better than wearing the shoes. "If it helps, I didn't want any of this either."

Mom gave me a compassionate smile and then looked at Alberto. "And who is your friend? Where is Noah?"

I updated her with what had happened and how I'd met my rescuers.

Mom grabbed Alberto's hands. "I can't thank you all enough for risking your lives to come here for my daughter. We owe you all so much!"

Alberto let my mom pump his hands up and down in a vigorous handshake, but the smile on his face sent a few chills down my arms. "It's alright. I have a feeling you'll be able to repay us soon."

Trina and I shared a worried look as my mom wished the necromancer goodbye, and he left me in the care of my mom and sister. Honestly, I was surprised he'd leave me with mere humans like that, but he must have figured I was safe enough for the moment.

"Where's Queen Gran?" I asked as soon as the guy was out of earshot, and we had started to head towards the car. "How's Caleb?"

"They're waiting for us over here. We figured showing the vampire queen to a necromancer probably wouldn't be a good move," Mom said as she led us around the car and into the wooded area behind it.

"Probably not." I nodded.

The sticks and leaves from the woods were pokey on my feet, and once I stepped on one in such a way that it stabbed one of my torn blisters, but I still refused to put those heels back on.

A little way into the trees, we came into a small clearing where Queen Gran was sitting very unqueenly-like on a log next to a dazed Caleb. He was rubbing his eyes and forehead, and by all accounts, looked like he'd just woken up from a long nap and couldn't remember what year it was.

"Do you feel any better?" Trina asked as we arrived.

Caleb groaned and dropped his hands into his lap. "She's never hit me like that before. It feels deeper than physical pain. I think she severed my bond with her and the seethe."

Queen Gran patted his leg with the queen's slender fingers and then stopped and studied her hands as if still surprised to see them. "I haven't had hands this smooth in many years." She turned back to Caleb. "It's probably a good thing to have ties broken with the seethe. Essentially, you just betrayed them and your queen all for the sake of my granddaughter."

They stared at each other, and I got worried if I'd have to watch my gran who was dressed as a vampire queen kiss my sister's friend who was a vampire but had maybe been in love with my gran at some point?

I wish I could say I was making all of this up.

"Logically, I know all that. I'm fine being away from the seethe, but I can't explain to you how it feels physically and emotionally. Vampire seethes, especially the queens, have a certain hold over their members. Sometimes when a vampire is cut off, he struggles so much with the loneliness that he'll try several methods of killing himself until something sticks."

Queen Gran frowned. "I'm sorry."

"But you've got a different seethe now," Trina said as she took a closer step towards them. "I'm sure Mom won't let you move in or anything, but you aren't alone."

Mom gave Trina a mixed look of confusion and surprise. "She certainly wouldn't. Although, we do owe you for your help today in my daughter's escape."

"And the several days of torture you endured so my identity could be safe," I said with a grateful smile.

Caleb's shoulders slumped. "Which was all for nothing since they figured it out anyway, which was also my fault."

"Yeah, good job, turd." Brandon bobbed his head, but I had a feeling that if Caleb had been able to hear him, Brandon probably wouldn't have been so harsh. He was as grateful as I was that Caleb had gone through so much to protect me, even if he couldn't admit it.

Queen Gran scooped his hand inside hers and held it tightly. "I don't care what that saying is about intentions, about how they pave the road to hell or whatever. They've got to matter. You didn't mean for them to catch Hanna, and you endured more than I can imagine to keep her safe. That's what matters."

Her words sparked a memory in my head about what Brandon had said to me after I'd realized I'd helped Rose enslave ghosts instead of helping them cross over.

"Caleb, I know we need to figure out what to do with a vampire queen's body since I imagine Gran doesn't want to parade around as her forever, but I have to ask before I forget again. Were you ever able to get more information on Rose?"

Caleb furrowed his eyebrows and shook his head. "I'm sorry. I don't know anything more about her than I did last week, which is to say that I know about as much as you."

Queen Gran pursed her lips thoughtfully. "I think the queen knows something. It's hard to know exactly what she knows since she's trying to block me from herself, and there's no amount of money anyone could pay me to go deep diving into a century's old vampire's vicious and dark memories, but, at the mention of Rose, something flagged inside my mind...er, her mind."

"What? Really?" I glanced at Brandon in excitement.

"You can read her thoughts?" Caleb looked at Gran with wide eyes.

"Only some of them, thank goodness. She's still fighting me inside here, but I can feel Trina's and Hanna's powers sustaining me. If there weren't three of us, I wouldn't have been able to take her. Lucky for the queen, she found a set of three Seers that probably hasn't come together in such numbers for generations, if ever."

"Right. Because there's only supposed to be one of us who can see ghosts." Trina glanced at me with a slightly apologetic smile.

I returned her smile, letting all my relief at having someone else to talk to about the ghosts shine through. Then I turned back to Queen Gran. "So what does she know about Rose?"

Gran scrunched the queen's face as if fighting through some cobwebs to get to the information. I wouldn't have been surprised at all to find out there were literal cobwebs inside the queen's brain. When she did find the information, it all came out in a rush as if she wanted to say it all before she forgot it or lost access to it. "Rose isn't her real name.

It's Ann Good. She was a child during the Salem witch trials in 1693. Her mother was executed, and her father smuggled her into the crowd to watch her burn. After that, she vowed to see witches come into their powers and become free to do as they wished. She's used ghosts these many years by siphoning their energy to keep herself young. She's gone by many names over the years, and, as far as the queen can piece together, she's been responsible for more than a few Seer's deaths."

The clearing was silent as we all stared at Queen Gran and processed this information.

"Wait. This human psychic lady is older than *I* am?" Caleb said.

"That's dark," Brandon muttered, glancing in my direction.

Mom's eyebrows drew together in confusion. "Okay. I feel like I'm missing something. Who is this lady and why do we care?"

"Oh, sorry. We'll have to explain later, but I need to find her and right some wrongs I may have helped her commit," I told Mom with a wince.

Trina and Mom exchanged looks.

"I promise I'll tell you the whole story when we finally get home and can relax over a warm cup of cocoa. As it is, I have to ask," I turned back to Queen Gran, "how does the queen know all this?"

"Apparently, she's been researching Seers for a long time, following their bloodlines and using them to do her bidding. Ann's life and story has crossed paths with the Seers many times, and the queen took a particular interest in her." Gran winced and rubbed the queen's forehead. "I think that's all we're going to get. I can feel my control starting to waver, or at least the part where I can invade her thoughts."

"Wow," I said, summing up everything I was thinking.

There was just enough room on the log for another person, and I slumped onto it next to Gran and stretched my legs out. Thankfully it was too dark to inspect the damage done to my feet, which was good because, frankly, I was afraid to see what they looked like. The cool night air had finally started to sink into me as the adrenaline ebbed and the exhaustion seeped in. I had no idea what time it was, but I knew it was late, and I was sure that the only thing any of us wanted was to curl up in our beds all warm and snuggly and not dream of sugarplum vampires.

"I think we can go off that and find more about her. Maybe we can even find her. Don't you have that magic Google thing you can use?" Brandon sat down on the ground next to me, and, while I appreciated his never-ending optimism, it was still a lot to think about right then.

Mom sighed and began combing back her hair with her fingers. "We need to figure out what to do with the queen and then get home to bed. This is way later than I've stayed up in a long time, and, as I'm supposed to be the responsible parent, I should probably be trying to get my girls in bed."

Queen Gran stood stiffly and looked down at herself. "As much as I've enjoyed being in such a powerful and beautiful body, I agree. We need to figure out what to do with her before she wins the mental battle and takes her body back. We're powerful Seers together, but despite being a soulless vampire, she has the laws of nature on her side. A ghost just isn't meant to inhabit a body like this, even one without a soul."

"Should we kill her?" Trina's voice was quiet as she suggested the idea. "I don't like murder or anything, but, if we leave her alive, what's to stop her from coming after us again? Especially since she knows there are two Seers now."

We were all quiet again as we thought about what could happen.

"Caleb?" I looked at him across the log. "I think this should be your decision. You've known her the longest, but you've also proven your loyalty here, so what do you think we should do? Will she come after us if we just let her free?"

He pressed his lips while looking at me and then turned to consider Queen Gran. "Kieran is like a spider. She sets traps and waits for people to fall into them. She won't come after you until she's confident she can win, and you all have shown today that you have powerful friends, including myself. The next time she and I meet, I won't be under her seethe control and will be much better equipped to stand up to her."

"It sounds like he's saying she should live." Brandon dragged in a dramatic sigh. "And here I was hoping for some vampire death."

"Haven't you seen enough death for one night?" Trina replied to him, surprising us into remembering she could hear and see him as well. She turned to me and gave me a flat look. "Where did you find this kid, anyway? He's like a walking narrator in some terrible sitcom or something."

Mom and Caleb looked at me and Trina oddly, but I figured they'd figure it out. "He is a bit...special."

"Hey, my material is good enough for a full movie, not just a sitcom, thank you very much," Brandon said as he stood with his hands on his hips.

"Right." Trina turned back to Caleb. "So, we just let her go free? What's to stop her from attacking us the moment Gran leaves her body?"

"I am." The log teetered slightly as Caleb stood and stared into Queen Gran's eyes. "You will all be very far from here, and the queen will leave this city and never come back."

Queen Gran's eyes were unfocused for a bit, and then she came back to Caleb's stony gaze. "She agrees. She knows she's beaten and regrets losing you from the seethe now that she doesn't have as much power over you. I have to say, I didn't realize how much power a queen had over her seethe members."

Caleb's expression softened, and he put a hand on Queen Gran's cheek. "It hadn't bothered me until a few decades ago when she prevented me from making my own choices about my own life."

Again, I worried they were going to kiss, and my eyes went to Trina. I wondered how she was dealing with all of this having just confessed to me a few days ago that she had a crush on Caleb.

Not everyone could say they had a crush on their grandma's ex-lover or boyfriend or whatever they had been.

Boy, did we all need therapy. Did therapists exist for the occult world of vampires and necromancers?

"Mom, before you go, I..." Mom's voice trailed off as she approached Queen Gran.

Caleb backed up and let them have a moment to talk.

Queen Gran's eyes crinkled at the corners, and I swore I saw more of Gran's face than the queen's at that moment. "I have to say this while you can hear me. I'm so proud of you, honey. Believe me when I say I've seen the pain and struggles you've endured these last several years. I'm so sorry you've been forced into a life of ghosts while being on the outside at the same time. I know your childhood was confusing and weird and now your daughters can both see ghosts. I'm sorry Josh left, and I'm sorry that I've tried to tell you how to be a wife all these years even though you haven't been able to hear me."

"But *I* could. Man, you can be bossy," I said to ease the tension a bit.

Gran put her hands on her hips and gave me a look. I smiled cheekily.

Mom choked out a combination of giggle and sob.

"However, in these last weeks, I've seen how strong you are. I've seen how you're pushing to be a good mom and make enough money to take care of your girls. I've seen how a woman can be strong and live her own life without needing the support of a man. I know you can do this, and I'm sorry I ever doubted."

Mom and Gran fell into an embrace while Mom's shoulders shook with sobs, getting tears on an already tattered vampire queen's dress.

"You don't know how nice it is to hear you say that, Mom, but I'd be lying if I said I didn't doubt. I doubt it every day." Mom's voice was muffled as she spoke, and I vaguely wondered what the vampire queen's body smelled like, although I was super happy that Gran and Mom were finally able to speak directly to each other.

They hugged for a while, and Trina came to stand next to me, once again linking our elbows together. Caleb stood quietly, but his anxious glances around the clearing told me he didn't feel patient.

"Aw, such a cute family moment. This belongs in an after-school special. Well, except for the whole zombie battle part and the bit about her actually being inside a vampire queen's body." Brandon was the only one who talked, but my smile told him I didn't mind too much.

Finally, they parted and looked fondly at each other. Again, I could see more of Gran's face than the queen's somehow. It must have been her facial expressions.

"I'm really proud of you, you know. I don't think I ever said that when I was alive or at least not enough," Gran said.

Mom smiled, and a few more tears leaked out. "It's okay. I know, but it is nice to hear."

Queen Gran's eyebrows furrowed, and she frowned. "I feel odd. The queen is winning. I think it's time to set her free."

Mom sniffed but nodded and stepped back.

"Maybe you guys should get to the car before she gets control back. You'll be at least a little safer there in case she decides she wants to attack," Caleb said to us with a worried look at his queen. "I'll keep watch to make sure she leaves town and doesn't disturb anyone."

Mom, Trina, and I looked at each other and nodded.

"Thanks, Caleb," I said while standing up from the log and wincing from my painful feet. "For everything."

He smiled. "Of course, doll."

Trina and Mom headed out of the trees and towards the car. Some instinct told me to stay behind for at least another moment.

The queen's expressions were all over the place as her body was being fought over for control. "I'm doing my best here, kiddo, but I won't last long. I think...I think it's my time for real."

"Oh snap," Brandon said, his eyes sad.

"What? You mean you're crossing over? Your unfinished business was to tell Mom you are proud of her?"

She shrugged with one shoulder while the other stayed stiffly still. "It was the last bit I needed to do I think. At first, it was to help you learn about yourself, then to see you have a supportive network of people who will help you, and then see Trina embrace her powers after I had helped her hide from them. Oh, and check under the third rock in the backyard of my old house. There is something there I need you to have."

"Oh, Gran! I love you! Thank you!"

Half of her face smiled, and she twitched. "Love you forever, peanut. Now, get out of here!"

I ran away then, through the pokey forest floor of sticks and away from the best ghost I had ever known.

Chapter 22

Dawn found me in the skatepark, still wearing my dirty and ripped homecoming gown with bandages all over my feet and a snug jacket around my shoulders. I hadn't even tried to convince my mom and Trina to let me out of the house after the entire seethe debacle, but they'd fallen into such a dead sleep that it was easy to sneak out after that.

It probably wasn't the smartest thing to be going outside on my own after being kidnapped, but I couldn't sleep despite the exhaustion that made my head feel like it weighed a hundred pounds.

I was hoping fresh air and a bit of pre-dawn quiet would help me decompress. Of course, with Brandon around it was anything but quiet.

"I think I need therapy after tonight," he said as we sat on our tabletop and watched the sky turn colors.

"I'm pretty sure I've always needed therapy. Heck, everyone probably needs therapy. Too bad there isn't such thing as a ghost therapist."

"Actually," he nudged me with his shoulder, and I almost felt it, "I think that's your job."

I sighed. "Gran's gone now."

He nodded, seeming to finally understand it was his turn to listen instead of rattling off distracting comedic quips.

"She had a *lot* of unfinished business to get through, and yet it all happened so fast. Well, fast in terms of all at once but also kind of slow since she had to wait eleven years for me to figure out what the heck I should be doing."

"It's okay. We all know you're slow."

"I'm going to miss her now more than I did when she died."

"Me too, oddly enough. Who is going to get mad at us for hanging out so much?"

"Trina?" We both chuckled softly at the idea of having my sister police us. That was, of course, if she chose not to wear the necklace. I wasn't convinced that one wild night would encourage her to brave the world of ghosts. It would probably do much the opposite, and I didn't blame her. However, I did know that after what I'd been through, I wouldn't want to wear that necklace at all.

Ghosts were becoming my life.

"I danced with a dead body today...well, I guess more like last night."

"Sexy. Want to dance with another one?"

I glanced at him in surprise and the corner of his mouth tipped up in a smile. "Just for a few moments?"

"Okay, but if you step on my sore toes, I'll poke you in the eye."

"Deal." He stood and extended a hand towards me.

I watched as his usual blue skin faded into a peach, starting with the tips of his fingers. Slowly, I reached out to him and touched his hand.

He helped me stand, and, by the time we'd stepped around the table, his body was fully alive-looking.

"Does it hurt at all? When I take energy from you like this?"

I shook my head, having a hard time finding my voice.

"I know you're worried about what will happen if we keep doing this, but I'm sure a few minutes won't be a big deal."

He pulled me closer, and I folded into his chest with my arms wrapped around his neck and shoulders. Whiffs of alluring cologne drifted to my nose, and I wondered if that's what the mall smelled like in the 90s.

"As much as I hate to admit it, I'm glad Noah was able to help you out today. I was really scared." His lips tickled the soft spot behind my ear as he wrapped one arm around my waist and the other across my back and into the tail ends of my wavy, long-since-gone-wild hair. The breath from his words sent shudders down my shoulders.

"Me too. Thank you for helping them find me. How did you get to them? I thought you couldn't leave me or the skatepark."

"Something guided your mom and sister here. Honestly, I'd popped back here in a desperate move to try and figure out how to break the entrancement on you and get help when not but an hour later, your mom and Trina stopped by looking for you. Even though Trina had seen you get abducted by some weird guys in suits, Mr. Tyler convinced her not to tell your mom but instead to make up a story about you getting upset and running away in anger. They were out looking for you and stopping by places you usually hung out at."

"I mean, okay...but why did Mr. Tyler get involved? When did they finally tell Mom the truth?" I pulled back a little so I could see Brandon's face and realized my mistake too late.

He watched my lips as he talked, and the growing light revealed his eyes were a deep green. "He knew exactly what was happening once he saw the four vampires take you away. He knew that it would scare your mom, but, when Noah showed up with a whole necromancer order behind him, Trina had to explain the truth. Your mom took it much better than anyone would have thought."

"Yeah, I noticed that."

Silence sunk in between us, and suddenly it didn't matter what had happened that night and how it had gone down. All that mattered was Brandon.

I leaned in, and we met in a soft kiss. Fire, need, and desire coursed through me as I felt the texture of his lips. My breath hitched as I pressed myself harder against him. Our soft meeting turned into a hungry, passionate kiss.

By the time we pulled apart, we were both breathing heavily, and I knew my heart was in trouble. Gran had been right about ghosts all along.

What kind of future could we possibly have?

Even if he managed to avoid completing his unfinished business, we couldn't keep using energy like this. There was no way we could have a full life of dating and sharing milkshake straws and stealing kisses in the backseat of a car.

As I looked into his eyes, I got the sense he was thinking about the same things. Then I decided none of that mattered right that second. The only time we had was what was in front of us, and, for just a moment, his body was real, and there was no one around to stop me from kissing him again.

To be continued

Don't Hunt Werewolves

Hanna's story continues in book 3, *Don't Hunt Werewolves*. Available Now!

After Halloween night reveals a death close to Hanna, she has to use her ghost powers to rescue some kids from school. While there, she runs into a tall stranger who she later finds out is Mr. Tyler's nephew, Gryphin.

Mr. Tyler and Gryphin enlist Hanna's help to find a dead werewolf from their pack. It is one thing for Hanna to talk to ghosts when she meets them, it's quite another for her to go hunting for a specific ghost.

With all the extra time Hanna is spending with the wolves, including the muscled Gryphin, Brandon starts having feelings that threaten to change the nature of their relationship in a terrifying way. Hanna will have to learn to balance using her powers to help ghosts with not neglecting the people she loves.

About the Author

Jeni Conrad is a wife, mother, teacher, writer, reader, and a human (honest, she can pass those robot tests almost every time!). She usually writes YA fantasy or paranormal stories . Since fifteen years old, she worked in the restaurant business while getting through high school, a BA in English, and then an MA in sociology. Now she works from home while wrangling two small girls, a dog, and two crazy cats.

www.jeniconrad.com

Also By Jeni Conrad

The Lost Guardian Series

Part 1- Game On

Part 2- IRL

The Hanna Sanchez Series

Don't Haunt Ghosts

Don't Bite Vampires

Don't Hunt Werewolves

Don't Summon Necromancers

Don't Hex Witches

The Mirror Islands Series

Peter in Wonderland

Alice in Neverland

www.ingramcontent.com/pod-product-compliance
Lightning Source LLC
Chambersburg PA
CBHW070441300726
48975CB00007B/2000